BY EVAN HUNTER

A HORSE'S HEAD

A NOVEL BY EVAN HUNTER

DELACORTE PRESS / NEW YORK

THIS IS FOR
HOWARD MELNICK
MY BROTHER-IN-LAW

See, see! what shall I see?
A horse's head where his tail should be.

A HORSE'S HEAD

1. JAWBONE

He came tumbling down the stairs head over heels cursing as his skull collided with each angled joining of riser and tread, wincing whenever a new step rushed up to meet him, and thinking all the while How *dare* he do this to me, a good old friend like me?

He was a lanky man of thirty-nine, needing a haircut, wearing a rumpled brown suit and a raincoat that had once been white, falling down the stairs with all the grace of a loose bundle of sticks, lurching and hurtling and banging every bone in his body. Oh you will pay for this, he thought, you will most certainly pay for this.

"And *estay* out!" a voice called from the top of the steps.

He could not believe he had reached the landing, everything still hurt as much as it had while he was falling. He got up and dusted off first the knees of his trousers and then the sleeves of his raincoat and then he picked up his battered fedora, which had preceded him down the staircase with perhaps even less grace, and rubbed the elbow of his coat across the hat and then set it on his head at what he assumed was a jaunty angle. It was while he was putting on his hat that he discovered his forehead was bleeding, which was really no small wonder, considering the number of steps he had hit on his descent. He thought it supremely rude of the proprietor of the place, a Puerto Rican gentleman named Hijo, which meant son (and he could guess son of *what*), to have thrown him down the stairs simply because he'd asked for a fifty-dollar loan. He wished he had half the money he had spent in Hijo's place over the past ten years, make that a quarter of the money, and then to be hustled out the door and hurled down the stairs. You'll pay for this, Hijo, he thought, and stuck out his tongue to wet the handkerchief, and then wiped at the blood, and then walked out into the daylight.

It was a rare spring day, April flaunting herself like a naked whore. Hello, April, he thought cheerily and then winced and felt his backside, certain he'd broken something. You dirty rat, Hijo, he thought, sounding like James Cagney in his mind, I'll get you for this, you dirty rat, and smiled. Oh it was a lovely day. Oh all the sweet young girls of New York were out in their summer dresses, having shucked their girdles and other restricting garments, wiggling along the avenue, prancing along as though having been led into the paddock to be ogled by horsebettors of all ages, Andrew Mullaney himself included.

Except, of course, that he himself had not been able to borrow fifty dollars from Hijo, son of, and whereas he had the twenty cents necessary for the purchase of a subway token to take him out to the Big Bold Beautiful Big A, he did not have the wherewithal to bet once he got there, great horseplayer that he was. The terrible pity about not having been able to raise the fifty was that Mullaney had received from a somewhat disreputable uptown dice player a tip on the fourth race, a filly named Jawbone who was supposed to be a hands-down winner. The disreputable dice player was a charter member of the Cosa Nostra, so it could be assumed that his information had come, if not directly from the horse's mouth, at least directly from the mouth of someone intimate with the horse's mouth. All of which left Mullaney out in the cold because the only thing you can do with a hot tip is play it. Nor can you tell anyone else how hot the tip is lest it suddenly cool; there's nothing so fickle as a pari-mutuel board. So Mullaney wasn't feeling particularly cheerful about his inability to raise the money. He had tried a faggot he knew in the Village, fellow who ran a jewelry store and from whom he had once bought a ring for Irene. The faggot had said No dice, Andy, business has been off, I don't know what it is, I'm designing the stuff same as I always did, maybe people are beginning to lose their good taste. Well, Mullaney said, I don't understand how anyone could pass this beautiful display of yours in the window without wanting to come in and buy up the whole sparkling lot, to which the faggot blushed, but did not give him the fifty dollars.

So Mullaney had gone uptown to Forty-second Street where there was a chess parlor and where he knew several of the chess hustlers there. Chess hustlers were usually very decent fellows, though usually broke as well. Still, there was no harm trying. He saw only one chess hustler he knew, a fellow named Archibald, whom everyone called Harry. Harry explained that he would have been only too delighted to give Mullaney fifty dollars if he had fifty dollars. But the chess-hustling business was very bad these days, what with smart-assed youngsters from the High School of Science coming downtown and playing amateurs for free, so what could he do? Mullaney sympathized and then suggested that he play his knight to queen four, thereby trapping

Black's rook, for which Harry thanked him—then played the knight and lost it.

So that was when Mullaney went downtown again to Fourteenth Street, and asked Hijo as nice as could be for fifty tiny little dollar bills, and Hijo threw him down the steps, Oh you dirty rat, I'll get you for this, he thought, feeling like James Cagney again. Under the influence, he winked at a nineteen-year-old girl and said, "Hello, Sweetie," as she went by in a huff, and then shrugged and thought what a beautiful day it was anyway, even if you had a hot nag named Jawbone, itching to be bet, and couldn't raise the money from any of your so-called friends, especially Hijo at whose poolhall he had spent perhaps a hundred thousand dollars in the past year, well at least a *hundred* dollars anyway. And whom he had taught to speak English, though it hadn't helped much when Hijo tossed him down the stairs, "And *estay* out!" he had yelled, reverting to type, you can take a boy out of Vega Baja.

The thought of Jawbone waiting to be bet, and the Biblical association with Samson made him think again of his own aching ass and the way he had bounced along on each of those thirty-seven steps, more than that even, he had stopped counting after he hit his forehead on number thirty-eight, one more and he could have made a Hitchcock movie. He was beginning to discover all sorts of little aches and bruises now that he was out in the warm spring sunshine. If I only had some hospitalization insurance, he thought, I could collect on it, and then put the money down on Jawbone. The trouble is they take a long time to pay off on those hospitalization bets, and besides I don't have any insurance. What I do have is twenty cents in my pocket, I wonder if anybody I know will be out at the track. I can risk the twenty cents and take the ride out, there's sure to be somebody there I know. I can stand outside the entrance—bound to run into *somebody* out there—and explain that this is really a sizzler of a tip, build it up a little, say I got it from the owner of a big stable down in Kentucky, instead of a small dice player with family connections, maybe promote the price of admission plus a small stake besides. It might be worth the risk. Fifty bucks or so on the nose of a horse which on the morning line was twenty to one, that's a thousand bucks, even if the odds don't climb, which they usually do on a longshot.

He was standing on the corner of Fourteenth Street and Fourth Avenue, trying to decide whether he should buy himself a couple of candy bars or a token instead, when the black Cadillac limousine pulled to the curb. He backed away from the curb at once because he had the sudden feeling that this was the President of the United States pulling up, that the doors would open and a few Secret Service men would emerge, and then the President himself would step out and go across the street to S. Klein, Always on the Square, to buy himself a ten-gallon hat that was on sale, maybe *several* ten-gallon hats to give away to Persian ministers of state. He was convinced this would be the President. He was very surprised when only a gentleman with a beard got out of the car, even though the gentleman looked like someone in very high diplomatic circles, not the President of course, and not even an *American* diplomat, but nonetheless a very bigwig indeed. Mullaney stepped aside to give the bearded gentleman room to pass, but the gentleman stopped alongside him instead and said directly into his right ear, "Get in the car."

For a moment, Mullaney thought he had also somehow injured his hearing on the trip down from the poolhall, but the bearded gentleman repeated the words again, "Get in the car," with a foreign accent Mullaney could not place. Only this time he pushed something into Mullaney's side, and Mullaney knew it wasn't a pipe. He had once been held up in Harlem after a crap game, and he knew the feel of a revolver against his ribs, and whereas this probably wasn't an American-make gun, considering who was holding it, it nonetheless had the feel of a very hefty weapon that could put several holes in a fellow if he wasn't too careful. So Mullaney said, "As a matter of fact, I was just thinking about getting into that car, sir," and immediately got in. The man with the beard got in after him and closed the door. The driver pulled the big machine away from the curb.

"Take me out to Aqueduct," Mullaney said jokingly, "and then you may have the rest of the afternoon off," but no one laughed.

"What kind of pistol is that?" Mullaney asked conversationally.

"It's a Luger. Shut up."

"Are you a spy?"

"Shut up."

"I'd like to know where we're going," Mullaney demanded.

"We're going to Kennedy International Airport," the man with the beard said.

"I'd rather go to Aqueduct," Mullaney said. "In fact, if you're interested in parlaying fifty bucks into a small fortune . . . "

"Shut up," the man said.

"You speak English very well for a spy," Mullaney said.

"He thinks we're spies," the man with the beard said to the driver, who was bald.

"Ha!" the driver said.

"Everyone thinks everyone is a spy," the man with the beard said.

"Ha!" the driver said again.

"Why are we going to Kennedy?" Mullaney asked.

"To put you on a plane to Rome," the man with the beard said.

They were heading through the Midtown Tunnel now, certainly enough on their way to the Long Island parkways and Kennedy Airport. First you, Hijo, you dirty rat, Mullaney thought, and then your two friends. This is Andrew Mullaney you're fooling around with here, what do you think?

"Do you know who I am?" he asked.

"No."

"I mean, you don't think I'm somebody else, do you?"

"We don't know who you are, and we don't think you're somebody else."

"My point is, I think you gentlemen are making a mistake of some kind . . . "

"There is no mistake."

". . . in that I'm Andrew Mullaney, and not whoever you think I am."

"We don't care who you are."

"My uncle is a judge," Mullaney lied.

"Ha!" the driver said.

It occurred to Mullaney that perhaps this was all some sort of elaborate joke perpetrated by one of his many friends about town. Knowing he was desperate for a little cash, they had got together to pretend they would not lend him the money, and then had hired a pair of Actors Equity members and a Carey Cadillac to take him out to Aqueduct (wasn't the race track, after all, on the way to Kennedy?), whereupon they would let him out of the car, shout April Fool! and present him with perhaps five hundred dollars in crisp new bills to lay on Jawbone's nose. The theory had possibilities, in spite of the fact that this was April fourteenth, some two weeks past All Fools' Day. But then, some of his friends couldn't even give you the right time of day, so how were they to know the exact date? He was beginning to enjoy the joke. He sat back against the cushioned seat.

"I think you guys should know," he said, going along with the gag, "that I don't have a passport with me."

"You don't?" the driver said.

"That's right," he said, thinking Got you, huh, Baldy? "Not only don't I have one *with* me, but I don't have one at *all* because I've never been outside of these United States."

"You won't need a passport," the man with the beard said.

"Then suppose you tell me how I'm going to get into Italy without a passport?"

"In a coffin," the man with the beard said, and somehow all the fun went out of everything right then.

The stonecutter's establishment was adjacent to the cemetery. An angry April wind, absent in Manhattan, sent eddies of lingering fallen leaves across a gravel path leading to a clapboard building. The path was lined with marble headpieces, some of them blank, some of them chiseled, one of them announcing in large letters across its black marble face IN LOVING MEMORY OF MARTIN CALLAHAN, LOVING HUSBAND, FATHER, GRANDFATHER, 1896–1967, Mullaney shuddered at the thought.

They had parked the limousine behind what appeared to be a bigger black hearse than Abraham Feinstein had been blessed with at his funeral. Feinstein had been the king of the Bronx blackjack players; Mullaney would always remember his funeral fondly. He wanted to tell the bearded gentleman that it wasn't really necessary to provide anything as ostentatious as Feinstein's funeral had been; Mullaney was, after all, just a simple horse-player. A plain pine box would suffice, a small headstone stating simply: MULLANEY. But the bearded gentleman again prodded him with the Luger and urged him along the gravel path to the cottage that was the stonecutter's office. Three men were waiting inside. One was obviously the owner of the establishment because he asked, as soon as they entered, whether any of them would care for a bit of schnapps. The bearded gentleman said No, they had business to attend to, there was no time for schnapps when business was at hand. The other two men who had been in the office when they arrived looked at Mullaney and one of them said, "Gouda, this is not the corpse."

"I know," the bearded gentleman answered. So he is Gouda, Mullaney thought, and winced when Gouda said, "But he will make a fine substitute corpse."

"Where is the original corpse?" the other man said. He was wearing a tweed jacket with leather elbow patches on the sleeves. He looked very much like a country squire from Wales.

"The original corpse jumped out of the car on Fourteenth Street," Gouda said. He was a man of excellent wit, Mullaney decided, even though his brown eyes were set rather too close to his nose. "O'Brien, there is no problem," he continued. "This gentleman will make a fine corpse."

O'Brien, who was the man with the leather elbow patches, studied Mullaney with too morbid interest. Mullaney, deciding this was the time to voice his own sentiments on the subject, said, "Gentlemen, *I* don't think I will make a fine corpse."

"You will make a fine corpse," Gouda insisted.

"Seriously, gentlemen," he said, "I can think of a hundred other people who would make finer corpses. I can, in fact, think of three people I contacted only today on a small financial matter who would make excellent corpses indeed."

"He's too tall," O'Brien said.

"That's right, I'm too tall," Mullaney agreed. "Besides, my uncle is a judge."

"Would anyone care for some schnapps?" the stonecutter said.

The third man who had been present when they arrived had so far said nothing. He sat on a corner of the stonecutter's desk, nattily dressed in a dark-blue suit, his silk-rep tie held by a tiny tietack, the letter K in gold. He kept staring at Mullaney, but he said nothing. Mullaney reasoned immediately that he was the Boss.

"What do you think, Boss?" O'Brien said, turning to him.

"He'll do," K said.

He spoke in a very low voice, all bosses speak in low voices. All bosses look like K, Mullaney thought, small and dapper and narrow as a stiletto, with an initial tietack, and cold blue eyes and hair going slightly thin, combed to the side over the encroaching baldness, all bosses look exactly like K.

"Suppose his uncle really *is* a judge?" O'Brien said.

"His uncle is not a judge," K said.

"He looks as if his uncle *could* be a judge or at least an alderman."

"That's right," Mullaney said.

"In fact, how do we know he *himself* isn't a judge or an alderman or an off-duty detective?"

"That's right," Mullaney said, "how do you know?"

"Do you realize what kind of trouble we'll be in if we've accidentally picked up somebody important?"

"Yes, consider that," Mullaney said.

K considered it, studying Mullaney thoughtfully. At last, he said, "He is nobody important."

"I beg your pardon," Mullaney said, offended.

"In any case," O'Brien said, "he's too tall."

"For the coffin?" Gouda asked, and Mullaney shuddered again.

"No, for the suit."

"We can alter the suit."

"I'm a very difficult person to fit," Mullaney said. "Gentlemen, seriously, I don't want you to go to any trouble on my part. If the suit won't fit me . . ."

"It'll fit him," K said in his very low voice.

"He'll split all the seams."

"It's only until he gets to Rome."

"You shouldn't have let the original corpse get away," O'Brien said to Gouda. "The suit was measured to order for him."

"He jumped out of the car," Gouda said, and spread his hands helplessly. "Could I chase him down Fourteenth Street? With a plane ready to take off?" He shrugged. "We grabbed the first person we saw." He appraised Mullaney, and then said, "Besides, I think he'll make a fine corpse."

"You could have picked someone shorter," O'Brien said petulantly.

"There were no short people on Fourteenth Street," Gouda said. "I *would* like some schnapps, after all."

"There's no time for schnapps," K said.

"That's right," Gouda instantly agreed, "there's no time for schnapps. Where's the suit, O'Brien?"

"Get the suit," O'Brien said to the man who had offered the schnapps. The man obediently went into the other room, but over his shoulder he called, "It won't fit."

The other men sat waiting for him to come back. The bald-headed driver was cleaning his fingernails with a long knife, What a dreadful stereotype, Mullaney thought. "What's your name?" he asked him.

"Peter," the driver answered, without looking up from his nails.

"Pleased to meet you."

The driver nodded as though he felt it wasteful to exchange courtesies with someone who would soon be dead.

"Listen," Mullaney said to K, "I really would *not* like to become a corpse."

"You have no choice," K said. "*We* have no choice, therefore *you* have no choice." It sounded very logical. Mullaney admired the logic but not the sentiment.

"Still," he said, "I'm only thirty-seven years old," lying by two years. Almost three years.

"Some people get hit by automobiles when they're only little kids," Peter said, still cleaning his nails. "Think of them."

"I sympathize with them," Mullaney said, "but I myself had hoped to live to a ripe old age."

"Hopes are dainty things ofttimes shattered," K said, as if he were quoting from something, Mullaney couldn't imagine what.

The stonecutter came back into the room with a black suit on a hanger. "I left the shirt," he said. "The shirt would *definitely* not fit him. What size shirt do you wear?" he asked Mullaney.

"Fifteen," Mullaney said. "Five sleeve."

"He can wear his own shirt," K said.

"I'd like to wear my own suit, too," Mullaney said, "if that's all right with you."

"That is *not* all right with us," K said.

"In fact," Mullaney went on, "I'd like to go home right now, or better still, I'd like to go to Aqueduct. If you gentlemen are interested, I have a very hot tip on a horse called . . ."

"He'll wear his own shirt," K said.

"A *yellow* shirt?" O'Brien asked, offended.

"It's not yellow," K said. "What color is that shirt?" he asked Mullaney.

"Jasmine."

"It's jasmine," K said.

"It looks yellow."

"No, it's jasmine," Mullaney said.

"Put on the suit," K advised.

"Gentlemen . . ."

"Put it on," Gouda said, and made a faintly menacing gesture with the Luger.

Mullaney accepted the suit from O'Brien. "Where shall I change?" he asked.

"Here," Gouda said.

He hoped he was wearing clean underwear; his mother had always cautioned him about wearing clean underwear and carrying a clean handkerchief. He took off his pants, feeling the sharpness of the keen April wind that swept over the marble stones in the courtyard and seeped through the crack under the door.

"He's got polka-dot undershorts," Peter said, and made his short laughlike sound. "A corpse with polka-dot undershorts, that's a hot one."

The pants were too short and too tight. Mullaney could not button them at the waist.

"Just zip them up as far as they'll go," K said, "that'll be fine."

"They'll fall down," Mullaney said, transferring his twenty-cent fortune from his own pants to the ones he was now wearing.

"You'll be lying in a coffin, they won't fall down," O'Brien said, and handed him the suit jacket.

The jacket was made of the same fine black cloth as the trousers, but was lined and therefore substantially heavier. There were three thick black buttons on the front, each about the size of a penny, and four smaller black buttons on each sleeve. The buttons resembled mushroom caps, though not rounded, their tops and edges faceted instead, a very fancy jacket indeed, if a trifle too tight. He pulled it closed across his chest and belly, and then forced the middle button through its corresponding button-hole. The shoulders were far too narrow, the armholes pinched, he let out his breath and said, "It's too tight."

"Perfect," K said.

"What's the lining made of?" Mullaney asked. "It rustles."

"It's silk," O'Brien said, and glanced at K.

"It makes a nice whispering rustle," Mullaney said.

"Those are angels' wings," Peter said, and again gave his imitation of a laugh. The other men laughed with him—all but Gouda, who, it seemed to Mullaney, had suddenly become very nervous and pale.

"Well," Gouda said, "let's get on with it, there isn't much time."

"Put him in the coffin," K said.

"Look," Mullaney protested, "I'm a married man," which was not exactly the truth, since he had been divorced a year ago.

"We will send your wife a floral wreath," Gouda said.

"I have two children." This was an absolute lie. He and Irene had never had any children at all.

"That's unfortunate," K said. "But ofttimes even little babes must untowardly suffer," again making it sound like a quote which Mullaney did not recognize.

"I'm a respected professor at City College," Mullaney said, which was also pretty close to the truth since he used to be an encyclopedia salesman. "I can assure you I'll be sorely missed."

"You won't be missed at all," Gouda said, which made no sense.

Somebody hit him on the back of the head, Peter he supposed, the dirty rat.

2. KRUGER

The stench was definitely chloroform.

His father had lied to him at the age of six, telling him he was going to get lots of ice cream after the tonsil operation, but neglecting to mention that chloroform was the vilest-smelling of anesthetics. He would never forget that odor, and there were definitely traces of it in the coffin now. He supposed, of course, that he should be grateful he was alive, if indeed he was alive. He certainly felt alive. He seemed to be breathing, albeit with difficulty because of the tight pants and jacket; he noticed that someone had left the coffin lid open perhaps an inch or so, very thoughtful because otherwise he might have suffocated. But then, he had known they weren't going to kill him because it would have been senseless and also a trifle wasteful to knock a man out if you were going to kill him. In the two seconds it took for everything to go black (everything actually went a sort of mauve, to be honest) he remembered realizing with soaring joy that they were not going to kill him, and then he fell to the floor.

Aside from the aroma of chloroform, the coffin was a very nice one indeed, lined with silk he could feel but not see since it was very dark in there even with the lid partly opened, roomy and quite comfortable. All in all, even though he wasn't dead, he had to admit they had given him a coffin every bit as nice as Feinstein's. In fact, and this was probably only pride of ownership, he had the feeling his coffin was even a little nicer than Feinstein's. He did not know whether or not he was still on the airplane to Rome because he didn't know how long he had been unconscious. He felt no sensation of movement, but maybe that was due to the comfortable padding of the coffin. He wondered why the original corpse had jumped out of the limousine on Fourteenth Street, and he also wondered who all those people in the stonecutter's cottage had been, people of taste no doubt, witness the fine comfortable coffin and the beautifully tailored suit.

It was very quiet in the coffin.

He began to like being there. It afforded him the opportunity for a little contemplation, a luxury that had been denied him from the moment he had first laid a bet on the trotters at Yonkers. That was two years ago and, worse luck, he had won a hundred dollars. Well, all water under the bridge, he thought. I would not be on my way to Rome right now (or already there, for all I know) if I weren't a horseplayer who'd been thrown down the stairs by Hijo, standing on the corner opposite S. Klein, Always on the Square. I would not be here right now if I were not Andrew Mullaney himself, which is after all the only thing to be, and a very nice thing to be when you own a comfortable coffin like this one. He was willing to bet not many people were blessed with such fine coffins, Irene should only see him now.

Since he had a lot of time on his hands and also a nice place for contemplation, he began thinking about Irene in earnest, and discovered as he always did that the image of her never varied. They had known each other for two years before getting married, and then had lived together in wedded harmony (he supposed) for an additional seven years before the divorce a year ago February; all in all, a good long time. But he always thought of her as she had looked when they met at the dance given by the Sons of Erin on Fordham Road, long red hair and sparkling green eyes, a saucy grin on her mouth, the absolute stereotype of every Irish girl whose skirts had ever been raised in a Dublin pub.

He thought how nice it would be if Irene were there in the coffin with him, they had never made love in a coffin. They had made love on a midnight train coming down from Quebec, where they had gone for a short vacation, and they had made love in the basement of their building at two A.M. while waiting for the clothes to get done, and they had almost made love on a Ferris wheel once, but Irene was afraid they wouldn't be able to keep track of where they were once they got started and might end up screwing in front of everybody at Palisades. Still, they had almost. Well, almosts don't count, Mullaney thought, a horse who *almost* shows doesn't almost *anything*. Still, they had almost. It would probably be great fun in a coffin, too. Maybe not this coffin, because of the chloroform smell, but take a coffin like Feinstein's, that would be a great coffin in which to make love.

Irene hadn't known Feinstein at all; there were a lot of his friends she never got to meet, primarily because he himself had only met them after the divorce. She probably would have enjoyed someone like Feinstein, though, a truly great blackjack player with a fine sense of humor, and a rare piety, which is how he happened to get killed, but that was another story.

He wondered again if he was in Rome, and decided to try lifting the lid of the coffin, an excellent idea that had not occurred to him before this, so engrossed had he been in recalling Irene and the highly comical sequence of events that had led to

Feinstein's death. He tried the lid now, somewhat regretfully since he was enjoying his retreat very much indeed, and discovered that it moved quite easily. Well, he thought, all good things must come to an end, and he raised the lid completely, and then sat up and looked around the room. There were two windows in the room. There was a dresser against the far wall. Above it there hung a picture of an old man with a beard, probably Sigmund Freud. There was a lamp on the dresser. There was a chair across the room from the dresser. A man was sitting on the chair.

The man looked a lot like an Italian Everett Dirksen. He had white hair like Dirksen, and nice kindly puffy eyes like Dirksen, and his tie was sort of sloppily knotted the way Dirksen's tie sometimes looked on television after a particularly heated session with Chet Huntley. The only thing about him, in fact, that did not look like Senator Dirksen was the gun in his hand, which, if Mullaney was not mistaken, appeared to be a very large American Colt .45 automatic.

"Boo!" he said to the man, thinking he might faint dead away on the floor, the way they do in movies when a coffin opens and there's a live person in it. But Dirksen just looked at him with his kindly puffy eyes, and nodded, as if he had known all along that Mullaney was only unconscious and that he would be waking up sooner or later. Mullaney shrugged. Dirksen got off the chair, went out of the room, and came back a moment later with another man who also looked like Dirksen.

"*È desto, eh?*" the new one said.

"*Si,*" the first one replied. "*A questo momento.*"

"*Va bene,*" the new one said and walked over to the coffin. "Out," he said to Mullaney in English. "Out of the box."

The coffin was resting on two sawhorses. Mullaney climbed out of it with great difficulty, cautiously looping one leg over the rim and then the other, certain he would split the tight pants.

"Where's the money?" one of the men said.

"Are you talking to me?" Mullaney asked.

"Yes. Where's the money?"

"What money?" Mullaney said, and realized instantly he had said the wrong thing. The man who had been talking to him suddenly made a face that indicated to Mullaney Oh are we going to play *that* game, where you pretend you don't know what I'm talking about and where I have to get rough perhaps, when you know very well what money I mean? That was what Mullaney read on his face, and all at once he didn't look at all like Senator Dirksen, neither of them did, they looked instead like people who could possibly get very mean if you didn't tell them where the goddamn money was.

"He doesn't know where the money is, Henry," the first man said.

"He doesn't know where the money is, George," the second man repeated.

They both had rather pained expressions on their twin faces, as if they were distressed by what they now felt they must do. It was obvious that what they now felt they must do was knock him around a little, Roman style. It seemed to him that he had been getting knocked around a little ever since Hijo threw him down the poolhall steps, and he really had no desire to get knocked around any further, in *any* style. At the same time, since he didn't know where the money was, or even which money they were talking about, he couldn't very well tell them what they wanted to know. It all looked hopeless. He decided to ask for the manager.

"Where's Gouda?" he said.

"Gouda is dead," Henry said.

"That's not true. I saw him only a little while ago."

"Was he alive?" George asked.

"Of course he was alive."

"He's dead now," George said.

"How did he die?"

"A terrible highway accident," George said, and looked at his twin.

"Terrible," Henry repeated.

The room was very still. Mullaney cleared his throat. "Well," he said, "I'm certainly sorry to hear that."

"Yes," George agreed. "Where's the money?"

"I don't know," Mullaney said.

"We figured it had to be in the coffin," Henry said.

"Well then maybe it is."

"No. We looked."

"Did you look carefully?"

"Very carefully. We even removed you and put you on the floor," Henry said. "The money is definitely *not* in the coffin."

"So where is it?" George asked.

"I told you. I don't know."

"We'd better take him to Kruger," George said.

"That would be a small man who wears a letter K on his tie, right?" Mullaney said.

"No. He's dead."

"He is?"

"They're all dead," Henry said.

"The accident," George said.

"Terrible," Henry said.

"Take him," George said, and son of a bitch if Henry didn't hit him on the head again.

The nice thing about getting hit on the head, Mullaney thought, is that it hardly hurts at all. It's over so quickly, whap, that you hardly realize it's happening. And while it's happening there are these really rather extraordinary colors that go shooting and bursting and rocketing all over the place, somewhat like a Greenwich Village event, though done with considerably more style. However, the *terrible* thing about getting hit on the head, Mullaney realized as he awakened in a moving automobile, was that whereas it didn't hurt much at the time, it sure as hell hurt a lot afterward.

"Ow," he said, and rubbed the back of his neck, and then

silently added Henry's name to the list of dirty rats who needed getting. "Why'd you do that?" he said.

"To transport you," Henry, who was driving, said.

"If you needed to transport me, all you had to do was ask. I'm a reasonable person, all you had to do was ask."

He didn't know where in Italy they were. They seemed to be coming through a suburban area that looked very much like New Jersey—the outskirts of Rome, no doubt. His head hurt, and he was angry with Henry and not exactly delighted with George, either, who sat silently on the back seat of the big Italian whatever-kind-of-car-it-was, holding a very un-Italian gun in his hand, a .38 Smith & Wesson Detective's Special which his cousins in the Bronx branch of the Mafia had undoubtedly heisted from the body of a good dead cop and then mailed in a candy box to Rome.

"What kind of gun is that?" Mullaney asked.

"A very good one," George said, thereby ending the conversation.

"What kind of car is this?" Mullaney asked Henry.

"Cadillac," Henry replied.

"Pretty fancy," Mullaney said.

He was in a very surly mood, and was beginning to feel highly uncooperative. In a few moments he planned to punch George right in the mouth, take the gun out of his hand, and hit Henry on the back of the head with it, see how *he* liked getting hit on the back of the head. In the meantime, he was resting, gathering his strength. What I'll do, he thought, is kick George in the leg instead. Then when he bends over to grab his shin, I'll throw him on the floor and take his gun away and then give Henry the old one-two right at the back of the head, *pow*, Henry, how do you like *that* little blow to the medulla oblongata? These Roman guys wanted to fool around with Andrew Mullaney, well, maybe they didn't know just who they were fooling around with here. Maybe he ought to inform them he was the only guy in his graduating class at C.C.N.Y. who could do seventy-four pushups, at a time when lots of kids were Communists. Or perhaps they would like to be told that he had once busted a very husky advertising man from Madison Avenue square on the jaw because first he had stated unequivocally that all girls with red hair were extremely passionate (which Irene was, but it was none of his damn business) and second that people who sold encyclopedias for a living were a little bit wrong in the head. Mullaney hit him with a devastating uppercut. And whereas the uppercut didn't exactly knock the advertising man unconscious, it certainly dazed him a little; there were perhaps a dozen witnesses who were willing to corroborate that fact, if Mullaney cared to take the trouble. So perhaps these young Mafiosi here driving him all over the suburbs of Rome did not realize they had got hold of a tiger. Well, he would show them soon enough. In the meantime, he kept marveling at the way American culture had engulfed Europe, billboards advertising American gasolines, signs in English catering to American tourists, ah, where were the glories of ancient Rome? The car was obviously closer to Rome itself now since Mullaney could see lights glowing on the distant horizon. He was pretty excited about the idea of being abroad, even if it had to be in the company of these two hoods taking him to see Kruger (there were bosses all over the world, it seemed). He could not wait to get out of the car and pinch his first Italian girl. He had once seen a movie with Jean Paul Belmondo, where Belmondo leaped out of the car and ran across the Champs Élysées and flipped a girl's dress right up over her head, oh that had been a wild escapade. (Irene hadn't liked it; suppose the poor thing hadn't had any panties on? she asked, practically.) This was before they got divorced, when they still used to go to movies and things together. But he had always remembered that crazy nut Belmondo running across the Champs Élysées, whoops, up go your skirts, dearie! As the lights of Rome came closer and closer, he felt some of the same wild exuberance Belmondo must have known. What he would do was smash old George here right in the *la panza,* and then grab the gun and give Henry such a clunk, oh boy, he could hardly wait. Then he would run out of the car and across the equivalent of the Champs Élysées and the first Italian girl he saw, he would throw her skirts up over her head and then run away laughing. Then he would pinch the next Italian girl he saw, live it up a little, because once they found out he didn't know where the money was, he was a dead duck anyway.

About that money, he thought, and he kept staring at the lights of Rome in the distance and thought how very much alike all big cities looked—but about that money—this city, this Rome, Roma Bella in the distance and fast approaching looked a lot like New York. But about that money, what am I going to tell them when they ask again and start putting bamboo slivers under my fingernails? Man, that Rome there sure looks a lot like New York, Mullaney thought, and then he recognized the toll booths, and realized they were approaching the Lincoln Tunnel.

"What the hell?" he said, startling even George, who he suspected had begun to doze on the back seat.

"What's the matter?" George shouted. "What is it? What is it?"

"Just where are we?" Mullaney demanded. It was one thing to get pushed around, but it was another to be welshed out of a trip to Rome.

"We're on our way to see Kruger," George said. "Stop making noise near the toll booths."

"Is this New Jersey?" Mullaney asked shrewdly.

"This is New Jersey."

"You're not even Italians!" Mullaney shouted.

"We are so!" George said, offended.

"Keep quiet while we go through the booth," Henry said, "or there'll be another terrible highway accident."

He was angry now, oh boy now he was really angry. They had really got his Irish dander up this time, hitting him on the head and giving him such a headache, and then not even shipping him to Rome as they had promised. His anger was unreasoning and uncontrolled. He knew he could not blame either Henry or George for the empty promises the others had made, but neither could he get angry with the others because (as George had pointed out) they were all unfortunately dead. But he was angry nonetheless, an undirected black Irish boiling mad anger that was beginning to give him stomach cramps. In about two minutes flat, as soon as they were past the toll booths (he didn't want any innocent people to get hurt if there was shooting), he was going to erupt into this automobile, rip George's gun in half, wrap it around his head, stuff it down his throat, oh boy, you started up with the wrong fellow this time! They were past the toll booths now and approaching the tunnel itself, the blue-and-white tiled walls, the fluorescent lighting, the cops walking on the narrow ramparts, waving the cars on; Mullaney waited, not wanting to cause a traffic jam in the tunnel when he incapacitated these two cheap gangsters.

There were a great many cars on the road, this was Friday night, the start of the weekend. He could remember too many Friday nights long ago, when he and Irene had been a part of the fun-seeking throng, but he tried to put Irene out of his mind now because somehow thinking of her always made him a little sad, and he didn't want to dissipate the fine glittering edge of his anger, he was going to chop through these hoodlums like a cleaver! But the traffic was dense even when they got out of the tunnel, and he didn't get a chance to make his move until the car stopped outside a brownstone on East Sixty-first, and then he realized they had reached their destination and it was too late to do anything. Besides, by then he wasn't angry anymore.

He got out of the car and thought They're going to ask me about the money again, I'd better think up a good one. He wondered how much money was involved here. Probably a couple of grand, maybe even more, otherwise they wouldn't be making all this fuss. He could feel George's gun in the small of his back as they climbed the steps in front of the building. Across the street, a girl in a green dress laughed at something her boy friend said. Henry rang the bell. An answering buzz sounded, and they went inside.

"Upstairs," George said.

The building was silent. Carpeted steps wound endlessly upward, creaking beneath them as they climbed. A Tiffany lamp, all glistening greens and yellows, hung from the ceiling of the second floor. As Henry walked beneath it, it bathed his head in a Heineken glow, giving him a thoughtful beery look. A flaking mirror in an ornate gold-leaf frame hung on the wall of the third floor. George adjusted his tie as he went past the mirror, and then began whistling tunelessly under his breath as they continued to climb. On the fourth floor, a bench richly upholstered in red velour stood against the wall, just outside a door painted in muted grey. Henry knocked on the door, and then patted his hair into place.

The door opened.

Mullaney caught his breath.

Kruger was a woman.

Into that hallway, she insinuated springtime, peering out at them with a delicately bemused expression on her face, cornflower eyes widening, long blond hair whispering onto her cheek. She might have been a fairy maiden surprised in the garden of an ancient castle, banners and pennoncels fluttering on the fragrant breeze above her. She turned to gaze at Mullaney, pierced him with a poignant look. A curious smile played about her mouth, the secret of her delicious joke erupting, Kruger is a woman, Kruger is a beautiful woman. He had once written sonnets about women like this.

He had once, when he was a boy and still believed in magic, written sonnets about delicate maidens who walked through fields of angel's breath and left behind them dizzying scents that robbed men of their souls. When he'd left Irene a year ago, she had asked (he would never forget the look on her face when she asked, her eyes turned away, the shame of having to ask), "Andy, is there another woman?" And he had replied, "No, Irene, there is no other woman," and had meant it, and yet was being dishonest. The other woman, the woman for whom he had left Irene a year ago, was this Kruger standing in the doorway with her shy inquiring glance, flaxen hair trapped by a velvet ribbon as black as a medieval arch. The other woman was Kruger; the other woman had always been Kruger. She leaned in the doorway. She was wearing a black velvet dress (he knew she would be wearing black velvet), its lace-edged yoke framing ivory collarbones that gently winged toward the hollow of her throat. Her hips were tilted, her belly gently rounded, her legs racing swift and clean to black high-heeled pumps. She leaned in the doorway and stopped his heart.

She was the gamble.

He had tried to explain to Irene, not fully understanding it himself, that what he was about to do was imperative. He had tried to explain that in these goddamn encyclopedias he sold to schools and libraries, there was more about life and living than he could ever hope to experience in a million years. He had tried to show her, for example, how he could open any one of the books, look, let's take BA–BL, just open it at random, and look, well here we are, *Balts, peoples of the East Coast of the Baltic Sea*, have you ever seen the people of the East Coast of the Baltic Sea, Irene? Well, neither have I, that's what I'm trying to tell you, that's what I mean about taking the gamble, honey.

I don't know what you mean, she said.

I mean the gamble, the gamble, he said, beginning to rant a little, he realized, but unable to control himself, I'm talking about taking the gamble, I've got to take the gamble, Irene, I've got to go out there and see for myself.

You don't love me, she said.

I love you, Irene, he said, I love you really honey I do love you, but I've got to take the gamble. I've got to see where it is that everything's happening out there, I've got to find those places I've only read about, I've got to find them. Honey, I've got to live. I'm dying. I'll die. Do you want me to die?

If you leave me, Irene said, yes, I want you to die.

Well, who cares about curses? he had thought. Curses are for old Irish ladies sitting in stone cottages by the sea. He knew for certain that somewhere there were people who consistently won, somewhere there were handsome sun-tanned men who held women like Kruger in their arms and whispered secrets to them and made love to them in the afternoon on foreign beaches, and later played baccarat and yelled *Banco!* and danced until morning and drank pink champagne from satin slippers. He knew these people existed, he knew there was a world out there waiting to be won, and he had set out to win it.

And had lost.

Had lost because Irene had said Yes, I want you to die, and slowly he had died, as surely as Feinstein had died (though that was really comical). He had taken the gamble, had thrown everything to the winds, everything, had been laying his life on the morning line for the past year now, had been clutching it to his chest across poker tables for the past year now, had been rolling it across green felt cloths for the past year now, and had lost, had surely and most certainly lost. This morning, he was down to his last twenty cents and squarely facing his inability to borrow even another nickel in this fair city of New York, and so they had put him in a coffin. He had very definitely lost.

Until now.

Now, this moment, he looked at Kruger standing in the doorway of the apartment and knew he still had a chance, knew by what he read on her face, knew that she was the lady he had set out to find on that February day a year, more than a year ago. He could not breathe; he had never stood this close to a dream before.

And then, because dreams never last too very long, a voice from behind Kruger said, "Is that you, boys?" and he looked past her into the room to see the ugliest, most evil-looking man he had ever seen in his life, and he realized at once that Kruger was not a pretty blond lady after all. Kruger was instead a two-hundred-

and-ten-pound monster who came lumbering toward the doorway in a red silk dressing gown, dirty black fingernails, hair
sticking up on his head and on his chest and growing like weeds
on his thick arms and on the backs of his hands and over his
fingers. *This* is Kruger, he thought, and if you don't tell him
where the money is, he is going to throw you to his crocodiles.
You lose again, Mullaney, he thought, and the girl said, "Do come
in."

They all went into the room.

He could not take his eyes off the girl. He followed her every
movement in terror because he knew that Kruger could bend
steel bars, Kruger could breathe fire, and he did not want Kruger
to see him sneaking glances at the girl. But the girl kept sneaking
glances back at Mullaney, like luck dancing around the edges of a
crap table when the dice are running hot and you can't roll
anything but elevens, dancing and tantalizing, and watching him
with that strange sweet wistful smile, walking as delicately as
though she were in a meadow of mist.

Kruger bit off the end of a cigar, spit it into the fireplace where
a real wood fire was blazing, and said, "Where's the money?"

Always back to that, Mullaney thought. There was a miasma of
evil emanating from Kruger, as strong as the stench of garlic,
wafted across the room, penetrating the woodsmoke smell, thick
and suffocating. Kruger could kill a bug by looking at it, he was
evil, and he was strong, and he was mean, and Mullaney was
afraid of him, and more afraid of him because he could not take
his eyes off the delicate blond girl.

"I don't know where the money is," Mullaney said. "Would you
happen to know who won the fourth race at Aqueduct today?"

"I have no idea who won the fourth race at Aqueduct," Kruger
said.

"Well, I have no idea where the money is," Mullaney said.

"I believe otherwise. I suggest you tell me, sir, or we may be
forced to kill you."

He spoke very well for a man who looked the way he did, his

cultured voice adding somehow to the terrible menace that rose from him like a black cloud from the smokestack of a steel mill, hanging on the air, dropping black particles of soot on Sunday church clothes. He stuck the cigar in his mouth, but did not light it. Mullaney had the feeling he was simply going to swallow it.

The girl was standing near the window, peering down into the street below, except occasionally when she turned to look at Mullaney with that same sad sweet smile on her face. He knew instinctively that she wanted him to save her from the clutches of such as Kruger. She wanted him to start a fight here, knock these fellows around a little, and then take her down to the casino, where he'd put twenty thousand francs on seventeen red and then maybe they'd go running barefoot along the Grande Corniche, that was what she wanted him to do. She wanted him to become what he thought he would become a year ago when he had flown the coop in search of some dizzy kind of freedom, finding nothing but cold dice and losing horses, dead hands and buried luck, finding none of the things he thought he was taking the gamble for, and managing to lose Irene into the bargain, the only thing that had ever mattered in his life until then. Now, here in this room, everything seemed within grasp once again. All he had to do was become a hero. All he had to ask of himself, all he had to expect of himself, was that he become a hero.

"If you kill me," he heard himself say, "you'll never find out where the money is."

"That's true enough," Kruger said.

"I thought you'd be reasonable," Mullaney said, and smiled like a hero.

"Oh, yes, I am a very reasonable man," Kruger said. "I hope you are equally as reasonable, sir, because I think you know how obsessed one can become by the idea of possessing half a million dollars."

"Yes," Mullaney said, and then said, "Half a million dollars?"

"Or didn't you realize it was that much money?"

"No, I didn't realize that, I certainly never realized that," he said, and knew at once that this was it, this was sweet luck keening to him from someplace, half a million dollars, if only he could be a hero. He felt himself tensing, knew instinctively that he would have to call upon every reserve of strength and intelligence he possessed if he was to get out of this room with what he wanted. He had come into this room thinking that all he wanted was to stay alive, but now he knew that he wanted the blonde as well, not to mention the money.

He suddenly knew where it was.

He knew with an intensity bordering on clairvoyance exactly where the money was. He almost grinned at his own ridiculously marvelous perception, he knew where the goddamn money was, he actually knew where it was.

"I know where the money is," he said aloud, surprised when he heard the words.

"Yes, I realize that, sir," Kruger said.

"And I'll be happy to get it for you."

"Good."

"But . . ." He hesitated. Kruger stood facing him across the room, the only other player in the game. Mullaney was holding half a million aces, half a million lovely crisp rustling American dollar bills, warm and safe and snug, the best hand he'd ever held in his life. He almost burst out laughing. The girl, leaning against the window drapes, watched him silently, anticipating his opening bet.

"I'd have to go for it alone," Mullaney said.

"Out of the question," Kruger answered, calling and raising.

"Then we'd better forget it."

"No, we won't forget it," Kruger said. "George," he said, and George moved a step closer to Mullaney.

"That won't help you a bit," Mullaney said.

"Perhaps not. I have a feeling, however, that it will help *you* even less."

"Well, if you want to get clever," Mullaney said, and then could think of nothing further to say. George was very close now.

The blued steel of the revolver glinted in the firelight. He flipped the barrel of the gun up so that the butt was in striking position. He smiled pleasantly, lots of people smile pleasantly before they commit mayhem, Mullaney reflected.

"Sir?" Kruger said.

"Just touch me with that gun . . ." Mullaney said.

"You realize, do you not . . ."

". . . just *touch* me with it, and . . ."

". . . that we can very easily drop you in the Hudson River . . ."

"I realize that."

". . . in little pieces?"

"Little pieces, big pieces," Mullaney said, and shrugged.

"So I suggest you tell me where the money is. *Now.*"

"And I suggest you bet your jacks," Mullaney said. "*Now.*"

"I beg your pardon?"

"Or get out of the game."

Kruger stared at him.

"Well?" Mullaney said.

Kruger was silent for a long time. Then he sighed and said, "How far is it?"

"How far is what?"

"Where the money is."

"It's near," Mullaney said.

"Take George with you," Kruger suggested.

"Out of the question."

"Henry then?"

"Neither of them. I go alone."

"Why?"

"Put yourself in my position," Mullaney said, not knowing what the hell he was talking about, "I need protection. I wouldn't mind giving up five hundred thousand dollars," —like fun I wouldn't, he thought—"after all, that's only money. But you can't ask me to risk my life getting it because what's the difference between that and getting killed right here in this room?" still not knowing what he was talking about, but realizing he was making sense because the men were studying him soberly and weighing his words, and the girl was glancing at him in approval and smiling encouragingly from where she stood in black against the red drapes. "If either George or Henry are recognized, I don't think I have to tell you what could happen to me," Mullaney said, not having the faintest idea what could happen to him especially since K and Gouda and the others were now dead, but figuring it never hurt to throw in dire predictions when you were dealing with people who had the power to make those predictions come true. "Think of my position," he said.

"He has a point," Kruger said. He kept studying Mullaney. "But think of *my* position," he said reasonably. "What guarantee do I have that you'll come back?"

"No guarantee at all. Except my word," Mullaney said.

Kruger coughed politely. "I'm afraid that's not enough for me," he said.

"Well, what can I tell you?" Mullaney said, and shrugged. Come on, Kruger, he thought, you are walking right into the sucker bet, it's sitting right here waiting for you, all you've got to do is come a wee bit closer, I'm going to let you pick up the bet all by yourself, come on, baby, come on.

"No," Kruger said. "I don't like the odds."

"They're the only odds in this game."

"You're forgetting that I can *end* this game whenever I choose."

"In which case you lose all the marbles."

"I'd be an idiot to let you out of here alone."

"You'd be a bigger idiot to throw away half a million dollars."

"If I let you go, I may be doing both."

"Not if I gave you my word."

"Please," Kruger said politely, and then began pacing before the fireplace, his huge hands clasped behind his back. Mullaney kept waiting for him to have the sudden inspiration he hoped he would have had long before now, but Kruger only kept pacing back and forth, thinking. "Suppose *I* go with you?" he suggested at last.

"No."

"Not too many people know me," Kruger said.

"No, I couldn't take that chance," Mullaney said, waiting for lightning to strike, wondering how many permutations and combinations Kruger had to examine before he fell over the sucker bet that was right there at his very feet.

"*I* know!" Kruger said, and turned from the fireplace. Mullaney held his breath. "The girl," Kruger said. "You'll take the girl with you."

It's about time, Mullaney thought. "Absolutely not," he said.

"Why not?" Kruger asked, frowning.

"That's the same thing as taking you or any of the others."

"No," Kruger said. "No, it isn't. I beg your pardon, but it isn't. The girl is not known."

"I'm sorry," Mullaney said. "I hate to be difficult, but either I go alone, or I don't go at all."

"Either you take the girl with you," Kruger said, looming large and hairy and black and menacing and shooting up cinders and sparks from the evil smokestack that he was, "or you leave here in a coffin."

"I arrived in a coffin," Mullaney answered, "so I might just as well leave in one."

"All right, George," Kruger said, "kill him."

"All right," Mullaney said, "I'll take the girl with me."

"Good. George, get her a gun."

George went to a cabinet against the wall, opened the top drawer, and removed from it a small pearl-handled .22. He showed the gun to the girl and said, "Do you know how to use this?"

The girl nodded, then took the gun and put it into her purse.

"If he does not go directly for the money," Kruger said, "shoot him."

The girl nodded.

"If he tries to contact either the others or the police," Kruger said, "shoot him."

The girl nodded.

"If he gets the money, and then refuses to come back here," Kruger said, "shoot him."

The girl nodded.

"Very well, go." They started for the door, and Kruger said, "No, wait." He walked very close to where Mullaney was standing, and said, "I hope you're not lying to me, sir. I hope you really know where that money is."

"I really know where that money is," Mullaney said, because he really did know.

"Very well. See that you bring it back. We'll get you if you don't, you know."

"I know," Mullaney said.

Kruger opened the door. Mullaney and the girl stepped into the hallway and the door closed behind them.

"Hello, honey," the girl whispered, and grinned.

3. MERILEE

It was nine o'clock on a Friday night, and all the gamblers were out.

Mullaney and the girl came down into the overspill uptown throng. He felt very much like a college freshman pledging for a fraternity, his trousers perhaps six inches too short, the cuffs riding high on his shins, his jacket sleeves reaching midway up his forearm, the jacket itself stretching tight to bursting across his shoulders, the big black buttons barely holding, the jasmine shirt ludicrously incongruous with the solemn burial garments. The fraternity brothers had given him the most beautiful girl in the world to carry on his arm and then had sent him into the clamor of Friday-night New York to get half a million dollars. There was no question that he already possessed both the money and the girl, so the secret now was to prolong this delicious suspense, to put off the moment of releasing—yes, that was the proper word—first the money, then the girl and himself. In the meantime, they walked idly down the street, he in his Ichabod Crane clothes, and she in her demure black velvet, laced at the throat, holding his arm with an intimate delicate-fingered knowledge—she too seemed willing to wait.

The gamblers, or more accurately the losers, were everywhere around them. They had saved their nickels and dimes to build their Friday-night stake, and now they were betting it on a single roll of the dice, the sucker bet supreme, a bigger sucker bet than even Kruger had laid. They hoped to win (he supposed) all the things *he* had hoped to win when he stepped out a year ago, but quicker and with a more dizzying sense of triumph, all of it on a single roll. Laughter awaited on the opposite side of that roll, dazzling good looks and keen intelligence, wealth unimaginable, luxury undreamt. So they all marched in their Robert Hall suits, and their heads swam with visions of cashmere lined with silk, expensive motor cars purring gently, Playmates of the Month spreading eager legs, the soft interiors of women they thought they had never known the likes of, all waiting, all beckoning, all belonging to the conqueror. Just a single winning roll and power would be theirs, lightning bolts to hurl, orgasms to waste, laughter to recklessly spend.

Mullaney had already won, had won in that apartment when he'd bluffed Kruger's hand. The cash was his, as was the girl, whenever he wanted them. Everybody else was a loser.

"Do you have any money?" he asked the girl.

"No," she said, and they both laughed.

"I have half a million dollars," he said.

"Oh I *know* you do, baby."

"Do you know where it is?"

"No, where is it?" she said, and laughed.

"What's your name?" he asked.

"First tell me where the money is."

"No. First tell me your name."

"Merilee," she said.

"That's very close to *my* name," he said, "which is Mullaney."

"That's very close indeed," the girl said.

"We are going to be very close indeed, Merilee."

"Oh yes indeed," she said, "we are going to be very close indeed."

"We're going to make love on a bed of five hundred thousand dollars. Have you ever made love on such a bed?"

"No, but it sounds like enormous fun," she said. "Where is it?"

"Your ass will turn green," Mullaney said, and laughed.

"Oh yes indeed it will. All that money will rub off on it, and I will absolutely adore the color of it. Where is it?"

"I wonder if it's in tens, or hundreds, or thousands," Mullaney said.

"Don't you know?"

"I won't know until I see it. I have a feeling, however, that it's in largish bills."

"A feeling?"

"Yes," he said, "a warm, enveloping feeling," and grinned at his inside joke.

"Do you know something?" she said.

"What?"

"We're being followed. No, don't look."

"How do you know?"

"I know. George and Henry are following us."

The girl was right; the twins were behind them. Mullaney caught a quick glimpse of them as he took her arm and led her onto Madison Avenue, and then spotted them again crossing the street near the IBM showroom on Fifty-seventh. He toyed with the idea of pulling something unexpected on the twins, playing some sort of fantastic trick that would leave them bewildered and lost, but he couldn't think of anything clever enough or devastating enough. So he simply continued walking up Fifty-seventh Street, toward Fifth Avenue, and then turned left on Fifth, all the while trying to think of a really clever gimmick he could pull on Henry and George, who were right there behind him, ambling along the avenue like a double vision of Friday-night delight, dirty rats.

Mullaney's poverty of invention was beginning to depress him. It seemed to him that someone in possession of half a million cool American dollars to warm the cockles of his heart, not to mention a rather beautiful young lady on his arm—

"How old are you?" he asked suddenly.

"Twenty-two," she said. "How old are you?"

"Thirty-one," he lied.

"That's a lie," she said.

"Right, I'm really thirty-three."

"Oh boy, what a liar," the girl said.

"I'll be forty years old in August," Mullaney said.

"You look older," the girl said.

"That's because I have half a million dollars. That kind of money can give a person worry lines."

"Oh yes indeed I'm sure," the girl said.

—someone in possession of such wealth and beauty and, yes, youth (she was only twenty-two, what a marvelous age to climb onto and into, all springtime taut and fresh), someone who owned all these things after a year of steady downhill plodding, well hell it just seemed impossible that someone so richly endowed could not think of a single solitary brilliant trick to shake those twins behind him.

"Listen," he said, "are you game?"

"I am game for anything, baby."

"No matter what?"

"Anything."

"Would you, for example, do it on a Ferris wheel?"

"I would, for example, do it on a roller coaster," she said.

"Then, sweetheart, let's *go!*" he said, and he grabbed her hand

and began running down Fifth Avenue. He glanced quickly over his shoulder and saw that he had taken the twins by surprise. The trick now was to maintain that element of surprise, lead them a merry chase around this fair Friday-night city, and then unleash all those crisp little mothers from where they were nestling so snug and warm, lay his shy blond beauty down upon the bills, hump her royally against a backdrop of cash, hang singles from her nipples, fivers on her navel, deck her halls with sawbucks and centuries, set her aglow with green like an April evening Christmas tree, humping her all the while, money and sex, winner take all, but maintain the element of surprise.

The first surprise was the Mercedes-Benz that stopped for a light on the corner of Fifty-fifth and Fifth. Mullaney pulled open the back door and shoved the girl onto the leather seat. To the driver, he shouted, "Get moving."

"Crazy," the driver said cheerfully, and stepped on the gas. "Did you just rob a bank?"

"Don't tell him," the girl said, and giggled.

"Lady, you are gorgeous," the driver said. "Where to?"

"Anywhere away from here," Mullaney said.

"Crazy," the driver said. "Let's go to Philadelphia."

"*Except* Philadelphia," the girl said.

"You know the Philadelphia jokes, huh?"

"Every one of them."

"None of them are jokes."

"I know."

"Lady, you are gorgeous," the driver said.

"I do it on roller coasters," the girl said, and giggled again.

"Front or back seat? There's a big difference."

"They're behind us," Mullaney said suddenly.

"Who?"

"Henry and George."

"Don't believe I know them," the driver said thoughtfully.

"They're killers," the girl said.

"Yeah?"

"Oh yes indeed."

"Lady, you are gorgeous."

"Let us out on the next corner," Mullaney said.

"Let you *out?* You just got *in!*"

"Surprises," Mullaney said, "that's the secret."

"Of what?" the driver asked, but they were already out of the car. Behind them, Mullaney could see the twins' cab pulling to the curb.

"Run!" he shouted to Merilee, and they began running again, laughing hysterically. He was suddenly afraid that the jacket would split up the middle. He tried to keep his shoulders back, to avoid putting a strain on the seam, but all the while he was certain the jacket would split.

"They're still with us," Merilee shouted. "Oh my this is fun!"

"We'll have to think of something clever," he said.

"Good," she said, "think of something clever."

"And unexpected."

"Oh yes unexpected, I *love* the unexpected!"

"Let's head for your apartment!" he said.

"Clever, clever," she said, "they'd *never* expect us to go there."

"Right!"

"Because I live with Kruger, you see."

"Oh."

"Yes."

They had reached Sixth Avenue now and he paused for just a moment on the corner, holding her hand, wondering whether to proceed directly west toward the honkytonk movie theaters or to turn uptown toward the camera stores and hardware stores and Howard Johnson's beckoning in the distance and beyond that Central Park and beyond that—

"Hurry!" she said.

"Yes, yes."

"They're coming!"

"Yes!"

"Can't we go to your place?"

"No," he said.

"Why not?"

"My landlady locked me out of it yesterday."

"For God's sake, hurry!" she shouted.

"The unexpected!" he said, and he tugged her hand and reversed direction and ran back toward Henry and George who were racing up toward the corner. There were a lot of people on the corner of Sixth Avenue and Forty-second Street, but not many of them paid too much attention to Mullaney and the girl, or even to Henry and George, who stopped dead in their tracks and then whirled about when they realized their quarry was heading in the opposite direction. Neither of the twins was exactly slim or svelte, and they were puffing hard and desperately out of breath as they once more took up the chase. Mullaney had another brilliant idea, which he planned to spring if things got too tight, and that was to run up Fifth Avenue again to the Doubleday's on Fifty-seventh Street, where he would lock the twins into one of the listening booths with a Barbra Streisand LP in stereo. But that was his ace in the hole, and he planned to play it only if the Public Library had already closed, which he hoped against hope it hadn't. He reasoned (correctly, he hoped) that the twins would never expect them to run into the Public Library, because who in his right mind would go into the Public Library on a Friday night?

"You're crazy," the girl said. "I love you you're so crazy."

He took a last look over his shoulder before running across the street, dodging traffic and coming once again onto Fifth Avenue. Pulling the girl along with him, he raced up the wide marble front steps of the library, past the MGM lions, and then ducked onto the footpath leading to the side entrance, and through the revolving doors and into the high hallowed marbled corridors, wishing he had a nickel for every encyclopedia he had sold to libraries all over the country (in fact he had once had even *more* than a nickel for every encyclopedia he'd sold). He caught from the corner of his eye a sign telling him the library closed at ten, and then saw the huge wall clock telling him it was now nine thirty-seven, which meant he had exactly twenty-three minutes to put his hands on the money, perhaps less if George and Henry found them first. He was fairly familiar with libraries, though not this one, and he knew that all libraries had what they called stacks, which was where they piled up all the books. This being one of the largest libraries in the world, he assumed it would have stacks all over the place, so he kept opening oak-paneled doors all along the corridor, looking into rooms containing learned old men reading books about birds, and finally coming upon a door that was marked STAFF ONLY, figuring this door would surely open upon the privacy of dusty stacks, convinced that it would, and surprised when instead it opened on a cluttered office with a pince-nezed old lady sitting behind a desk, "Excuse us," he said, "we're looking for the stacks."

The stacks, he thought, would be symbolically correct for unleashing those stacks of bills, which he had been very close to all along, but which he was now very much closer to, actually within touching distance of, actually within finger-tingling stroking distance of, five hundred thousand dollars' worth of unmitigated loot. The girl's hand was sweating in his own as they went rapidly down the marble corridor, as if she too sensed that he was about to unlock that avalanche of cash, turn her backside green with it as he had promised, allow her to wallow in all that filthy lucre. He spotted another door marked PERSONNEL and tried it, but it was locked, so he kept running down the corridor with the girl's sweaty hand in his own, the smell of money enveloping both of them, trying doors, waiting for the door that would open to their touch, open upon rows and rows of dusty books in soaring stacks behind which they would allow the bills to trickle through their fingers, floating noiselessly on the silent air, if only Henry and George did not get to them first.

And then, unexpectedly (the only way he was beginning to expect), one of the doors opened on more books than he had ever seen in his life, stacked from floor to ceiling in metal racks stretching as far as the eye could see. He closed the door behind them, and then locked it. Taking her hand, he led her between the columns of books, wondering if any of them were the very encyclopedias he used to sell before he took the gamble, the gamble which was now to pay off in half a million lovely dollar bills.

"Oh my," the girl said, "but it's spooky in here."

"Shhh," he said, and clung tightly to her sweating hand. In the distance, he could hear footsteps, a library page running to get another book on birds for one of the learned old gentlemen reading in one of the wood-paneled rooms. He led her away from the footsteps, led her deeper and deeper into the labyrinth of books, doubting he would ever be able to find his way out again, but not caring because the money smell hung heavy on the air now, mingling with the musty aroma of old books. The patter of feet disappeared in the distance. There was suddenly a cul-de-sac as private as a woodland copse, books stacked on every side of them, surrounding them, a dim red light burning somewhere over a distant exit door, their escape when they needed it.

"Are you going to lay me now?" the girl asked.

"Yes," he said.

"First the money," she said.

It galled him that she said those words because they were only the ancient words whispered in cribs from Panama to Mozambique, and he did not expect them from this girl who had said she would do it on roller coasters.

"I have the money," he said.

"Where?"

"I have it," he insisted.

"Yes indeed, baby, but where?"

"Right here," he said, and kissed her.

He thought, as he kissed her, that if she still insisted on the money first, he would probably produce it because that's what money was for, to buy the things you wanted and needed. He thought, however, as he kissed her, that it would be so much nicer if she did not insist on the money, but instead offered herself to him in all her medieval, black-velveted, delicate charm, offered herself freely and willingly and without any promises, gave to him, simply gave to him without any hope of receiving anything in return; that, he thought, would be very nice. He almost lost himself in that single kiss, almost produced the money the instant his lips touched hers because the money no longer seemed important then, the only important thing was the sweetness of her mouth. The girl too, he thought, was enjoying the kiss as much as he, straining against him now with a wildness he had not anticipated, her arms encircling, the fingers of one hand widespread at the back of his neck the way he had seen stars doing it in movies but had never had done to him even by Irene who was really very passionate though sometimes shy, her belly moving in against him, her breasts moving in against him, her thighs, her crotch, everything suddenly moving in freely and willingly against him, just the way he wanted it, "The money," she whispered.

He pressed her tight against the wall and rode the black skirt up over her thighs. She spread her legs as he drove in against her, and then arched her back and twisted away, trying to elude his thrust, rising onto her toes in retreat, dodging, and giggling as her evasive action seemed to work, and then gasping as she accidentally subsided upon the crest of another assault. "The money," she said insistently, "the money," and tried to twist away as he moved in against her again, rising on her toes again, almost losing a shoe, only to be caught once more by a fierce and sudden ascent, her own sharp twisting descent breaking unexpectedly against him. "The money," she moaned, "the money," and seized his moving hips as though to push him away from her, and then found her hands moving with his hips, accepting his rhythm, assisting him, and finally pulling him against her eagerly. Limply, clinging to the wall, one arm loose around his neck, the other dangling at her side, she sank to the jacket he had spread on the floor and said again by tireless rote, softly, "The money, the money." She was naked beneath her skirt now, its black velvet folds crushed against her belly. His hands touched, stroked, pretended, possessed. She stretched her legs as though still in retreat, protesting, trying to sidestep though no longer on her feet. Weaponless, in angry reprimand, she snapped her groin up sharply against his demanding hand, a short petulant whiplash, and then sighingly moved against him in open surrender, shaking her head, breathing the words once in broken defiance, "The money." Lifting herself to him, she tilted groin and buttocks up, opened skirt and legs, funneled him toward her and onto her and into her, "Turn you green," he whispered, "Yes yes turn me," she said, "Spread you like honey," he whispered, "Oh yes spread me," she said, and he rushed deep inside her with a sureness he had dreamt long ago, and remembering she murmured, "Oh you louse you promised."

He had not, of course, broken his promise. He had told her he would cause her to lay down in green pastures, and that was exactly what he had done, though not letting her in on the secret, even lovers had to keep their little secrets. But he had most certainly done what he'd promised. Suddenly, he began chuckling. Holding her close, his lips against her throat, he began chuckling, and she said, "Stop that, you nut, it tickles."

"Do you know what we just did?" he said, sitting up.

"Yes, I know what we just did," Merilee answered, demurely lowering her skirt.

"Do you know *where?*"

"In the New York Public Library."

"Right. Do you know on what?"

"On the floor."

"Wrong."

"Excuse me, on your jacket."

"Wrong."

"On what then?"

"On half a million dollars," Mullaney said, and got to his feet and dusted off his trousers and then offered his hand to the girl. "May I?" he asked.

"Certainly," she said, puzzled, and took his hand. He helped her to her feet, grinned, and picked up the jacket. As he dusted it off, he said, "Do you hear anything?"

"No."

"Listen."

"I still don't hear anything."

"Listen," he said, and deliberately brushed his hand over the jacket in long sweeping palmstrokes, striking dust from the shoulders and the back and the sleeves, and keeping his head cocked to one side all the while, grinning at the girl, who kept listening and hearing nothing, and watching him as though making love had done something to his head.

"I don't hear anything," she said.

"Don't you hear the rustle of silk?"

"No."

"Don't you hear the flutter of angels' wings?"

"No."

"Don't you hear, my dear sweet girl, the sound of money?"

"I don't hear anything," she said.

"Have you got a knife?" he asked.

"No."

"A scissors?"

"No."

"Have you got a nail file in your bag?"

"All I've got in my bag is a driver's license and a pearl-handled .22. Where's the money?"

"I'll have to tear it."

"Tear what?"

Mullaney grinned and turned the jacket over in his hands. He could feel the stiffness of the bills sewn into the lining, could almost feel the outline of each dollar-sized packet nestling between the outer and inner fabric. He debated whether he should take the packets out one at a time and spread them across the floor at Merilee's feet, or whether he should simply slit the hem at the bottom of the jacket and allow the packets to fall helter-skelter-come-what-may, as if it were raining money. He decided it would be nice to see it rain money, so he grinned at Merilee again (she was watching him intently, her blue eyes narrowed, a feral sexy look on her face) and then he began plucking at the lining thread at the jacket's hem. The jacket had been excellently tailored, he had known immediately that K and O'Brien and all the others were gentlemen of taste, with good tight stitches placed close together, all sewn by hand, all designed to withstand any possible accidents on the way to Rome. Mullaney finally had to rip the first few stitches with his teeth, something his mother had warned him never to do, and then he thrust two fingers up into the torn opening, and began ripping the stitches all the way down the line, keeping the jacket bundled and bunched because he didn't want the bills to fall out until he was ready to let it rain. When he had ripped the lining clear across the bottom, he rose from his squatting position and, still holding the jacket so that nothing could fall out of it, held it at arm's length in both hands and said, "It's going to rain money, Merilee."

"Oh yes indeed let it rain," Merilee said.

"It's going to rain half a million dollars' worth of money."

"Oh yes yes yes."

"It's going to rain all over this floor."

"Let it rain, baby," the girl said.

"And then we'll make love again," Mullaney said.

"Half a million times," the girl said, "one for each dollar bill."

"Are you ready?"

"I am *ready*," she said, her eyes glowing.

"Here-it-comes," Mullaney said, "five-hundred-thousand-dollars-in-American-money, ta-ra!" and he allowed the lining to fall away from the jacket.

4. CALLAHAN

The packets of bills fell to the floor just like the rain Mullaney had expected, plop, plop, plop, great big drops of bills falling to the stone floor of the library and raising a cloud of dust which at first obscured his vision a bit, and caused him to believe that perhaps he was not quite seeing what he thought he was seeing. Plop, plop, plop, the packets kept falling out of the jacket and pattering all around while he and the girl stared down at their five-hundred-thousand-dollar rain, and the dust settled, and they kept staring down at the packets, and Mullaney wanted to weep.

The packets were worth exactly ten cents because that is how much *The New York Times* costs on a Friday, and that is exactly what these were made of, *The New York Times*. Mullaney kept staring down at the packets, which someone had cut very nicely into the shape of dollar bills, and then stacked and bound neatly with rubber bands, each packet slim enough to be sewn into a funeral jacket. He did not raise his eyes from the slowly settling dust because, to tell the truth, he was a little embarrassed about facing the girl.

"It seems to be newspaper," he said, and cleared his throat.

"Yes indeed," Merilee said.

They kept staring at the cut stacks of newspaper.

"Boy," he said.

"Newspaper," the girl said.

"Boy."

"*The New York Times,* no less," she said. "I don't even *read The New York Times.*"

"Boy."

"You know who must have done this?" she asked.

"Who?"

"Somebody who reads *The New York Times.*"

"I'll bet," Mullaney said.

"Oh my," the girl said. "Oh my my my my my."

"Mmm,' Mullaney said.

"Oh my."

They were silent again.

Into the silence there came the unholy clamor of a ringing bell, startling Mullaney so much that he leaped back against the wall and then was surprised to find himself shaking. He had not realized until just this moment that the worthless collection of clipped newspapers at his feet represented something more than just the end of a gambler's dream. This pile of garbage containing yesterday's baseball scores and war casualties, yesterday's stock prices and theater reviews, this worthless pile of shredded garbage lying in the dust at his feet also contained, if Mullaney was willing to read it correctly, an obituary notice announcing the untimely demise of one Andrew Mullaney himself, to take place in the not unforeseeable future. It was one thing to consider running out on Smokestack Kruger when you were in possession of half a million dollars and a beautiful blonde. It was another to think of running out on him when you had only a mangled copy of this morning's *Times* and a blonde who was beginning to get a distinct hangdog expression. He could not understand the hangdog expression, but there it was, spreading across her mouth and drawing down the corners of her eyes, Oh boy, Mullaney thought, I'm going to be in pretty big trouble soon, his innate optimism refusing to allow that he was *already* in pretty big trouble, in fact in *very* big trouble.

"That's why you should always get the money first," the girl said suddenly, as though she had been mulling it over for quite some time.

"I guess so," Mullaney said. The jacket was still in his hands. He glanced at it sourly, and then threw it to the floor. It lay inert and worthless at his feet. Angrily, and for good measure, he kicked it. Twice.

"Oh boy Kruger's going to kill you," Merilee said.

"Mmm."

"Kruger's going to absolutely murder you."

"Listen, did you hear a bell?" Mullaney said.

"What?"

"Just a few minutes ago? I think it's closing time. I think we'd better get out of here."

"I think you'd better get out of New York," the girl said. "I think you'd better get off the planet earth, if you want my advice, because Kruger is going to kill you."

"Well . . ." Mullaney said, and he hesitated because he was about to make a speech, and he rarely made speeches. He was going to make a speech because he incorrectly assumed everything was ending instead of just beginning, and he thought it would be nice to say something to commemorate the event. He started thinking about what he was going to say as he led the girl toward the red light burning over the exit door at the far end of the labyrinth. By the time they reached the door, he knew what he wanted to tell her. He put his hand on her arm. The girl turned and stared up at him, her flaxen hair aglow with spilled red light, her eyes wide and solemn and fitting to the occasion.

"Merilee," he said, "I really thought the money was inside the jacket, and I can't tell you how sad it makes me that it was only paper scraps. But in spite of that, I remember what happened *before* I opened that jacket. I remember you, Merilee. And so whatever happened afterwards doesn't matter at all, the disappointment doesn't matter, the possibility that I'm in danger doesn't matter, none of it matters except what happened with you. *That* was good, Merilee, that was something I'll *never* forget as long as I live because it was real and honest and, Merilee, it was just really really good, wasn't it?"

"No," the girl said, "it was lousy."

The guard at the front door of the library bawled them out for lagging so far behind all the others and causing him to unlock the door after he had already carefully locked it for the night, did they think he had nothing to do but lock and unlock doors all night long? Mullaney supposed the guard did have a great many other things to do, so he didn't argue with him, he just meekly allowed himself to be let out of the library and then he walked down the steps and stood with the girl near one of the lions and figured they would have to say goodbye. She would go back to Kruger, he supposed, and he would go he didn't know where.

"Well . . ." he said.

"I'm supposed to shoot you, you know," she said.

"You might just as well," he answered.

"I'm terribly sorry the relationship didn't work out," she said.

"So am I."

"But I don't think I could shoot you."

"I'm grateful," Mullaney said.

"When they get you—they'll get you, you know . . ."

"I know."

". . . you just tell them you escaped, okay? That's what I'll tell them."

"Okay, that's what I'll tell them, too."

"Well," the girl said, and glanced over her shoulder.

"It was very nice knowing you," Mullaney said.

"Oh yes indeed," she answered, and walked away.

We'll meet again, he thought, not really believing that they would. He thrust his hands into the pockets of the too-short trousers, and began walking downtown on Fifth Avenue. A breeze had sprung up and he was a bit chilly now that he no longer had his paper-lined jacket. He began wondering about that jacket. He was very good at making deductions based on the condition of the track and the number of times out and the number of wins and losses and the weight of the jockey, and all that. He was also very good at figuring the true odds on any given roll of the dice as opposed to the house odds, and he could calculate within reason the possibility of, say, drawing a diamond to a flush, very good indeed at doing all of these things—which was why he'd lost his shirt over the past year. Well, hadn't actually lost his shirt, was actually still in possession of his jasmine shirt, which was a bit too flimsy for a cool April night like this one. Nor was he really convinced that he was not a very good gambler; he was simply a gambler who'd had a run of bad luck. Being equipped, therefore, with a coolly calculating mind that was capable of figuring combinations, permutations and such, he put it to use in speculating about the jacket and the odd fact that *The New York Times* had been sewn into it, rather than the half-million dollars everyone had been expecting.

The first obvious truth about the jacket was that Kruger had not known the money (or even the facsimile of the money) was sewn into its lining. Henry or George, he forgot which, had mentioned that the money was supposed to be in the coffin, but whereas they had thoroughly searched the coffin, they had not thought to search the person *in* the coffin. Which meant, following a logical progression of thought, that whoever had told them the money was in the coffin had neglectfully forgotten to mention it was sewn into the corpse's jacket.

Very good, Mullaney, he thought, you're getting very close. To what, he didn't know.

Kruger knew the money was in the coffin, but did not know it was in the jacket.

Excellent.

On the other hand, K and O'Brien and all the others knew the money was in the jacket, but apparently did not know the money in the jacket was only *The New York Times.* They had concocted an elaborate scheme whereby they were prepared to ship a coffin and a corpse (was it to be a real corpse, and was that why the original victim had jumped out of the limousine on Fourteenth Street?) to Rome, where an informed party no doubt was to have opened the coffin, removed the body, slit the jacket's lining, and become richer by half a million dollars. But somewhere along the line, someone had decided it would be a good joke to substitute newspaper strips for cash and, all unbeknownst to K and his fellows, had tiptoed away with the loot and stitched the morning paper into the garment.

Very good.

Now, Mullaney thought, we come to the difficult part, difficult because Kruger and his fellows didn't tell me anything much about it except that there had been a terrible highway accident. Was it reasonable to assume that the hearse and the coffin had been hijacked on the way to Kennedy and then shuttled out to Secaucus or environs awaiting the resurrection of the corpse? But how had Kruger and his fellows learned about the money in the first place? And who had substituted the newspaper strips for the cash?

Mullaney suddenly remembered something that caused the sweet aroma of money to flood once more into his nostrils. He suddenly remembered that O'Brien had sent someone else to get the suit of clothes from the other room, and he suddenly remembered who that someone had been. The man who kept offering the schnapps. The stonecutter or whatever the hell he was. He had very definitely gone into the other room to get the jacket and pants, leaving the shirt behind because he was certain it would not fit Mullaney. Was it not possible, then, that the stonecutter was the man with the shifty fingers, the man adept at cutting up *The New York Times?* The only trouble was that Mullaney didn't know where he had been this morning, other than that it was on the edge of a cemetery. Wait a minute, he thought, wasn't there a sign, didn't I notice a sign, something that caused me to think of Feinstein's funeral (it was *so* funny the way he died) no, the hearse in the backyard made me think of his funeral, an excellent hearse, that and the marble stones, IN MEMORY OF, wait a minute, one of them had a name on it, now hold it what was the name on that stone, just a minute, the large black marble stone, and across the face of it, IN LOVING MEMORY OF . . .

Who?

In loving memory of all the pleasures I will no longer enjoy on this sweet green earth.

In . . .

    loving . . .

        memory . . .

Got it! he thought as it came to him in a terrifying rush, IN LOVING MEMORY OF MARTIN CALLAHAN, LOVING HUSBAND, FATHER, GRANDFATHER, 1896–1967, crazy! and hoped it wasn't just a dummy stone left around the yard for prospective customers to examine for chiseling styles.

He found an open drugstore on Thirty-eighth Street and looked up the name Martin Callahan in the Manhattan telephone book, discovering that there were two such Callahans listed and thinking So far, so good, I've got twenty cents, and a phone call costs a dime, and there are only two Martin Callahans, so I can't lose. He went into the phone booth and dialed the first Martin Callahan and waited while the phone rang on the other end. There was no answer. This was Friday night. If this was the quick Callahan, he might very well be out stepping. Mullaney hung up, retrieved his dime (which was one-half of his fortune) and dialed the second Martin Callahan.

"Hello?" a woman said.

"Hello," he said, "my name is Andrew Mullaney. I was out at a cemetery this morning . . ."

"What?" the woman said.

"Yes, and happened to see your husband's beautiful stone . . ." He paused.

"Yes?" the woman said.

"Your husband *was* Martin Callahan, wasn't he?"

"Yes, he died last month, poor soul," she said.

"Well, I'd like to get a stone just like his," Mullaney said, "but I can't remember where I saw it. Would you remember the name of the stonecutter?"

"Is this Phil?" the woman said.

"No, this is Andrew Mullaney."

"Because I don't think it's a very funny joke, if this is you, Phil."

"No, this isn't Phil."

"I thought you were coming here at ten o'clock," the widow Callahan said.

"Well, you see, this isn't Phil."

"I got all ready for you," she said, petulantly he thought.

"Would you remember the name of the stonecutter, ma'am?" he asked. "It's really very important."

"Are you sure this isn't Phil?"

"Oh, I'm positive. Positive, ma'am. Andrew Mullaney, M-U-L-L . . ."

"Oh," the woman said. She paused. "The stonecutter's name is Roger McReady, and he's of McReady's Monument Works in Queens," she said, and hung up.

"Thank you," Mullaney said in retrospect, and hung up. Since he was very hungry, he spent his last dime on a Hershey bar, which he consumed in three bites. Then he went out into the street and began walking crosstown toward the Queensboro Bridge. He had no plan in mind. Vaguely, he assumed it would be best to keep on the move, but he figured he had at least a little time before Merilee found her way back to Kruger's apartment on East Sixty-first. So he walked at a normal pace, ambling along and looking at the Lexington Avenue chippies and the Third Avenue fags and the Second Avenue winos, then cutting uptown and thinking all the while what a nice city New York was if only a person had some money to spend in it. Irene had never been a one to worry about money, couldn't matter less to her whether he'd earned ten thousand a year (which he hadn't) or twenty thousand (which he most *certainly* hadn't). "The best things in life are free," she was fond of chirping around the house while he wrote out checks for the mountain of bills that seemed to accumulate each month, "all the world loves a lover, and *boy* do I love you!" or words to that effect, all of it sounding to him like the jabberwocky of a happy schizophrenic. He would gnaw his pencils down to a nub and mutter to himself about freedom and realization, thinking of the several times he had been out to the racetrack and won, or thinking of the few five-and-ten-cent poker games he had busted, or thinking of the impromptu crap game in which he had won thirty-two dollars from his startled friends—break out, he had muttered to himself, break out, cut loose, be a gambler!

So here he was, big gambler, just having lost half a million dollars, but hot on the trail of it again. Or at least hot on the trail of the stonecutter who might or might not have a clue as to how all that newspaper had happened to get inside the jacket. The problem now was one of transportation. He paused at the approach to the bridge, saw a sign reading FOOTWALK TO WELFARE ISLAND, and remembered that it was possible to walk to the island, and then across it, and then onto another bridge that led to Queens. The idea of such a long walk did not appeal to him, but the only other choice he could think of was walking all the way up to 125th Street and then across the Triboro Bridge, which seemed even longer to him. So he went down the cobbled path below the arching roadway overhead, and paused at the steps leading to the walkway. There were several signs affixed to the stone wall there. One of them, in white letters on a red enameled field, read:

NO STANDING

ANY

TIME

A sign alongside it, in black letters on a white field, read:

NO BABY CARRIAGES
BICYCLES DOGS OR SKATERS
PERMITTED ON FOOTWALK

He was standing there reading the second sign when a police car pulled up behind him. There were two patrolmen in the car. The one sitting alongside the driver rolled down his window and said, "Can't you read that sign?"

"What sign, officer?" Mullaney said.

"That sign right behind you there," the patrolman behind the wheel said, pointing. "I guess he can't read the sign, Freddie."

Mullaney turned and read the sign again. He was neither a baby carriage, a bicycle, a dog, or a skater, so he couldn't understand why the policemen had stopped, or why they were now questioning him.

"Well, I can read the sign," he said, "but I don't see . . ."

"The *other* sign," Freddie said.

"Oh, I see," Mullaney said, and turned to look at it again. "It says No Standing Any Time."

"Oh, he sees," the patrolman behind the wheel said, "it says No Standing Any Time."

"Yeah, Lou, he sees," Freddie said, both of them beginning to sound very much the way Henry and George had sounded, though these two didn't look at all alike. "What are you doing here?"

"I was just . . ."

"Are you *standing* here?"

"Yes, but . . ."

"Does the sign say No Standing Any Time?"

"Yes, but that applies to auto—"

"Then what are you doing standing here?" Lou asked.

"I have to get to the cemetery," Mullaney said, which was the truth so far. He decided to embroider upon the truth a little because both Freddie and Lou looked as if they just might pull him in for standing or loitering or hitchhiking or skating across the bridge without skates or raping somebody, it being Friday night, and there not being enough trouble to occupy them anywhere else in the city. "A very good friend of mine passed away just last month," Mullaney said, "name of Martin Callahan. I was just talking to his widow a few minutes ago, and she seemed all broken up because the stone is ready, but she can't bear to go out and look at it, being grief-stricken. So she asked me if I'd go out to take a look at it, see that they spelled his name right and all that, and I promised I would and then like a fool left my wallet in my jacket. At the gym. In my gym locker."

"At the gym?" Lou asked.

"Yes, I go there to work out with the medicine ball. I've got a desk job, you see, keep the old bod in shape with a medicine ball."

"What gym?"

"You know. Over on Fifty-third," he said, wondering if there *was* a gym someplace on Fifty-third.

"Oh yeah, *that* one," Freddie said. "What kind of work do you do?"

"I sell encyclopedias," Mullaney said.

"Yeah, huh?"

"Yeah. So here I promised her I'd go out tonight and take a look at the stone for her, and I didn't want to go all the way back to the gym, so I thought I'd walk across the bridge."

"That's a very interesting story," Lou said.

"How did he die?" Freddie asked.

"Who?"

"Hoolihan. Your friend."

"Callahan, you mean."

"Yeah, Callahan, him."

"Well . . ." Mullaney said, and paused, unable to remember how Callahan had died, but remembering very clearly how Feinstein had died, and figuring he might as well give them that story since they had thought his first story so interesting. "Actually," he said, "it was very comical the way he . . ."

"Never mind," Lou said, "I don't like to hear about how guys died. Get in the car, and we'll drop you off at the cemetery."

"Thank you," Mullaney said, and got into the squad car. "Where I'm going, actually, is to the stonecutter's just outside the cemetery. McReady's Monument Works."

"I know where that is," Freddie said.

"He thinks this is a taxi," Lou said.

"Yeah," Freddie said, "he thinks this is a taxi."

But, being New York's Finest, they nonetheless drove him over the bridge and into Queens, where they dropped him off on the sidewalk just outside McReady's Monument Works.

5. McREADY

A cold wind blew in off the cemetery, keening relentlessly over gravestone and urn, eddying against the black iron fence, rising to a vivid scream that dropped again in moaning obbligato, a tortured cry of unknown horror and graveside lament.

Mullaney was cold and he was frightened.

A light was burning in the stonecutter's cottage. He crept around the side of the house, the gravel crunching underfoot, the wind billowing into his jasmine shirt. There were ghosts in the adjacent cemetery, he knew, tall apparitions in soiled winding sheets, eyesockets staring, skeletal fingers grasping. Bony women cackled on the wind, withered lips pulled back over toothless gums, their voices echoing on the fitful air. As Mullaney approached the lighted window, a shutter banged, and banged again, and his heart thumped, and he almost ran. A tree in new April leaf suddenly whipped its branches across the sullen night, rattling fresh leaves. Somewhere a cat shrieked in terror and was still again.

Teeth chattering, Mullaney peered into the cottage.

McReady the stonecutter was sitting at a small table. He was eating a sandwich and pouring schnapps from a brown bottle. Mullaney watched as the old man bit into the sandwich. It was a deliciously monstrous concoction, a huge wedge of French bread stuffed with what seemed to be at least fourteen different kinds of meats and cheeses. Mullaney, remembering again how hungry he was, watched enviously as the old man clamped his teeth into the crisp brown bread. Savagely, McReady tore loose an enormous bite, chewed it with obscene enthusiasm, and then washed it down with a huge swallow of whiskey. Smacking his lips, he wiped the back of his hand across his mouth, and then brought the sandwich into biting position again.

Mullaney's eyes narrowed.

He was hungry, and frightened, and cold, and whereas he philosophically reasoned that most cruel acts in this world were perpetrated by people who were either hungry, frightened, or cold, the knowledge did not prevent him from devising a cruel little act of his own.

He had already relegated blame for the switched money to McReady, arguing that he would now be in possession of half a million dollars had McReady not performed his sleight-of-hand. But worse than the money swap was the solitary and selfish indulgence taking place inside this cottage on the edge of the cemetery. McReady's feast was assuming the dimensions of an onanistic orgy. Relentlessly, he chewed and swallowed, poured and drank, licked his lips and belched in contentment. What I'm going to do to you, Mullaney thought in rising anger and greed, is scare you out of your wits, old man. I am going to rap on the window here and pretend I'm one of the ghosts howling out there in the cemetery, come to get you for your many many sins among which are substituting paper scraps for money and making a pig of yourself swilling good food and liquor before the very eyes of a starving horseplayer.

The anger with which he had conceived his malicious plan gave way to the sheer enjoyment of contemplating its execution. Chuckling, he hunched down below the window, his eyes level with the sill, so that he could watch McReady's reaction unobserved. Oh boy, he thought, this is going to be good, and he raised his knuckles toward the pane, giggled, and rapped sharply on the glass.

McReady looked up.

The expression on his face was similar to the one that had been on Henry's when Mullaney yelled "Boo!" from the coffin. He nodded. Then he took another bite of his sandwich. Then he put the sandwich down on its plate. Then he rose. Chewing, he walked leisurely to the door and opened it. Around a mouthful of food, he asked, "Who is it?"

"It's *me!*" Mullaney bellowed, and stepped into the light streaming through the open door.

"Oh, hello there," McReady said, "come in." He backed away from the door. "It certainly is a brisk night, isn't it?" he said. Mullaney entered the cottage. McReady closed the door behind him and walked back to the table. "Sit down," he said. "Sit down. I was just having a little snack, helps the long night to pass." He picked up the remainder of his sandwich and devoured it in two enormous gulps. Pouring more whiskey into his glass, he asked Mullaney, "A little schnapps?"

"Thank you," Mullaney said.

The stonecutter rose and walked to a small cabinet set on the wall. Mullaney noticed that the wall was covered with posters advertising marble and granite. A calendar near the cabinet was printed with the words "Elegant . . . Exotic . . . Eternal," and a photograph of what appeared to be the tomb of Tutankhamen. McReady came back to the table with a plastic water tumbler. He poured it almost full to the brim, raised his own glass, and said, "*L'chaim.*" The men drank.

McReady smacked his lips and said, "I'm very happy you stopped by to see me. I was wondering what happened to you."

"I'll bet you were," Mullaney said.

"When I heard about the accident on the radio . . ."

"Was it on the radio?"

"Yes, a terrible accident."

"Are they dead?"

"It would appear so."

"I know who killed them," Mullaney said.

"Ahhh."

"A man named Kruger."

"Ahhh."

"And two people who work for him. Henry and George."

"Ahhh."

"Do you know them?" Mullaney asked.

"Have a little more schnapps," McReady said, and poured the plastic water tumbler to the brim again. The men lifted their glasses. "*L'chaim,*" McReady said. They drank. The whiskey was good, and it was very cozy inside the cottage. Outside, the wind howled and the cemetery demons tossed restlessly. But within the cottage, there was the smell of cheese and good whiskey, the aroma of McReady's tobacco as he lighted his pipe and exhaled a cloud of smoke. Mullaney felt himself relaxing. It had been a long day, and the possibility existed that it might be an even longer night, but for now there was whiskey and cheese and—

"Is there more cheese?" he asked.

"Why certainly," McReady said, "are you hungry, you poor man?"

"I'm famished," Mullaney said.

McReady rose and went to a small refrigerator, set under what appeared to be a door serving as a desk, one end of which was

supported by the refrigerator, the other end by a green filing
cabinet. He stooped, took from the refrigerator a wedge of cheese
and a long salami, opened the filing cabinet to remove a knife,
and came back to the table. Mullaney fell upon the feast without
ceremony.

"I like to see a man eat," McReady said.

"Yes," Mullaney agreed, eating.

"Would you perhaps know what happened to the jacket?"
McReady asked.

"Yes."

"What happened to it?"

Mullaney swallowed more of the whiskey, washing down his
food. "There was only *The New York Times* in it," he said.

"Ahhh," McReady said.

"Which I'm sure you knew, anyway," Mullaney said.

"Ahhh?"

"Yes."

"Paper scraps, do you mean?"

"Yes."

"Cut into the size of bills?"

"Yes."

"Sewn into the jacket?"

"Yes."

"I knew nothing about it," McReady said.

"You were the one who gave the jacket to me."

"That's true."

"There was supposed to be half a million dollars in it," Mullaney said.

"You've learned a lot since the accident," McReady said, and
his eyes narrowed. He had, until that moment, seemed like only a
pleasant-looking old pipe smoker, his head partially bald, a fringe
of white hair curling about each ear, his nose exhibiting the rosy
tint of the habitual drinker, leisurely puffing on his pipe, puff,
puff, and gulping his whiskey, a nice pleasant stonecutter of a
man feeding a starving horseplayer and making pleasant chitchat

in the night while the wind howled outside and the cemetery horrors moaned. Until he narrowed his eyes. When he narrowed his eyes, Mullaney suddenly wondered what a nice guy like McReady was doing in a place like this, cutting stones for corpses and substituting paper scraps for money. I'll bet this whiskey has been poisoned, he thought, or drugged, but he took another swallow of it nonetheless.

"Half a million dollars," he repeated.

"Give or take a few thousand," McReady said, and puffed on his pipe with his eyes still narrowed. "Who told you all this?"

"Kruger."

"Ahhh," McReady said.

"You still haven't said whether or not you know him," Mullaney said.

"I know him."

"He wants that money," Mullaney said. "So do I."

"What gives you any claim to it?" McReady asked reasonably.

"I almost became a corpse for it."

"You may still become one," McReady said, again reasonably. He seemed like a very reasonable fellow, except for the way he kept his eyes squinched up so narrow, never taking his gaze from Mullaney's face. The cottage was still. Outside, the cemetery ghouls groaned into the wind. Mullaney took another swallow of whiskey.

"Would you like to hear my theory?" he asked.

"Yes, certainly," McReady said.

"It's my theory that *you* substituted the paper scraps for the money."

"Me?"

"You."

"No," McReady said.

"It's my theory that *you* have that five hundred thousand dollars."

"No," McReady said, and shook his head for emphasis, and puffed on his pipe again, and again said, "No."

"I went to a lot of trouble finding you," Mullaney said, and swallowed more whiskey, emptying the glass. McReady poured it full to the brim again. Mullaney lifted it, and said, "By the way, that was a nice job of chiseling on Martin Callahan's stone."

"Thank you," McReady said.

Mullaney drank. "So?" he said.

"So what?"

"If *you* didn't put those paper scraps in the jacket, who *did?*"

"Let us say that where there is cheese, there is also sometimes a rat," McReady said.

"What's that supposed to mean?"

"It's supposed to mean that half a million dollars can be a very tempting sum."

"Very tempting indeed," Mullaney said. "If *I* had it, I would take it to Monte Carlo and play seventeen red."

"Black," McReady said.

"What?"

"Seventeen is black."

"Then that's what I would play," Mullaney said. "If I had the money."

"Unfortunately, you *don't* have it."

"Do you?"

"Not yet," McReady said.

"What does that mean?"

"Ahhh," McReady said, and puffed on his pipe.

"Why were you sending it to Rome?" Mullaney asked.

"Ahhh," McReady said.

"This is a big international gang, isn't it?" Mullaney said shrewdly. "This is an enormous criminal cartel, isn't it? This is a big heroin operation, right? Or white slavery, right, am I right, McReady?"

"You are wrong," McReady said.

"Then what is it?" he asked, and suddenly realized he was drunk.

"It is none of your business," McReady said, "that is what it is."

"It's my business because you made it my business."

McReady put down his pipe. Mullaney saw that his hand was very close to the knife on the table, which was a very large and sharp-looking kitchen knife, something he had not noticed while he was slicing the salami. McReady's eyes were still narrowed. Mullaney was beginning to think he was simply nearsighted.

"I would like to ask you some questions," McReady said.

"Oh, would you now?" Mullaney said, feeling suddenly very exuberant, feeling again the way he had felt when he'd stood up to Kruger back on Sixty-first Street, somewhat like a hero, albeit a drunken one.

"Yes, and I would like you to answer them."

"Well now, maybe I'll answer them, and maybe I won't," Mullaney said.

"We shall see," McReady said, and Mullaney was positive now that he was a member of an international crime cartel because all the members thus far had the same corny way of sounding terribly menacing when they talked to you, as if they had all learned to threaten in the same exclusive school run by Fagin or somebody, Three six nine a bottle of wine, Mullaney thought, I can lick you any old time. But McReady's hand was on the knife.

"Did you open the jacket?" McReady asked.

"I did."

"And found the paper scraps?"

"I did."

"Where?"

"Inside the jacket. Sewn into the jacket."

"I meant . . . where did you make this discovery?"

"Oh, I get it," Mullaney said. "I get it now, pal. Go ahead, torture me, I'll never tell you where I left those heroin-impregnated scraps of paper. Or is it LSD? Huh? Is that what *The New York Times* was soaked in? LSD? I wouldn't be a bit surprised."

"You have a vivid imagination," McReady said.

"Where'd you learn to talk that way?" Mullaney said. "Did

Fagin teach you to talk that way at his international crime school, all menacing like that?"

"Mr. Mullaney . . ."

"Oh, so you know my name, huh?"

"Yes, we got it from your driver's license."

"*We* is it, huh? Big criminal organization, huh? Go ahead, torture me, I can take torture of any kind, Irene and I once lived in an apartment that had ten thousand cockroaches, you think I'm afraid of torture? I'll *never* tell you where I left those paper scraps!"

"I don't *care* where you left the paper scraps," McReady said. "All I want to know is where you left the *jacket*."

"So that's it, huh?" Mullaney said. "It's the jacket that's important, huh? Go ahead, torture me."

"Have some more schnapps," McReady said quickly.

"Oh no you don't!" Mullaney snapped. "Trying to get me drunk, huh, so I'll spill everything I know, huh? No you don't," but he poured himself another drink and raised his glass and said, "*Skoal*, buddy, I could have won a fortune at Aqueduct today if you louses hadn't come along and spoiled it. You happen to know who won the fourth race?"

"No, I don't."

"Jawbone, right?"

"I have no idea."

"I thought so," Mullaney said. "Jawbone, huh? I knew it."

"Where did you leave the jacket?"

"Ha ha," Mullaney said, and shoved back his chair defiantly and exuberantly, and then almost fell flat on his face. He staggered back from the table, suddenly ashamed of himself, not because he was drunk but only because he had become drunk in the presence of someone he did not like. There are many many ways to get drunk, he thought, and one way is as good as any other way; the only thing that can be bad about getting drunk is the company you're in while you're doing it. He did not like McReady any more than he had liked K or Gouda or Kruger or any of the other members of this vast cartel, perhaps two cartels (so the *jacket* is important, huh? he thought, never tell a book by its jacket), and yet he had allowed himself to get drunk in the man's presence, which was a mean and despicable thing to do.

The most fabulous drunk in his life, the only one he could really distinguish from every other drunk in his life, small or large, was the one he had thrown with Irene in their apartment the day she discovered the Cache. She only discovered the Cache because they were at that time waging war against the ten thousand cockroaches who shared their place on East Sixteenth Street, which meant they were opening cabinet doors and dispensing roach powder, lifting dishes and pots and pans, and spraying sharp poofing puffs of poison into dark corners and niches, watching the cockroaches flee in disorganized retreat. The Cache consisted of four ten-dollar bills which she had hidden in a casserole against a rainy day, and then completely forgotten. She had tilted the casserole so that he could get a better shot at the nest of little scurrying bastards hidden in the corner, and suddenly the money had fallen out of it, payment for mercenaries, and it began raining. They had by now sprayed everything in sight or out of it, and since it had begun raining, and since the money had been put aside for a rainy day, Mullaney suggested that they spend the afternoon (it was Saturday) getting delightfully crocked, which suggestion Irene thought was capital, repulsed as she was by the hordes of insects breeding in their closets. They had taken a taxicab up to Zabar's on Eightieth and Broadway, where they bought a tin of Beluga caviar, and then had come back downtown and bought two fifths of Polish vodka and a box of crackers, and had spent the rest of the afternoon and evening eating caviar and drinking the vodka neat. It had been a marvelous drunk. They tried to make love several times during the afternoon and evening, but neither could manage it because they were positively squiffed, laughing and reeling all over the apartment, drinking to the cockroaches and also to the Beatles (who were fairly new at the time) and drinking to Queen Eliza-

beth ("Up the Irish!" Irene shouted) and also to Khrushchev
(Mullaney took off his shoe and banged it on the counter top, less
in imitation of the Russian premier than in an attempt to squash a
poison-drunk cockroach who was making his dizzy way toward
the sink—and missing) and they drank to J. D. Salinger for
having listed all the ingredients in Zooey's or Franny's or somebody's medicine cabinet, without which literary feat American
fiction that past year might have been barren and bleak, and oh,
it had been a marvelous drunk.

This drunk was a lousy one because it was taking place in the
presence of McReady, a joyless staggering dumb intoxication. Its
only saving grace was that in talking to the hopeless drunk who
was Mullaney, the pipe-smoking McReady had inadvertently
revealed the fact that the *jacket* was important, the *jacket*, though
Mullaney could not for the life of him see how.

"I need air!" he shouted, suddenly desiring to be sober, and
staggered across the room to the window and threw it open. A
gust of cemetery wind rushed into the room, a blast of chilling
tombtop air that smelled of rot and decomposition. Behind him,
the front door of the cottage was suddenly blown open by the
gust of air that rushed through the window, though it seemed to
Mullaney that such a gust would have blown the door *closed*
rather than open. Drunkenly, he turned to see how such a remarkable thing could have occurred contrary to all the laws of
physics, and realized at once that the door had been *thrown* not
blown open and realized in the next drunken shuddering horrible
moment it had been thrown open by a ghost.

6. K K was pale and covered with dust, K was wrapped in tattered, torn and trailing rags, K wore upon his face a haggard look of weariness, evidence of a journey from some distant purgatory, K was a spectral image standing just inside the cottage door, a terrifying poltergeist that raised its arm and pointed a long bony blue finger at Mullaney in mute accusation. Beyond the open window, Mullaney could hear the fearsome wailing of a thousand other ghosts, the clatter of bones, the clanking of chains, all the promised horrors his grandmother had conjured for him when he was but a wee turnip sitting on her knee. The stench of them rushed through that open window, stale and fetid from the grave, while standing just inside the door was

another of their gruesome lot, closer, more frightening, pale and
ragged and dead, oh my good sweet Jesus save me, killed in a
terrible highway accident, dead, and closing the door gently now,
the door squeaking on its hinges, closing the door and taking a
step into the room, and raising its arm once again, the blue bony
finger extended, and pointing directly at Mullaney who swayed
in drunken terror near the open window where, beyond, the thousand other keening members of the union shrieked their dirges to
the night.

He jumped through the open window head first, arms extended, hands together, fingers touching, as though he were going
off the high board at Wilson's Woods swimming pool, where he
and Irene used to swim a lot before they were married. He hit the
gravel outside hands first, absorbing the shock with his arms,
rolling over into an immediate somersault, and then coming up
onto his feet and breaking into a run the moment he was erect.
He intended to run toward the sidewalk, out of this grisly place,
away from the shrieking, melancholy voices in the cemetery, but
his drunken state had been intensified by the plunge through the
open window and the head-over-heels somersault he had performed with considerable style and grace, and he detected with
horror that he was running not for the open gate of McReady's
Monument Works but instead for the open gate of the cemetery.
He stopped himself with effort, and was turning in the opposite
direction when the door of the cottage opened, and K stepped
into the light with his dusty rags trailing, leaping off the doorstep
and bounding across the yard toward Mullaney.

There is nothing to be afraid of, Mullaney said to himself,
knowing he was lying, and turned toward the open cemetery gate
again, reasoning it might be safer to face a thousand caterwauling
but possibly benign specters rather than one obviously enraged
and accusing demon, which K most certainly was. As he ran into
the cemetery, he began to regret his decision. He tried to tell
himself that his grandmother's tales had only been fictions calculated to delight a young and excitable wee turnip like himself

("You're a wee cowardly turnip," she would laugh and say, after he had almost wet his pants in her lap), but whereas he was willing to exonerate old Grandma of any malicious intent, he was now beginning to think her stories had contained the unmistakable ring of truth. Yawning pits opened before his feet, gravestones moved into his path, trees extended clutching branches and roots, faces materialized on the air, laughter sounded in his ears and faded, screams permeated the night, dogs howled and bats hovered, skeletons danced and specters drifted on the wind, oh my God, he was scared out of his wits.

This is not what I bargained for when I said I'd take the gamble, he thought, beginning to sober up and becoming more and more frightened the more sober he got. I did not bargain for the mummy's curse or the witch's tale or the monkey's paw. All I bargained for was a life of romantic adventure, and not K loping along behind me there wrapped in ceremonial funeral rags and shouting whatever the hell it is he's shouting. I did not bargain for things that go bump in the night, or in the daytime either, I did not bargain for terror, I do not want terror in my life, I want peace and happiness and calm, I want it to be dawn, I want all these crawling things to go back into their holes, I want the sun to shine, "or I'll shoot!"

He caught the words carried on the wind, words shouted in K's unmistakable voice, and then heard the full sentence shouted again, "Stop or I'll shoot!" and wondered why a ghost would have to shoot, and simultaneously became cold sober, and simultaneously realized that K, whatever else he was, was definitely not a ghost. He realized, too, that if *anybody* shot him, K or Kruger or anybody else, then *nobody* would ever learn where he had left the jacket, which was undoubtedly very important to all concerned, though he still couldn't understand why, especially in its torn and tattered shape. The jacket, of course, was back in the stacks of the New York Public Library, resting on the dusty floor where he and Merilee had made love only a short time ago, and that's where it would stay until tomorrow morning when the library opened. The trick then, he thought, as K shouted again behind him, was not to avoid getting *killed* by these people because he was certain they weren't going to kill the only person who knew where the jacket . . .

Merilee, he thought.

Merilee also knows where the jacket is.

Well, he thought, that's okay because Kruger only knew the money was supposed to be in the coffin, but not in the jacket. So chances are six to five he doesn't know what else is important about the jacket, as neither do I. Besides, why shouldn't he imagine the jacket is still on my back, which is where he saw it last, unless Merilee decides to tell him about our brief, ecstatic (for me, anyway) episode on the library floor? Well, hither thither willy nilly, let's say he *does* ask her why the back of her velvet dress is covered with dust, and let's say she *does* tell him what happened, which is doubtful, why should she mention the jacket at all, except to say that I had slit it open and found only cut-up newspapers in the lining? Why would she possibly mention I had left it on the floor back there, when she—no more than Kruger—has any knowledge of its importance?

Things were getting terribly complicated, and besides K was once again shouting "Stop or I'll shoot!" which Mullaney knew very well he would not do.

A shot rang out.

The shot, carried on the wind, broke into a hundred echoing fragments of sound, put to rout the screaming banshees of the night, rushed away on the crest of its own cordite stench, and left behind it a stillness more appropriate to cemetery surroundings. Mullaney knew the shot had been intended only to frighten, but he was now impervious to fear because of his knowledge of the jacket's whereabouts. Besides, he was beginning to realize something he had suspected all along, that his grandmother was simply full of shit, there *were* no ghosts, in or out of cemeteries. And since there were no ghosts to worry about, and since K could not harm him without eliminating the sole source of information about the jacket, he decided to play the same trick he had used to such marvelous advantage on Forty-second Street. He decided to reverse his field and charge K, knock him head over teacups and then run out of the cemetery and vanish until tomorrow morning. The wind was blowing fiercely as he turned, billowing into his jasmine shirt, causing the fabric to balloon out from his body. K stopped some twenty feet away from him and extended his arm again, the blued revolver in his hand pointing like an accusing finger. You can't scare me, pal, Mullaney thought, and permitted himself a grin as he rushed toward K. An orange spark flared in the night, there was the sound of the gun going off and then nothing, and then a whistling tearing rush of air, and Mullaney was surprised to see a neat little bullet hole appear in his jasmine shirt where it ballooned out not three inches from his heart. He was surprised to see the bullet hole because if K was trying to frighten him, he was carrying things just a trifle too far. Didn't K realize Mullaney was the *source?* Didn't K realize Mullaney knew where the jacket was?

A third shot sounded on the air, and this time the bullet whistled past Mullaney's left ear in terrifying proximity. He decided he had better knock K down before K did something he would be terribly sorry for later, like maybe killing Mullaney and therefore never finding out where the jacket was. Mullaney stepped to the left in a broken-field tactic he had learned from the encyclopedia, FA–FO, just as K fired again. Then he threw a block he had learned from the same volume, shoulder low, legs piston-bent, shoving up and back, catching K in the ribs and sending him tumbling over, the gun going off wildly in his hand for the fifth time, more than enough for an empty revolver if the gun was any one of a half-dozen or so in the Smith & Wesson line, but leaving yet another shot or more if the gun was one of the *other* Smith & Wessons, or a Colt, or a Ruger, or—oh boy there were too damn many of them, volume PA–PL, see also *Handguns, Revolvers, Weapons* and *Warfare.*

Mullaney ran.

He ran with uncontrollable glee, cavorting between the grave-stones, laughing to the night, delighted to have learned that his grandmother was full of shit, delighted to have knocked K on his ass, and delighted to be the only person in the entire world who knew the jacket was important and who *also* knew where it was—which was to say, delighted to be himself, Andrew Mullaney.

It was funny the way Mullaney got to be a fugitive from the law within the next ten minutes. Oh, not funny the way Fein-stein's death had been, but funny in a fateful sort of way that caused him to reflect later upon the vagaries of chance and the odds against drawing to an inside straight.

He had come perhaps six blocks from the monument works when he realized that an automobile was following him. Glancing rapidly over his shoulder, he saw only the car's headlights on the dark street, about half a block behind him. He quickened his pace, but the car maintained its distance, rolling along slowly beside the curb. He was in a suburban area of two-family houses that spread out in monotonous sameness from the cemetery's boundaries, and whereas there were lights on in many of the houses, the thought of knocking on one of those doors and telling someone he was being followed by a car possibly containing people who wanted to know where he had left the jacket he'd been wearing when they placed him in the coffin—the thought was ludicrous. Besides, as the car passed under a street lamp, Mullaney noticed that it had a distinctive green-and-white color combination and that it also sported a dome light, and it occurred to him just as the dome light came on and began revolving in a Martian manner, that the car was a police car.

"Hey you!" a voice behind him shouted, and he recognized the voice as belonging to one of the cops who had picked him up at the approach to the Queensboro Bridge. "You with the funeral story!" the voice continued, as if Mullaney needed further proof that these were his old friends Freddie and Lou, returning to correct their oversight of an hour before. The oversight, as Mullaney saw it, was that they had neglected to arrest him. They had undoubtedly taken a coffee break after dropping him off at McReady's friendly establishment, and had discussed the fellow in the jasmine shirt over their steaming cups of brew, coming to the conclusion that he had looked highly suspicious and dangerous and was undoubtedly armed and wanted for any number of crimes in California and some of the border states. They had then finished their prune and cheese Danishes and had come back to Queens to track him down, checking McReady's spooky courtyard first, and then cruising the streets where, worse luck, it had been comparatively simple to spot a man in a jasmine shirt.

So now they were behind him with their dome light revolving and their spotlight suddenly in action, bathing him in its glare as if he were trying to jump the wall at Sing Sing, and shouting, "You! You with the cockamamie story! Stop or we'll shoot!" which everyone seemed to be yelling at Mullaney lately, and which left him no choice but to cut around the corner toward the cemetery fence again, and leap the fence, and start running once again among the gravestones, though this time neither with fear nor jubilation. This time he ran with all the experience of a graveyard veteran, all the concentration of a steeplechase racer, dodging in and out of the stones, ducking, weaving, bobbing, running for a distant fence beyond which he could see a row of lighted apartment buildings. He had no idea where Freddie and Lou were, whether they had abandoned the squad car and were chasing him on foot, or whether they were simply cruising the cemetery's boundaries waiting for him to emerge again. That was a chance he would have to take. He felt certain that they were here to arrest him, and felt more than certain they would do exactly that the moment they saw the bullet hole K had put in his nice shirt. So he ran without fear and without joy, simply doing what had to be done, trying not to knock over any of the older, smaller gravestones, but concentrating on getting out of the cemetery and away from Freddie and Lou because tomorrow morning he hoped to get back to the New York Public Library to retrieve the jacket and wring from it its secret. The trick was to stay alive and out of sight until tomorrow morning at nine or ten or whenever the hell it was the library opened (he would get there at *eight*, to make sure) and that meant staying away from K's fellows and also Kruger's fellows, and now the Police Commissioner's fellows because he did not want to be arrested as a vagrant and have to spend however many days on Riker's Island. A fellow was a vagrant only if he didn't know what he wanted to do with his life, and Mullaney knew *exactly* what he wanted to do—or at least thought he did.

So he ran until he was out of breath, and then he rested behind one of the larger tombs (though not as large as Feinstein's) and then began running again toward that distant fence beyond which the apartment lights beckoned. When he reached the fence, he paused again, crouching behind a large marble slab, listening. He could hear nothing but the sound of a solitary cricket. Across the street, the apartment houses rose in illuminated majesty, and beyond them was the entire borough of Queens, which was certainly a large enough place in which to hide. Cautiously, quietly, he climbed the fence and dropped to his knees. He crouched a moment longer, still listening. Then he rose.

The spotlight came on the moment he stood erect.

"There he is!" Lou shouted.

"Shoot him!" Freddie said.

Mullaney broke into a run as the spotlight picked him up, beginning to feel the same indignation he had felt when Hijo threw him down the poolhall steps, wanting to turn and tell these fellows they were civil-service employees who were supposed to *protect* citizens like himself, not go turning spotlights on him, and not—for God's sake, they were shooting! They were both of them *shooting* at him, one of them standing outside the car and resting his revolver on his bent arm, and the other one manipulating the spotlight and getting off a shot every now and then, though neither of them were as good shots as K had been, neither of them came anywhere near putting a bullet in him or even his shirt. Out of breath, angry, indignant though unafraid, Mullaney ran across the street and into the nearest apartment building, saw the open and waiting elevator and was about to enter it when the doors closed. He looked up at the indicator, saw it marking the elevator's slow rise, calculated immediately that Freddie and Lou would assume he was in the elevator, and decided to take the steps up instead. He found the service stairway, opened the door (A sign warned KEEP THIS DOOR CLOSED FOR PROTECTION AGAINST FIRE, but it said nothing about PROTECTION AGAINST POLICE) and ran up the steps to the third floor. On the third floor, he opened another fire door and stepped into the corridor.

He had no idea what he would do next.

He heard music coming from the end of the corridor, voices, laughter. A party, he thought, and he decided to crash it, and then decided he could not take the chance because suppose they called the police and said somebody was trying to crash their party? He would then have not only Freddie and Lou chasing him but the whole damn Queens police force, and besides he wasn't in a party mood. In fact, it made him even more angry and indignant to realize that these happy Queens residents could be enjoying themselves at a party, drinking and laughing and dancing and having a grand old time while he, Andrew Mullaney, was being chased all over the city by gunmen of every persuasion. He had never been able to successfully crash a party in his life, but his anger now provided him with exactly the motivation he needed. He thought, as he marched angrily and indignantly to the apartment at the end of the hall, how marvelous it was that human beings could always find motivation whenever or wherever they needed it. Still marveling, he raised his fist, certain that he knew exactly how to crash the party. He banged on the door and waited. He heard the sounds of music within, and laughter, and then the clattering approach of high heels, and the chain being drawn back, and the door being unlocked.

The door opened.

"I live in the apartment downstairs," Mullaney said angrily and indignantly. "You're making too much noise, and I can't fall asleep."

"Well then come on in, honey, and have a drink," the girl said.

7. MELANIE

The girl was Nefertiti, the girl was Cleopatra as she must have really looked, the girl was colored, her skin as brown as nicotine, her eyes glowing and glinting and black, her hair cropped tight to her skull, huge golden earrings dangling, mouth full and parted in a beautiful wicked smile over great white sparkling teeth, the better to eat you with my dear, he had written sonnets about girls like this.

There was behind her the insinuating beat of a funky jazz tune, Thelonious Monk or Hampton Hawes, there was behind her the smoky greyness of a room indifferent to skin, the insistent clink and clash of whiskied ice and laughter, the off-key humming of a sinewy blonde in a purple dress, the fingersnapping click of a lean dark Negro in a dark blue suit, there was behind her the aroma of bodies, the aroma of perfume. And—also behind her, also seeming to rise from far behind her where lions roared to the velvet night and Kilimanjaro rose in misty splendor—rising from far behind her like mist itself, and undetected by her as she stood in smiling welcome in the doorway, one long brown slender arm resting on the door jamb, was a scent as comforting as a continent, he had written sonnets about girls like this.

"Well, come on in, honey, do," she said, and turned her back and went into the room.

He followed her in, immediately closing and locking the door behind him, shutting out the menace of Freddie and Lou, shutting out the menace of the sharpshooting K and the smokestacking Kruger, the memory of Merilee, the promise of whatever secret the jacket would reveal. He enclosed himself in a warm protective cocoon and watched the girl's lovely sinuous behind in the tight Pucci dress as she walked across the room ahead of him. She turned a small pirouette, lifted one hand in introduction, wrist bent, and announced, "The cat downstairs. He can't sleep."

"Give the man a drink," someone said, and Mullaney thought Here we go again.

"Is that a bullet hole in your shirt?" the girl asked.

"Yes," he answered. "How can you tell?"

"When you've seen one bullet hole," she said, "you've seen them all. Sit down and tell me how you got it."

He sat in an easy chair near the window where the borough of Queens winked its nighttime sky against the greater Friday glow of Manhattan, and the girl sat on the arm of the chair with her thigh in its Pucci silk tight against his arm, and the scent rising again from her, strong and intoxicating; he did not need the drink someone pressed into his hand.

"I was cleaning my revolver . . ." he started.

"Oh, you were cleaning your revolver," the girl said.

"Yes, and it went off."

"You must be more careful," the girl said. "Are the fuzz after you?" she asked.

"Yes," he answered honestly.

"I thought they might be. The reason I thought they might be is because the person who lives downstairs is an old lady of seventy years of age who can hardly walk because of her arthritis, and not a man in a pretty yellow shirt with a bullet hole in it."

"If you knew I wasn't the lady downstairs, why'd you let me in?"

"I'm partial to blue eyes."

"My eyes are brown."

"That's why I let you in."

"But you said . . ."

"I'm drunk, who knows *what* I'm saying?"

"What's your name?"

"Rose."

"Really? My mother's name was . . ."

"No."

"It's *not* Rose?"

"No. It's Abigail."

"All right, why'd you let me in, Abigail?"

"Don't call me Abigail. My name is Melanie."

"Is it really?"

"Absolutely. Melanie is from the Greek, it means black."

"But is it your name?"

"I just said so, didn't I?"

"You also said it was Rose and Abigail."

"That's right, it's Melanie Rose Abigail. Do you like that name?"

"I like it."

"Which one?"

"All of them."

"I like Melanie best."

"Why'd you let me in the apartment, Melanie?"

"I didn't want the fuzz to get you, that's right, call me Melanie, say Melanie. I don't like the fuzz to get anybody, not even murderers. Are you a murderer?"

"No, Melanie."

"Then why are the fuzz after you?"

"Because they think I look suspicious."

"You *do* look suspicious."

"That's because I'm a gambler, and also because I have a bullet hole in my shirt."

"No. It's because you have the look of a man who is searching for something, and Mother always taught me to regard such a man with suspicion and doubt."

"Is that how you regard me?"

"Yes. Who put the hole in your shirt?"

"A man named K."

"Who is a lousy shot."

"I don't think he was trying to hit me."

"Then why did he shoot at you?"

"To scare me."

"Did he?"

"No."

"What are you searching for?"

"Half a million dollars."

"Will you settle for a clean shirt that doesn't have a bullet hole in it?"

"Do you have one?"

"You didn't answer my question."

"If you have one, I'll settle for it. For the time being."

"Oh my, what will the man want next?" Melanie said, and rolled her eyes. She extended her hand to him. "Come," she said.

"Where?"

"To where I may have a shirt or two laying around."

"Which is where?"

"Questions, questions. Don't you trust me?"

"The police are in the building. *Should* I trust you?"

"Honey, who are you *going* to trust? When the fuzz come

busting in here, which they will most certainly do if they're already in the building, do you want them to find a suspicious-looking man with a bullet hole in his pretty yellow shirt, or do you want them to find a contented-looking man in a white shirt and a silk rep tie and perhaps a jacket that is still hanging in the closet of my bedroom that used to belong to a bass guitar player I kicked out last month, though not of your color? Would you like them to find a fellow whose pants look like they shrunk up three sizes too small for him, or would you like to find a well-dressed Ivy League type in nice pleatless slacks made for my bass guitar player friend at Chipp's, now which is it you prefer, and how can you afford *not* to trust me?"

"I trust you," Mullaney said.

"That's fine," Melanie answered, "because I have never trusted a white man in my entire life."

"Then why are you helping me?"

"It's the blue eyes that get me," Melanie said. "Also, I like gamblers."

"They're brown."

"Yes, but I'm drunk."

"Which is probably the only reason you're helping me."

"No. I don't like you to look so suspicious. I want you to look contented, man, contented."

"How will we manage that?" Mullaney asked.

"I have never kissed a man who did not look extremely contented afterwards."

"Oh, do you plan to kiss me?" Mullaney asked.

"I **plan** to swallow you alive," Melanie said.

He felt very well-dressed in his pleatless trousers and vented jacket, wearing the white shirt and gold and black silk-rep tie Melanie had provided, very collegiate, although he had never dressed like this when he was attending City College from 1949 to 1951, and again from 1954 to 1956, after he had served his two-year stint in the Army. He missed the old maroon sweater he used to wear religiously to classes in those days, and he also missed what the sweater represented, an attitude he had tried to recapture when he began taking the gamble a year ago, an attitude exemplified by the sweater, which was theadbare at the elbows and beginning to unravel at the cuffs, exemplified too by the fact that he owned only one key and even that didn't open anything he *really* possessed, it was to the lock of his mother Rose's apartment. He missed the maroon sweater and the reckless who-gives-a-damn attitude he had worn all through college, the knowledge that he would not be called upon for any responsibilities deeper than having his assignments in on time, or wearing a rubber when he screwed some hapless girl from Hunter. These Ivy League garments were very chic and very well-tailored, but they did not come anywhere near being as debonair as his maroon sweater.

He missed his jasmine shirt, too, which had been a gift from Irene on his thirty-eighth birthday, and which he had cherished over the interceding year and a half, almost two years. The maroon sweater had disappeared a long time ago, gone the way of all shabby sweaters and attitudes, and now the jasmine shirt had a bullet hole in it, and it too had been replaced with a bass guitar player's excellently tailored threads, and Melanie had promised to swallow him alive.

The suspense was killing him.

The suspense at first was compounded of two equal parts: the possibility that Freddie and Lou might at any moment knock on the apartment door, and the further possibility that Melanie might at any moment swallow him alive. There was something very strange about Melanie in that she had told him she did not trust any white man (he believed her) and yet she would not let him out of her sight, would not let go of his hand, would not stop rubbing her long sinuous cat's body against him at every opportunity. He was beginning to suspect that she was naked beneath the clinging Pucci silk, and the notion of exploring this darkest heart, the possibility of being swallowed alive by a race and an intelligence that went back millenniums, consumed as it were by someone or something that simultaneously hated him and desired him was tantalizing and terribly exciting. But conversely, and contradictorily, and contrarily, he was terrified that she would indeed envelop him in her blackness, completely enclose him in the centuries-old vastness of her mother womb, absorb him, cause him to disappear from view entirely, swallow him alive exactly as she had promised.

Adding to the suspense was the advancing hour. He had crashed the party at perhaps twenty minutes past midnight, and it was now ten minutes past one, with still no sign of the diligent Freddie and Lou. This was a large apartment building, of course, and it could be assumed that if they were knocking on every door it would take them quite a while to work their way around to Melanie's apartment, by which time she might already have feasted upon him and drunk his blood. Or, worse fate, Freddie and Lou might break in on the moment of climax, catch them *in delicto,* as it were, adding Indecent Exposure to their charges, or perhaps Disorderly Conduct, or perhaps extraditing him to Alabama and slapping him with a retroactive charge of Miscegenation, there were all sorts of possibilities to the law now that he was a fugitive.

By this time, many of Melanie's guests, both black and white (the white ones puzzled him since he couldn't understand why someone who didn't trust white men would have three white men and two white women among her Friday-night party guests), were beginning to say their farewells and go off into the night to pursue their separate desires. He knew for certain now that Melanie was naked beneath the silk. He touched her breast and saw the nipple rise against the fabric and then she pulled away from him and smiled in wicked encouragement, and he saw desire and hatred mingled again on her face and wanted to love her and simultaneously wanted to destroy her, it was all very confusing.

In one moment, he hoped that Freddie and Lou would arrive

quickly, revolvers drawn, handcuffs waiting, to carry him away from this dangerous, hateful cannibal who would most surely destroy him. But in the next moment, he devoutly wished that they would *never* find him, that he could take this exciting, beautiful, passionate and wanton woman, ravage her repeatedly, hate her, love her, possess her, be possessed by her, merge with her, become one with her, become some vaguely defined beige mixture of arms and legs and lips, settle the entire civil-rights movement there on her bed without assistance from Martin Luther King or anyone, thrash out the hate and leave only the love, and yet knowing this was impossible because too much of it was compounded in hate. Suspensefully, Melanie took his hand between her own two hands, palms full and cushioned and moist, and brought them to her mouth and nibbled at his fingers while he watched the clock. Help me Freddie and Lou, he thought, why is there never a cop around when you need one?

He noticed a rather fat and frizzled Negro woman sitting in an easy chair near the record player, moving her crossed leg in time to the music, so that her sandaled foot tapped out the beat on thin air. The woman was perhaps fifty or fifty-five, and she was wearing a black muu muu, white pearls around her throat, hair cut just like Melanie's, in close tight African style. She kept beating her foot on the air as though she were squashing white missionaries and Belgian nuns, her skin very black, her teeth very white, her black eyes darting around the room as the number of guests dwindled, until finally it was a quarter-to-two, and the only people in the room were Melanie, the very black and menacing woman in the muu muu, and he himself, Andrew Mullaney.

It occurred to him along about then that Freddie and Lou were not going to find him this night, and so he began resigning himself to the pleasurably hateful fate of making love to Melanie. Suspense being a delicate thing at best, however, he realized that whereas Freddie and Lou were no longer a qualifying element, the large woman in the muu muu definitely was. He wondered if she was planning to spend the night, and then wondered how he could delicately ask about her.

Melanie saved him the trouble by saying, "I don't think you've met my mother."

"I don't think I have," Mullaney said. "Pleasure."

"The white man is a horse's ass," Melanie's mother said, not meaning anything personal.

"Don't mind her," Melanie said. "Would you help me take out the garbage?"

"The white man is fit for taking out the garbage," Melanie's mother said.

"Don't mind her," Melanie said. "The incinerator is down the hall."

"The white man is fit for the incinerator," Melanie's mother said, which sent a shiver up Mullaney's spine.

They gathered up the bags of garbage in the kitchen, and carried them to the front door. At the door, Melanie said, "Why don't you go to sleep, Mother," and Mother simply replied, "I'm not sleepy."

"Very well," Melanie said, and sighed, and opened the door. She preceded Mullaney down the empty hallway toward the small incinerator room. He pulled open the furnace door for her, and she dropped the bags of garbage down the chute. Below, somewhere in the bowels of the building, there was the sense if not the actual sound and smell of licking flames, a hidden well of fire destroying the waste of a metropolis. He released the handle, and the door banged back into place. Below, the building throbbed with consuming fire, a dull steady roar that vibrated into the soles of his feet and shuddered through the length of his body.

"Kiss me," Melanie said.

This is the gamble, he thought as he took her into his arms. This is why I took the gamble a year ago, I took it for this moment in this room, this girl in my arms here and now, I have written sonnets about girls like this. I took the gamble so that I could make love to women in the stacks of the New York Public Library, I took the gamble so that I could make love to women in incinerator rooms, black or white, yellow or red, lowering her to the floor and raising the Pucci silk up over her brown thighs and reaching his hand into the thick tangled black hair suddenly revealed, the pink wet wonder of her parting to receive him, "I hate you," she said, "Yes," he said, "love me," and she wrapped her long legs around him. He reached for the top of her dress, lowered it off her shoulders and kissed the dark nipples against the dark skin, "I hate you," she said again, "Love me," he said, "I hate you, I hate you, I hate you," her teeth clamped into his lips, he could taste blood, he thought She will kill me, and thought This is the gamble, and remembered he had once very long ago when he was a soldier made love, no, had not made love, had laid, had humped, had *fucked* a Negro prostitute in a curbside crib while his buddy waited outside for his turn, and had not considered it a gamble. And had later told Irene that he had once laid a colored girl, and she had said, "How lucky you are," and he had not known whether or not she was kidding. Here and now, here with the fires of hell burning in the building below, here with a girl who repeated over and over again as he moved inside her, "I hate you, I hate you, I hate you," he wondered about the gamble for the first time in a year, and came without her. "I hate you," she said, with excellent reason this time.

He told her he was sorry, which he truly was, and which he thought was a gentlemanly and certainly American thing to admit, as she pulled her dress down over her long brown legs, and stood up. She said his apology was accepted, but that nonetheless he had been an inadequate and disappointing partner, whereas she had been hoping for someone with skill and virtuosity enough to perform on Ferris wheels, for example.

"I would be willing to do it on a *roller* coaster!" he shouted in defense, and then lowered his voice because it was, after all, the wee small hours of the morning, whispering, "I'm truly sorry, Melanie."

Yes, she said, but you must admit there is something about the white man that can only engender hatred and distrust, dusting off her Pucci dress, and tucking her breasts back into the bodice. The white man has been taking for centuries and centuries, she said, and he doesn't know how to give, you see, nor even how to accept graciously. The white man (he was beginning to feel as if he'd been captured by the Sioux) knows only how to grab and grab and grab—which is why you have that look on your face that Mother always warned me about—but he doesn't know what he really wants or even why the hell he's grabbing. The white man is a User and a Taker and a Grabber, and he will continue to Use and Take and Grab until there's nothing left for him to feast upon but his own entrails, which he will devour like a hyena, did you know that hyenas eat their own intestines?

"No, I did not know that," Mullaney said, amazed and repulsed.

It is a little known fact, Melanie said, but true. You must not think I'm angry at you, or would harbor any ill feelings toward you, or seek any revenge other than not permitting you to spend the night in my apartment, which would be impossible with Mother here, anyway. She despises the white man, as you may have gathered. I, on the other hand, *like* the white man, I really do. As a group, that is. And whereas it's true that I've never met one individually or singly of whom I could be fond, this doesn't mean I don't like them as a group. I am, for example, keenly disappointed in you personally, but this needn't warp my judgment of the group as a whole, do you understand? In fact, I suppose I should be grateful to you for proving to me once again just how undependable the white man really is, as an individual of course. Trust him, let him have his way with you, and what does he do once again but leave you with empty promises, though I wouldn't march on Washington for something as trivial as this, still I think you know what I mean. Now I suppose you think I'm going to ask you to give me back those clothes you're wearing, send you out into the night wearing your own flimsy yellow shirt with the bullet hole in it, but no, I'm not the type to seek revenge or to harbor any ill feelings, as I've already told you. I *like* the white man, I do. So you can keep the clothes because they once belonged to a Negro who is ten times the man you are, though I don't wish to offend you or even cause you any embarrassment. But perhaps they'll remind you as you go through life that you once took a little colored girl in an incinerator room, grabbed her and took her and used her, and left her not hating you, certainly not hating you, but nonetheless feeling a very keen disappointment in you, which I should have been prepared to expect. But grateful to you nonetheless for ascertaining it once again to my satisfaction. I am, in fact, *extremely* satisfied. Your performance was exactly what I expected, and therefore I am satisfied with my disappointment, do you understand what I'm saying?

"Oh, of course," Mullaney said, relieved.

"Well, good then," Melanie said, and offered her hand and said, "Good luck, I hope the fuzz don't get you, I take the pill."

"I beg your pardon?"

"I take the pill, don't worry, and I hope the fuzz don't get you."

"Thank you," Mullaney said.

The fuzz were waiting for him outside the building.

In fact, Freddie, or Lou, or perhaps both of them, hit him on the head with a blackjack or some similar weapon or weapons.

8. BOZZARIS

At eight o'clock on Saturday morning, Mullaney was brought up to the lieutenant's office, together with the eight other prisoners who had spent the night downstairs in the precinct's detention cells.

The lieutenant's name was Bozzaris, and he sat behind a scarred wooden desk in the only two-window office in the squadroom, puffing on a cigar and studying the men who stood before the desk in various attitudes of discomfort. He had very black hair parted in the middle. The part seemed to lead directly into a rather long cleaving nose which bisected his face, pointing toward the long cigar in the exact center of his mouth, which seemed in turn to join the cleft in the exact center of his chin, so that Bozzaris seemed to possess a face that had been formed by folding an ink blot in half, thereby producing two equal and identical sides.

"Well," he said, "I don't know how many of you folks who were arrested last night are familiar with the procedure here in New York City, but I thought I might fill you in on it for your own benefit and also because I have always been a maverick, witness my name."

Mullaney had never heard of a maverick named Bozzaris, but he made a mental note to look it up in his encyclopedia when he got the chance and also when his landlady let him back into his room.

"We used to have a thing here in New York, oh maybe two three years ago, which has now been abolished, but which was a very good thing while it lasted. I am referring to the lineup, which I am sure at least some of you folks are familiar with, and which has been discontinued oh these past two three years. Now the lineup was a very good thing, I will repeat that, a *very* good thing, because it enabled detectives from squads all over the city to go down to Police Headquarters on Centre Street and get an actual glimpse of all the people who were committing crimes all over this fair metropolis, that was the purpose of the lineup. As some of you folks here may know, only felony offenders were taken to the lineup, and a felony is a crime punishable by death or imprisonment in a state prison, so we used to get quite a show down there every morning from Monday to Thursday. But unfortunately that's all been done away with, be that as it may, we won't go into police policies right now, let's just say the loss has been keenly felt, especially by nonconformists like myself, witness my name.

"Well, I want to tell you that whereas the Police Department of the City of New York may have done away with the lineup, Detective-Lieutenant Alexander Bozzaris has not done away with it here in his private bailiwick, which happens to be this squadroom in this precinct right here. Every morning before we take you people down to the Criminal Courts Building to be arraigned, I have my own personal lineup for the felony offenders we pulled in the night before, just for the enlightenment of all the hard-working detectives on my squad. Now I want to assure you folks that this is just an informal little gathering, but in keeping with the landmark ruling of the Supreme Court of our land, I am compelled to mention several things to you which you may or may not care to take advantage of. I must advise you, first of all, that you don't have to answer any questions I ask you, and also that anything you say can and will be used against you in court, though I'm sure you know we won't take unfair advantage, nossir. Next, in keeping with the protection afforded to you by the Fifth Amendment of our Constitution, which gives you the right to choose between silence and speech, I have to tell you that you can ask for a lawyer, and if you can't afford one, the state will have to get one for you, though I'm sure none of you is going to need a lawyer at this informal little get-together. And lastly, I want you to know that if you make any statements without a lawyer being present, the burden's going to be on us to prove that you waived your rights. So, as you can see, we're pretty much hamstrung here, and I'm sure none of you is going to have any objections about this little private lineup, do any of you have any objections?"

Mullaney thought for a minute that he might object, but then saw that none of the other prisoners were objecting, and decided he wouldn't be a spoilsport.

"Okay then," Bozzaris said, "if there are no objections, and I appreciate that, folks, I sincerely do, then I guess we can get on with our little lineup here. Please take seats on that bench over against the wall there, and I'll bring my fellows in, and we can get this show on the road, I hope you all had a good night's rest downstairs in our comfortable detention cells."

Bozzaris pushed a button on his desk, and a detective appeared at the door. "All right, Sam," he said, "bring the other fellows in, and let's get this show on the road."

"Right," Sam said, and went out, and came back again not two minutes later with five other detectives who nodded at the lieutenant and then began to perform certain routine chores and duties around the room. One of them drew the green shades on the mesh-covered windows; another of them turned out the overhead light; yet another pulled down a white screen that was hanging on the wall opposite the lieutenant's desk. Even in the semidarkness, Mullaney could see that the screen was marked with graduated height readings: five-foot-four, five-foot-six, five-foot-eight, and so on. The detective named Sam turned on a spotlight that hit the screen in a sudden explosion of intense whiteness, and then the lieutenant cleared his throat and said, "Well, let's begin."

"Ready to begin, sir," the detective named Sam said.

Bozzaris cleared his throat again. "Well, let's see what we have here this morning," he said in a friendly cheerful manner, and then called off the name and the age of the first offender.

The man who got off the bench and walked to the screen was nattily dressed in a dark brown suit, white shirt, yellow tie, and polished brown shoes. He looked like a jockey. He stood against the screen and Mullaney saw that his height was just five feet six inches. In the same cheerful friendly voice, Bozzaris told the assembled detectives why the man had been arrested, and then said, "No statement," which Mullaney took to mean the prisoner hadn't said anything when they'd apprehended him, a gambit he himself had employed the night before, mainly because he had been unconscious at the time.

"Well now," Bozzaris said, "it seems that you picked somebody's pocket last night, Jerry, is that right?"

"No," Jerry said, "I'm innocent."

"Be that as it may," Bozzaris said in his friendly familiar voice, "two off-duty detectives saw you stick your hand into a man's pocket and remove his wallet from it, isn't that right, Jerry?"

"No, I'm innocent," Jerry said, which Mullaney wished he wouldn't say quite so often or quite so strenuously.

"Well, Jerry," Bozzaris said, "when you were arrested we found a man's wallet in your pocket, and the name in that wallet was David Gross. Now your name doesn't happen to be David Gross, does it, Jerry?"

"No, it's Jerry Cooke," Jerry said, sounding astonished.

"That's what I thought, Jerry."

"Yes, that's what it is," Jerry said, sounding even more astonished.

"So how did this wallet with a driver's license for a man named David Gross, and a Diners Club card for this man David Gross, and oh all sorts of identification for this man David Gross, happen to come into your possession? Would you happen to know, Jerry?"

"Gee, I wouldn't happen to know," Jerry said.

"Unless you picked it out of his pocket, isn't that right, Jerry?"

"Gee, I wouldn't know," Jerry said.

"Well, what do you think, Jerry?"

"I think I'm innocent."

"You didn't pick Mr. Gross's pocket?"

"No, sir. That I definitely did not do."

"Are you a pickpocket, Jerry?"

"Yes, sir, I am. And a very good one, I'm proud to say."

"Jerry, I have your B-sheet here, and I think these gentlemen might be interested in knowing that you have been arrested for picking pockets on three separate occasions, and convicted on two of those occasions, so just how good a pickpocket you are would seem to be a matter for debate. Did you or did you not pick Mr. Gross's pocket?"

"No, sir, I did not. I am innocent."

"Jerry, you had better have new stationery made," Bozzaris said. "Next case."

One of the detectives took Jerry's arm and led him to the door, where a uniformed policeman was waiting to escort him out. Mullaney watched with rising anticipation, knowing very well that he, personally, had not committed a felony or, for that matter, *any* crime—and hoping to tell that to Bozzaris at the earliest opportunity. But there were eight other prisoners in the room (including a woman, he now saw), and he wondered how long it would take Bozzaris to get to him.

"Harrison, Randolph, age twenty-six," Bozzaris said, "beat a man over the head with a stickball bat. No statement."

Harrison got off the bench and walked over to the white screen, shading his eyes with his hand and trying to see past the glaring spotlight. He was a man of medium height and build, wearing a plaid sports jacket and dark-blue slacks. His white shirt was open at the throat, and he wore no tie.

"Well now," Bozzaris said, "why did you hit a man over the head with a stickball bat, Randy?"

"Who says I did?" Randy answered.

"Well, the man you hit over the head with the bat, for one."

"If I hit him with anything at all, which I didn't, it was definitely not a stickball bat."

"What was it?"

"A broom handle."

"What's the difference between a stickball bat and a broom handle?"

"A stickball bat has had the broom part taken off of it, whereas what it is claimed I hit him with had the broom part still attached. Therefore, if I hit him, it was with a broom handle which was never a stickball bat."

"Be that as it may, why did you hit him?"

"If I hit him, which I didn't, it was because of a tip."

"A tip?"

"On a horse."

"You gave him a tip on a horse."

"No. *He* refused to give *me* a tip on a horse."

"So you hit him."

"I persuaded him to give me the tip."

"On which horse?" Bozzaris asked, and Mullaney looked toward the desk, where he saw Bozzaris picking up a pencil and moving a small pad into place.

"Well, I don't know if I should reveal such a confidence," Randy said, "especially since it is claimed I hit a man with a stickball bat."

"Perhaps the charge will be dropped, who knows?" Bozzaris said.

"Who knows indeed?" Randy said. "But in the meantime, why should I give away a perfectly good tip on a horse which was supposed to run yesterday and got scratched, but which is running today instead. At twenty-to-one on the morning line."

"Twenty-to-one?" Bozzaris asked.

"Twenty-to-one," Randy said.

There was a new flurry of activity in the room. Mullaney noticed that all the gathered detectives were opening their black books in which they took notes on criminals and criminal activities, and reaching for pens and pencils.

"Where is this horse running?" Bozzaris asked.

"Aqueduct."

"Which race?"

"The second race."

"And the horse's name?"

"It is too bad about this charge against me," Randy said.

"It certainly is," Bozzaris agreed, "but people are talking to the D.A. all the time, and who knows what will fall upon his ear? I personally, in fact, do not see how anyone could get hurt with a broom handle. It had been my impression that this person was assaulted with a stickball bat, which is a horse of another color."

"A stickball bat *can* be a very dangerous weapon," Randy agreed.

"Certainly. But I don't see how a broom handle, especially with the broom attached, could be at all dangerous."

"Neither do I."

"Ask him the horse's name," one of the detectives said.

"By the way, what *is* the horse's name?" Bozzaris said.

"I will tell you in confidence if you promise to respect the confidence," Randy said.

"I will certainly respect the confidence," Bozzaris promised.

Randy walked to the desk, bent over it, and whispered something into the lieutenant's ear. Bozzaris nodded and scribbled a word onto the pad in front of him. Mullaney tried to see what was written on the pad, but the room was too dark and the desk too distant.

"Thank you," Bozzaris said, "I certainly appreciate this confidence."

"Please say hello to the district attorney for me," Randy said.

"Next case," Bozzaris said. "Hawley, Michael, age fifty-seven, and Ryan, Diana, age fifty-five, broke into a jewelry store on West Forty-seventh Street, no statement. How about it, folks?"

There seemed to be a new excitement in the air, and Mullaney realized it had nothing to do with the tip Randy had just given the lieutenant, which tip was still secretly nestled under Bozzaris' large protecting hand. The detectives were leaning forward avidly, their eyes fixed on the man and woman who now stood against the illuminated white screen. Mullaney found himself leaning forward as well, intently studying the pair and trying to determine what accounted for their undeniable star quality. There was no question that they were the leading performers thus far, though not next-to-closing, and Mullaney could not imagine why. They seemed to be the most ordinary sort of aging couple, the man a lanky fellow in a dark-green raincoat, his hands in his pockets, his hair long and unruly, a dazed look on his face; the woman a frizzled redhead wearing too much makeup, a wrinkled blue dress, and the same dazed expression. Yet every detective in the office was giving them his undivided attention, and even Bozzaris' voice dropped a decibel or two, so that it now seemed he was talking to a pair of honored guests in his own living room, the governor and his wife perhaps, his voice friendly and warm, the port sparkling in the light of a cozy fire, intimate and relaxed; Mullaney heard himself sighing.

"What were you doing in that jewelry store, Mike?" Bozzaris asked.

"Looking," Mike said.

"For what?"

"A ring." Mike smiled in embarrassment. "For Diana," he said.

"For who?"

"Diana."

"Me," the woman said. "He was looking for a ring for me."

"At three o'clock in the morning?" Bozzaris said.

"Yes," Diana said, and blushed.

"Why?"

"Because we just got engaged," Diana said, and smiled.

"What?"

"Last night. And we needed an engagement ring."

"At three o'clock in the morning?"

"Yes. Well no. We got engaged at two-thirty. So Mike said we needed a ring."

"So we went out shopping for one," Mike said.

"But all the stores were closed," Diana said.

"So you decided to open one," Bozzaris said.

"That's right," Mike said. "But we didn't mean any harm."

"It's just we're in love," Diana said, and squeezed her fiancé's hand.

"Let me get this straight," Bozzaris said. "You got engaged . . ."

"I love you, darling," Diana said.

"I love you, too, sweetheart," Mike said.

". . . last night at two-thirty and decided you needed a ring . . ."

"Yes, to seal the engagement. I love you, honey."

"Oh darling, yes, I love you, too."

"Now cut it *out!*" Bozzaris said. "There happens to be a law against breaking into jewelry stores."

"What do jewelers know about love?" Mike asked.

"Or policemen, for that matter," Diana said.

"Be that as it may, you'd better listen to me, you two, because this is something pretty serious here, and I want some honest answers."

"All our answers so far have been honest, Lieutenant," Mike said sincerely, and blew a kiss at Diana.

"Good, and I hope they'll continue to be that way because we appreciate honesty here, don't we, fellows?"

The detectives grunted.

"I love you," Mike said.

"I adore you," Diana replied.

"This is what I want to ask you," Bozzaris said, "and I'd appreciate an honest answer: Did you know that a large jewelry concern on Forty-seventh Street was broken into on Thursday night?"

"What's that got to do with *last* night?" Mike asked.

"I love you," Diana said.

"Last night was *Friday* night," Mike said.

"That's true, and I'm glad you're still being honest with us," Bozzaris said. "But I'm asking you about Thursday night, and I want to know whether or not you were aware of the information I just gave you."

"What information?"

"That a large jewelry store on Forty-seventh Street was broken into on Thursday night."

"No, I was not aware of that information," Mike said.

"Now that you're aware of it, what do you think?"

"I don't know anything about it," Mike said.

"Neither do I," Diana said. "All I know is I love him, oooh, I love him, love him, *love* him."

"Would it surprise you to learn," Bozzaris asked, "that several very expensive gems were stolen from that concern on Thursday night?"

"It would surprise me," Mike said, "because I have no knowledge whatever of the heist."

"I adore you," Diana said.

"The stolen gems were diamonds, Mike."

"That's very interesting."

"There were three very *large* diamonds stolen, Mike, each about ten carats, and there were also eight smaller diamonds stolen, about five or six carats each."

"I'm sorry to hear that," Mike said, "but what's it got to do with love?"

"Lots of money involved here, Mike."

"Can money buy love?" Mike asked.

"I worship you," Diana said.

"Mike, when our patrolman found you and Diana there in the jewelry store with the alarm ringing, you were stuffing your pockets with diamond rings, kid stuff compared to the Thursday-night heist, oh maybe one or two carats each, some a little larger, maybe something like twenty thousand dollars involved, small potatoes. But don't you think it's possible, Mike, that someone who knocked over a place on Thursday night—and got away with it—might decide to come back to the same street on Friday night and knock over *another* place?"

"It's possible," Mike said. "Are you saying *I* knocked over that place on Thursday night?"

"You just said it was possible."

"Why would I do a thing like that?"

"Why not?"

"We weren't even *engaged* on Thursday night. In fact, we hadn't even *met* on Thursday night."

"Kiss me," Diana said.

"Why'd you need so many rings?" Bozzaris asked.

"I beg your pardon?"

"You had seven or eight rings in your pockets. Why'd you need so many?"

"A girl like Diana should have a choice," Mike said.

"He's mad about me," Diana said.

"I'm mad about you," Mike admitted.

"So your story is you know nothing about that other heist, huh?" Bozzaris said.

"What's your favorite color?" Mike asked Diana.

"Yellow," she said. "What's yours?"

"Blue. Who's your favorite singer?"

"Sinatra. Who's yours?"

"Yes, oh yes! Do you want boys or girls?"

"Three of each."

"Get them out of here," Bozzaris said.

"Do you like walking in the rain?"

"I love it. What's your favorite pie?"

"Blueberry."

"I love you."

"I adore you."

Mullaney watched as they led the engaged couple out of the room, trying to figure out how he could sneak over to Bozzaris' desk for a look at the nag's name on the pad there under his hand. If this really *was* a bona-fide tip, and if the jacket at the library really *did* contain the clue to the whereabouts of five hundred thousand dollars, " . . . age thirty-nine," Bozzaris was saying, "charged with Burglary in the First Degree. No statement."

The room was silent. No one rose from the bench to walk toward the screen.

"Is he here?" Bozzaris asked.

"Mullaney, Andrew," the detective named Sam said. "Are you here?"

"Present!" Mullaney said, and rose swiftly.

"All right, Andy, let's get up there," Bozzaris said.

Mullaney nodded and walked toward the screen. The spotlight was blinding, he could see only the detective sitting closest to the screen; beyond him, the room was a black void. Bozzaris' voice came out of that void, friendly and familiar. "Shall I read that again, Andy?"

"Please," Mullaney said.

"Mullaney, Andrew, age thirty-nine," Bozzaris said. "You're charged with Burglary One, what do you have to say?"

"I don't understand the charge," Mullaney said.

"I will explain the charge, or at least the part that applies to you," Bozzaris said. "You are charged with violation of Section 402 of the Penal Law of New York State, Burglary in the First Degree, which is defined thusly: A person who, with intent to commit some crime therein, breaks and enters in the night time, the dwelling house of another, in which there is at the time a human being and who, while engaged in the night time in effecting such entrance, or in committing any crime in such a building, or in escaping therefrom, assaults any person. That is the charge as it applies to you, Andy. How about it?"

"I didn't break and enter any building."

"You broke and entered a cottage owned by a Mr. Roger McReady of McReady's Monument Works in the borough of Queens, at or about midnight last night."

"I was invited into the cottage."

"You broke and entered in the night time the dwelling of another at which time Roger McReady, who I'm told is a human being, was present. And in attempting to escape from this dwelling, you assaulted a friend of Mr. McReady's by tackling him and knocking him to the ground in the cemetery where he was giving chase. What do you say, Andy? Burglary One happens to be punishable by no less than ten and no more than thirty."

"Years?" Mullaney asked.

"Years."

"That's a long time."

"That's a very long time. What do you have to say, Andy?"

"What is it I'm supposed to have burgled?"

"You're supposed to have burgled a considerable amount of whiskey, as well as some very good cheese and salami. Is this your first offense?"

"I've never had any trouble with the law before," Mullaney said.

"In that case," Bozzaris said, "the arraigning magistrate may wish to set bail for you since this is your first offense. So what we'll do is take you downtown to be mugged and printed, and then you'll go over to the Criminal Courts Building where you'll be arraigned and a date for your trial will be set. Do you have anything to say before you go?"

"Yes, but I would like to tell it to you in confidence," Mullaney said, "if you promise to respect the confidence."

"I will most certainly respect the confidence," Bozzaris said.

Mullaney walked to the desk and bent over it. He stepped carefully to Bozzaris' left, so that Bozzaris had to lean over slightly, his hand moving away from the pad upon which he had scribbled the horse's name. Mullaney put his mouth close to the lieutenant's ear, and then glanced swiftly at the penciled lettering on the pad:

JAWBONE

"I'm innocent," Mullaney whispered.

"Be that as it may," Bozzaris said.

The name Jawbone was blinking on and off inside Mullaney's skull as he was led to the door and out of the office, letters ten feet high, JAWBONE, jawbone, JAWBONE, jawbone, the nag who was supposed to have run in the fourth race yesterday, apparently scratched—according to Harrison, Randolph, age twenty-six—and running today instead, twenty to one on the morning line. If that jacket at the library could really tell him where to find the five hundred thousand dollars, and if Aqueduct would take all the money he could bet in the half hour between races—Mullaney was so lost in thanking God for the good fortune that had caused him to get arrested, so lost in counting the profit he would make on that wonderful marvelous horse Jawbone, that he scarcely realized he was being led with the other prisoners into a police van and taken downtown to 100 Centre Street, where they were photographed and fingerprinted, JAWBONE, jawbone, JAWBONE, and then marched across the street for arraignment. The

presiding magistrate was a man who looked like Spencer Tracy in
Judgment at Nuremburg. Apparently thinking Mullaney was
Heinrich Himmler, he sternly read the charge against him and
asked whether Mullaney understood it. Mullaney said he did.
The judge then asked Mullaney how he chose to plead, and
Mullaney said, "Not guilty." The judge then asked him whether
or not he could afford a lawyer because if he couldn't the court
would supply one from the Legal Aid Society, but Mullaney said
he would find his own lawyer, thanking the judge just the same,
and having in mind Marvin Pitkin who had done so well for
Feinstein before his comical demise. The judge then told Mullaney that he personally considered First Degree Burglary a
heinous crime since it involved the violation of a man's *sanctum
sanctorum,* the breaking and entering into his home of homes, his
dwelling place, in the night time, all of which sounded very
familiar to Mullaney and almost put him to sleep. Because of the
serious nature of the crime, the judge said, he was going to set an
extremely high bail for a first offense, and that bail would be five
hundred dollars. Mullaney was about to tell the judge that
meeting such a bail was an impossibility, when a voice at the
back of the courtroom said, "I'll pay this man's bail, your Honor."

"Your name, sir?" the judge asked.

"Arthur Purcell, your Honor," the voice from the rear of the
courtroom said.

Mullaney turned and saw Purcell—a blond, pleasant-looking
man of about thirty-three, wearing a grey suit, white shirt and
black tie—walking toward the front of the courtroom. The judge
told him to settle things with the bailiff, and Purcell immediately
went to the right-hand side of the courtroom where someone,
presumably the bailiff, was sitting behind a desk covered with
rubber stamps and inked pads, and officially banging away at all
the documents spread before him. Mullaney saw Purcell reaching
into his back pants pocket for a wallet, and then the judge
cleared his throat and Mullaney turned toward the bench again.
The judge informed him that he was expected to appear in court

on May seventeenth, and that if he did not appear on that date, the bail would be forfeited and a warrant issued for his arrest. He asked Mullaney whether or not he understood that. Mullaney said that he understood it completely. Very well, the judge said, you are released on five hundred dollars bail until the seventeenth of May, try to stay out of trouble until then. Mullaney assured the judge that he would try very hard to stay out of trouble, meanwhile thinking of the jacket in the library and of how many tickets on Jawbone he could buy and of how he would spend the money plus all of his winnings on a life of romantic adventure in Monaco, Rio de Janeiro or perhaps even Jakarta. Purcell fell into step beside him as he walked toward the leather-padded doors at the rear of the courtroom.

"Thank you very much, Mr. Purcell," Mullaney said. "I certainly appreciate your generosity and kindness."

"Don't thank *me*," Purcell said, and held the door open for Mullaney to precede him into the marble corridor.

"Who *should* I thank?" Mullaney asked, and immediately saw K standing by the corridor window.

K no longer wore his torn and tattered rags of the night before. Instead, he was dressed in a freshly pressed blue suit. He looked very grim, if extremely neat, the small gold K still holding his tie in place. He beckoned to Mullaney, and Mullaney figured there was no sense arguing with him now, especially since Purcell had a rather large and unsightly bulge on the left-hand side of his coat, which could not have been caused by his wallet because Mullaney remembered that he kept his wallet in the back pocket of his trousers. He also remembered that K had put a hole in his jasmine shirt the night before (something for which he would never entirely forgive him). Someone—probably Feinstein—had once taught him never to argue with gentlemen who were heeled, so he decided to chat instead and desperately searched for an opening conversational gambit that might possibly eradicate the very grim look K—and now even Purcell—was wearing.

"I heard you were dead," Mullaney said at last.

"No, I am alive," K assured him.

"I see that."

"Yes."

"That's a very nice suit."

"Thank you. It was made for me by the same person who tailored your burial garments."

"Oh," Mullaney said.

"Yes. Which brings up a small matter . . ."

"You weren't dressed nearly as well last night," Mullaney said.

"That's because I was in an automobile accident and then was forced to make my way through the brambles and bushes lining the parkway in order to avoid getting killed by the people who had engineered the accident."

"I see," Mullaney said.

"Yes. Some people by the name of Adolph Kruger and his fellows, with whom I understand you have become acquainted."

"I didn't know his name was Adolph," Mullaney said.

"Well, there is oft ignorance afoot," K quoted, "but it neither dims nor extinguishes the true light."

"I'm sure," Mullaney said.

"About the jacket . . ."

"But on the other hand . . ."

". . . Roger McReady tells me that you know where the jacket is, and that . . ."

". . . on the other hand, there is oft true light afoot, but it neither dims nor extinguishes the ignorance."

"On the other hand," K said, "people have oft had their heads broken for not listening to reason and answering questions that have been put to them."

"What was the question?" Mullaney asked.

"The question was: Where's the jacket?"

Mullaney suddenly remembered that he was inside a court-house (a sign over the entrance doors advised him that this was PART 1A, and a second sign on a metal stand to the left of the doors read JUDGE LUTHER HORTON PRESIDING) and further remembered that this was a *criminal* courthouse. It was then that he noticed how many policemen of every stripe were swarming all over this second-floor corridor, and wondered whether K or Purcell would risk shooting at him with so many uniformed minions of the law abounding, not to mention untold invisible plainclothesmen. How *could* they risk shooting, how could they even risk giving chase?

"Why should I tell you where the jacket is?" Mullaney asked, stalling while he made his decision. He didn't feel like running again (he had been doing so goddamn *much* running lately), but neither did he feel like getting shot at again, or even hit on the head again.

"You should tell us where the jacket is," K said logically and smoothly and calmly, "because if you do, I will induce Mr. McReady to drop the criminal charges against you, which charges —as you may or may not know—could lead to at least ten years in a state penitentiary."

"Yes, I know that," Mullaney said, thinking furiously. "But what's so important about that jacket?"

"Let us say it has sentimental value," K said.

"Let us say bullshit," Mullaney said.

"Mr. Mullaney," K said, "the possibility also exists that we will kill you if you do not tell us where the jacket is. Have you weighed that possibility?"

"Yes," Mullaney said, thinking Why, I don't have to run at all! All I have to do is turn swiftly and economically and begin walking toward the elevator bank in the middle of the corridor. "I have weighed the possibility," he said, "and I've decided you can't lay a finger on me."

He smiled politely, and would have tipped his hat if he were wearing one. Then he turned swiftly on his heel and began walking as fast as he could toward the elevators. Behind him, K and Purcell held a hurried, whispered consultation, and then immediately began walking after him, as fast as they could without attracting the attention of any of the corridor policemen.

Mullaney reached the elevator bank just as the doors on one of the cars were closing. He walked in swiftly, caught a quick glimpse of K and Purcell just before the doors closed, heard another elevator operator in another car shout "Down!" and realized they would not be very far behind him when he reached the street floor. His heart was pounding, and his hands were sweating, but he stood very calmly in the midst of lawyers and clients and policemen and bailiffs and judges while the car dropped soundlessly in its shaft. Ignoring the several ladies present, he stepped out of the car before them the moment it stopped, and walked rapidly toward the entrance doors and the street. He did not look back at the building until he had reached the corner of Leonard Street, and then he turned and saw K and Purcell bounding down the steps. *The horses are on the track,* Mullaney thought, trying to sound like Freddie Capossela in his mind, *It is now post time.* He took a deep breath, said aloud, "They're off!" and began running.

It was a nice day for a run.

If a fellow has to run, Mullaney thought, he certainly couldn't wish for a nicer day than this one. He could remember fishing for blue crabs one night off a Fire Island dock, Irene luring the crabs in with a flashlight and he scooping them up into a net before it began raining. They had run that night because the rain was suddenly upon them in torrents and they were positive they could be drowned just standing still on the dock. The house they had rented for the month of August was at the far end of the boardwalk, adjacent to Saltaire, and they were both barefoot and afraid they would pick up wood splinters, neither of them dressed for the sudden summer storm, there had been stars and a moon in the sky when they'd begun their solitary crabbing. But they ran nonetheless into the pelting rain and were drenched within minutes. And then, suddenly, there was no point in running any longer, they were both as wet as they ever would be. So they said the hell with it, and joined hands and idly ambled up the boardwalk, laughing and singing, and waking at least two irate neighbors who shouted for quiet, thereby waking at least two more. They were wet to the marrow when they finally reached the house, shivering on the front porch while Mullaney tried to extricate the key from the sodden pocket of his dungaree trousers. They each drank a shot of medicinal brandy, and Mullaney lighted a fire in the old fireplace, filling the house with smoke that sent them out laughing into the rain again.

He could remember that night's running with great pleasure, and he wondered now whether they hadn't done the very sensible thing, whether it wasn't advisable to stop running when you really had nothing further to lose, and realized that what he had to lose right now was his life, and tried again to understand what was so terribly important about that jacket lying in the stacks of the New York Public Library, and couldn't. He knew he should hurry back there to pick it up before someone found it, but he also knew he could not go there with K and Purcell in hot pursuit. So he kept running east, away from the library, coming out into Chinatown, and then continuing eastward and northward until he hit Houston Street, and then running past the pushcarts and the dry-goods stores and the catering places and the delicatessens, and looking behind him to see that K and Purcell were still with him, closer than they were before. He was convinced that they would get him now. For the first time since last night in McReady's cottage, when he thought he was looking at K's ghost, he knew fear—fear that this would be the end of everything, the end of all hope, he would not escape them, he would be unable to circle uptown to the library to claim the jacket and unlock its secret, he would never place his monstrous bet on Jawbone or flee to Rio or Jakarta where dusky sloe-eyed maidens would drop grapes into his mouth—all at once the man with the beard stepped into his path.

The man had black beetling brows and burning black eyes. His beard was wild and unkempt, black too, he was dressed entirely in black except for a white handkerchief knotted cowboy-fashion around his neck, black coat, black hat, black shoes, black socks,

Mullaney's fear rocketed into his skull. Behind him he could hear K and Purcell rounding the corner, It's an international ring, he thought, there's no escape, there's no goddamn escape, they've got me surrounded.

The man clutched Mullaney's arm and leaned closer.

He'll kill me, Mullaney thought. He'll kill me on the spot and take my head to K.

"Are you Jewish?" the man asked.

"Yes!" Mullaney shouted, hoping he would pass.

"Good," the man said. "We need you for a *minyen.*"

9. SOLOMON He heard footsteps clattering on the sidewalk outside as the synagogue door whispered shut behind him.

"This way!" K's voice shouted.

"Where is he?" Purcell shouted. "Where did he go?"

"This way! This way!"

He leaned against the closed door with his eyes shut, breathing hard, listening as the footsteps faded, echoing on the street, "Where did he go?" Purcell shouted again.

Mullaney opened his eyes.

The bearded man was studying him closely.

"The *goyim?*" he asked, and because he sensed that *goyim*

meant enemy, and since K and Purcell were most certainly that, Mullaney nodded, and sucked in a deep breath. Both men were silent, listening. The voices outside were indistinct now, distant. K shouted something, but the words were unintelligible. They kept listening. At last, the street outside was silent. The bearded man smiled, his grin cracking into his black beard, as white as the handkerchief knotted around his neck. He beckoned to Mullaney, and Mullaney followed him down the long flight of steps just inside the entrance door.

He had been in a synagogue only once before in his life, and that had been for Feinstein's funeral services, a very classy synagogue befitting his station in life. The underground temple in which he found himself now was small and dim, with two high windows at street level, and another two opening on what appeared to be the brick wall of the tenement next door. Three dozen or more folding wooden chairs faced what he assumed to be the altar, a carved wooden stand upon which rested a candelabra holding six lighted candles. Behind the altar was what Mullaney first thought was a picture, and then realized was another small window, stained glass, set very high up on the wall, also at street level. He could not tell what the window depicted; it seemed to be only an interesting design of blues and greens behind which were darker blues and blacks pierced by a yellow pane of glass that descended vertically from the top of the window. To the right of the window, and almost on the same level, a candle—or at least a flame—flickered in a small metal cage that hung from the ceiling on a brass chain. A pair of red velvet curtains were on the wall below and behind the hanging cage, and a rack on the adjoining wall was draped with what appeared to be fringed silk scarves.

"I'm Goldman," the man with the beard said abruptly and handed a black skullcap to Mullaney, who held it on his open hands and looked up into Goldman's face.

"And your name?" Goldman said.

"Mullaney," he said.

"Come, Melinsky, you'll meet the others."

"Mullaney," he corrected.

"Come, take a *tallis*, we've been waiting here all morning. To get a *minyen* in this neighborhood, you have to have a big shining temple. Come, Melinsky, come."

"Mr. Goldman . . ."

"This is Melinsky," Goldman said to the other men in the room. "Solomon, get him a *Siddur*, let's begin here."

The other men—there seemed to be six or seven, or perhaps more—were rather old, some of them bearded, some of them bald, most of them wrinkled. They were standing before the rack of silk scarves, all of which were identical, white and striped with the palest blue, fringed with long white knotted tassels. As Mullaney watched, the men began taking scarves from the long wooden rack bar, and draping them over their shoulders. He suddenly knew that they were prayer shawls, not scarves, and further knew he could not go on with this hoax.

"Mr. Goldman . . ." he started, but Goldman turned away from him and began walking toward the front of the temple.

"You have to yell at him," a voice at his elbow said. "He's a little deaf."

Mullaney turned at the sound of the voice, and then looked down to find a short old man wearing a white skullcap perched on the back of his bald head. The man was smiling, his mouth was smiling, his eyes were smiling behind thick-lensed rimless spectacles. He had a tiny mustache that echoed the white of the prayer shawl draped over his shoulders. His suit was brown, and he wore a brown tie and a yellow sweater under his jacket. He extended his hand.

"I'm Solomon," he said.

"How do you do?" Mullaney said. "Mr. Solomon . . ."

"Come, I'll get you a *Siddur*," Solomon said. "You're from the neighborhood?"

"No. As a matter of fact . . ."

"You'll forgive me, Melinsky," Solomon said, "but you forgot to put on your *yarmoulke*," and tapped the top of his head.

Mullaney hesitated a moment. Then, thinking a bare head

might defile the temple, and not wishing to offend either Solomon or especially God, he quickly put the skullcap on and said, "Mr. Solomon, there's something . . ."

"We're Orthodox, you know," Solomon said.

"No, I didn't know that."

"Yes. So you'd suppose, in *this* neighborhood especially, it would be easy to find ten men for a *minyen, nu?*"

"I suppose so," Mullaney said.

"Especially on the *shabbes*."

"I suppose so, yes."

"But it's very difficult. Believe me, you are performing a real *mitsva*."

"Yes," Mullaney said.

"You didn't take a *tallis*. Take a *tallis*, hurry. Goldman gets impatient. We've been waiting here since seven o'clock this morning. These days, religion is a difficult business. Nobody cares, nobody comes, only the old men who are already dying. Look, we have to send somebody out on the street yet to find a Jew so we can pray. *Ach*," he said and shook his head.

"I see," Mullaney said, beginning to understand at last.

Solomon took one of the silk shawls from the rack and draped it over Mullaney's shoulders. "Don't be embarrassed," he said. "We all know you're a stranger." He smiled. "It's no sin to pray with strangers."

"I guess not," Mullaney said.

"I'll get you the *Siddur*," Solomon said, moving toward a shelf of books on the left-hand side of the room. "Do you remember your Hebrew?"

"Well . . . well, no. No, I don't. As a matter of fact, Mr. Solomon . . ."

"It's in English also, you'll be able to follow. Besides, it all comes back. You'll be surprised how it all comes back."

"I'll be *very* surprised," Mullaney said.

"Why? When was the last time you were inside a temple?"

"When Feinstein died."

"Isadore Feinstein from Washington Heights?"

"No, Abraham Feinstein from the Grand Concourse."

"Anyway, a person shouldn't have to die for people to pray. It's almost too late already by then."

"I guess so," Mullaney said.

"Come, we're starting. Goldman is a good reader. He could have been a *khazn*."

"Mr. Solomon," Mullaney said, "I really feel I should tell you . . ." and suddenly heard footsteps on the street upstairs. He hesitated. The other old men had taken seats already and were watching Goldman, who had his back to them, a book open on the altar before him. The room was silent as they awaited the opening words of the service. Into the silence came not Goldman's voice, but K's from the sidewalk outside the open windows.

"Where'd the bastard go?" he shouted, and the words would have sounded obscene even if they hadn't been.

"How about that store across the street?" Purcell answered.

"You think he's in there?"

"I don't know. Let's take a look."

"Wait! What's this door here?"

Mullaney held his breath.

"I think it's a synagogue," K said.

"Shhh."

"I don't hear anything," K said.

"Don't they pray in synagogues?"

In that moment (and Mullaney could have kissed him, beard and all) Goldman began reciting the opening words of the service. His voice rang out in clear and vibrant tones, the Hebrew filling the room in ancient meter, carrying across the heads of the old men sitting in their prayer shawls, rising to the high open windows at street level.

"It's a synagogue," K said, "I told you."

"Let's try that store," Purcell said.

Mullaney let out his breath.

"Page eleven," Solomon whispered beside him.

He listened to their retreating footsteps. Over the sound of the footsteps, fading, came Goldman's resonant voice, and the answering chant of the old Jewish men. He found page eleven. Each right-hand page of the prayer book was printed in Hebrew, he saw, each left-hand page in English.

"Here," Solomon said, and pointed to a line on the English page.

Mullaney realized at once that, despite the English translation, he would have difficulty following the service, the Hebrew words tumbling in ritual splendor from the front of the temple, the mumbled answers coming discordantly and out of phase from the congregation—he wondered suddenly where the rabbi was, wasn't there supposed to be a rabbi around? Solomon, ever helpful, turned pages for Mullaney, pointed out new lines to him, and each time Mullaney nodded, and read the words in English and finally despaired of keeping up, and decided instead to conduct his own service because he hated to see a sabbath go to waste. He roamed through the prayer book at will, learning, for example, that the prayer shawl around his shoulders was called a *tallith* (though it most certainly had sounded like *tallis* when both Goldman and Solomon pronounced it). He was amazed by the numerical significance attached to the threads of the fringe, because apparently four threads were separated from the others and then twisted tightly seven times around the remaining seven threads, after which a double knot was tied. It was then twisted another eight times and fastened with a second double knot; eleven more times and yet another knot; and then another thirteen times and a final double knot. Seven plus eight, Mullaney learned, equaled fifteen, which was the numerical value of י״ה, a Hebrew symbol he could not translate. Eleven, on the other hand, equaled ו״ה, and thirteen equaled אחד, meaning "The Lord is One." Furthermore, Mullaney learned, the numerical value of the word ציצית was 600, which, together with the eight threads and five knots, made a total of 613, the exact number of the 248 positive and 365 negative precepts of the *Torah*. He did not know what the *Torah* was, but he was enormously impressed by the very logical mathematical precision of the religion. So engrossed was he in learning all about the *tallith* (he would have to tell Solomon how to pronounce it correctly) that he did not realize the congregation was standing, and only joined them after Solomon tugged at his sleeve. He had always been a sucker for God, Mullaney supposed as the Hebrew words rang around him, always a sucker for the Latin mumbo-jumbo of the Catholic church in which he'd been raised, the trappings of the priests, he had to admit Catholics knew a lot more about show biz than Jews, at least when it came to costume design; you couldn't compare any of these *talliths* (was that how the word had got corrupted) with what Catholic priests and altar boys wore during mass. The church, on the other hand, had never come up with a triple parlay like 600, and 8, and 5, combining to form the exact number of precepts in the *Torah*, whatever that was. He could remember even now, and he missed the aroma here in church on the sabbath, the musky smell of incense, the priest swinging his thurible, and the words *et cum spiritu tuo*—the congregation was sitting now, he wished there were some incense here.

"Page twenty-six," Solomon whispered, and when Mullaney had found the page, he pointed to a line in the English text.

"Thou wast the same," Mullaney read silently, "before the world was created; thou hast been the same since the world has been created; thou art the same in this world, and thou wilt be the same in the world to come," a premise he could not buy because it seemed to negate the motivation for taking any gamble; if nothing ever changed, if you remained the same now and always, then what was the sense of—and then, reading back, saw that the passage was prefaced with the words "Blessed be the name of his glorious majesty forever and ever," and realized they related to God, and thought again of the incense flooding over the altar railing and wafting back over the pews, *et cum spiritu tuo.*

It had been so simple then to accept without question, why

does the world get so complex? Mullaney wondered. Well, he thought, it gets complex because sooner or later you've got to say No, you have got to shake your head and say No, I will *not* accept this, I will *not* be bound by this, I will be free. And so, despite your mother's sorrowful look (oh those soulful brown eyes, I think she'd wanted in her heart of Irish hearts for me to become a priest like my Uncle Sean in County Wicklow) you must break the old lady's heart by saying No, my dear Mother darling, I do not wish to accompany you this Sunday to St. Ignatius, I am terribly sorry but this Sunday I would like to sleep till noon, and then write myself a sonnet or two and then stroll in the park by the river and build a castle on the further shore, *that* is what I wish to do—you must say No sometime in your life. And, perhaps, I don't know because I am new at this game of Taking the Gamble, I have only been at it for a year now, and losing steadily, but perhaps you have got to take the gamble more than once, turn your back more than once, say No, and No again, rush out into the wind and find whatever it is out there that's beckoning you. Because, you see, you're not really his glorious majesty, you are only Andrew Mullaney and you were *not* the same before the world was created, nor will you be the same in the world to come. Say No to Irene who begged you to stay, with her mascara running down her face and looking very much like a little girl who had put on her mother's heels and makeup, weeping in the chair as I took a last look back at her and started to say something, but could not because Goodbye is very final, and I loved that woman, you do not say Goodbye to someone you love, and yet not sufficiently debonair to say *au revoir* or *ciao* (I have never yelled *Banco!* in my life, how could I even *pretend* to say those other things) and knowing that So long was far too casual for a woman who had given me seven years of very happy times—but you've got to say No sometime, you have got to say No or die, and I could not die, not even for you, Irene my love.

So Solomon, where are we now? where are you pointing now with your old and withered finger? what are you showing me in your ancient book, is this the *Siddur,* does *Siddur* mean prayer-book or missal or some such, what are the words? let them speak to me, Solomon, because I am, and always have been, a sucker for God, though a gambler besides.

"Here," Solomon said.

Here, Mullaney thought, and read *On your new moon festivals you shall offer as a burnt-offering to the Lord two young bullocks, one ram, seven yearling male lambs without blemish,* numbers again, Mullaney thought, *and a partridge in a pear tree,* he thought and remembered the third Christmas they were married, he and Irene, when he had given her the Twelve Days of Christmas, carrying each of the days in his head for a month before the twenty-fifth, he could still remember each and every damn word of that song, it had driven him crazy for the better part of December. But oh the joy on that Irish phizz of hers when she opened them all on Christmas morning, each package wrapped and appropriately numbered. "One," of course, was the partridge in a pear tree, he had bought her a small flowering pear and a tiny cotton-stuffed bird whose wire feet he had attached to the uppermost branch. For "Five," he had bought five gold rings in Woolworth's, enormous rings with rubies and emeralds that looked like the real McCoy, and diamonds every bit as genuine in appearance as the collection that had been stolen on Forty-seventh Street Thursday night—"Lots of money involved here," Bozzaris had said—the whole thing had cost him two dollars and nineteen cents, Irene's face worth a million dollars when she opened the box and the rings came tumbling out. For "Eight," he had bought eight paperback novels with the bustiest half-clad beauties he could find on the covers, maids with milking breasts bursting out of peasant blouses, unimaginable titles like *Up in Mabel's Cooze* or whatever; he had felt like a complete pervert buying the novels in a Times Square bookshop where scurvy characters thumbed photographs of long-legged girls in black lingerie, and he a respectable encyclopedia salesman. The Twelve Days of Christmas, one to twelve, each box numbered and each gift clever, if he had to say so himself, though inexpensive because that was a prime requisite in those days, clever but cheap. He had hated that bloody song ever since because in order to remember that "Nine" was nine drummers drumming, for example, he always had to sing the whole damn thing from the top, oh, what a Christmas that had been.

"They want you to hold up the *Torah*," Solomon said.

The men had parted the red velvet curtains under the hanging caged candle and had taken from the wooden cabinet there a large—well, he didn't know quite *what* it was at first, a red velvet case or cover with two carved silver handles protruding from its top. And then someone removed the velvet cover, but Mullaney still didn't know what it was until Solomon said, "The Holy Book, they wish you to hold it up."

"Why?" Mullaney said.

"It is an honor," Solomon said.

"I appreciate it," Mullaney said, "but no. Thank you, I don't think it would be right. For a stranger," he added hastily. "Thank you, Mr. Solomon, but it would not be right."

Solomon said something in Yiddish to the old man who was anxiously leaning over them. The man smiled, and nodded, and then chose someone else to come to the front of the temple. The man walked to the altar, seized the *Torah* by both silver handles and held it up for the congregation to see the holy words. The service was coming to a close. Someone was reading more Hebrew, Mullaney no longer tried to follow even the English translation, some of the older men were impatiently beginning to take off their *talliths* (See, Mullaney thought, I learned a word). And then the *Torah* (another word) was rolled up and put back into its cover and carried back into the wooden cabinet behind the velvet drapes, and the drapes were closed, and there were more words in Hebrew, and the men were rising, and Solomon said, "Now that wasn't so bad, was it, Melinsky?"

"No, that was very nice," Mullaney said.

"Not like maybe at a big fancy temple," Solomon said with a wink, "but not bad for a bunch of old Jews, huh?"

"Not bad at all," Mullaney said, giving him a wink of his own, and following him toward the left-hand side of the temple where the other men were taking off their prayer shawls and carrying them to the scarred wooden rack on the wall. The flickering light on its long chain hung motionless from the low ceiling, casting dancing shadows on their faces as they folded the shawls over the long wooden bar. Mullaney followed Solomon to where the others were standing, being careful to imitate the exact way Solomon draped his *tallith*, the Hebrew lettering to the right, though he wasn't at all sure this was part of the ritual.

"Would you like a little schnapps?" Goldman asked, and Mullaney suddenly thought of McReady and the burglary charge and of the jacket at the New York Public Library.

"Well, I really ought to be going," he said.

"Come," Solomon said, "it's a *b'rokhe*."

Mullaney followed Solomon to a round table at the rear of the temple. The table was set with a white cloth. A small dish of cookies rested on the table alongside a fifth of Four Roses. Two dozen shot glasses were turned upside down in a loose circle around the bottle. An old man there was already pouring for some of the others.

"Come," Solomon said, "it's very good for the intestinal tract."

"Well, just a little," Mullaney said. He was still wearing the *yarmoulke*, and he wondered whether he was supposed to take it off now that the service was over. None of the other men seemed to be removing theirs, however, so he touched the back of his head once again (the *yarmoulke* sat so feathery light on his skull that he was certain it had fallen off), adjusted the cap, and then accepted the glass Goldman offered. The synagogue seemed so suddenly dark, had it been this dark when he'd entered not an hour ago?

"*L'chaim*," Goldman said. "To life."

"*L'chaim*," the men repeated, and raised their glasses. To life, Mullaney thought. McReady had used those identical words in the cottage last night, *l'chaim*, to life.

"To life," he said aloud, and drank.

The stained-glass window above the altar suddenly erupted in dazzling brilliance, showering incandescent bursts of color into the room (The earth was without form and void, Mullaney thought in that instant, darkness was upon the face of the deep, and the Spirit of God was moving over the face of the waters— and God said, "Let there be light," and there was light), blue and purple, green, a penetrating shaft of yellow, glowed intensely for only an instant, illuminating the faces of the men and the whiskey glasses they held to their lips. And then an explosion rent the silence of the room, just above the temple's low ceiling, and Mullaney pulled his head into his shoulders and thought They've come to blast me out with bombs and mortars, I'm finished.

"Rain," Goldman said, and shook his head. "Why does it always rain on the *shabbes?*"

"It is the Lord's will," Solomon said, peering through his thick glasses, tilting his head to one side, listening as the rain drops began pattering on the temple roof. The men sipped their whiskey silently. Another streak of lightning illuminated the magnificent stained-glass window, the rolling blue and green sea capped with white, the darker blue beyond, the nascent world's blackness, the dazzling yellow pane of light, let there be light. Thunder boomed above. The drops fell more heavily now, beating on the roof of the old building. Solomon poured more whiskey into Mullaney's glass and said, "You know what happened to my Uncle Aaron, he should rest in peace?"

"We *all* know what happened to your Uncle Aaron," Goldman said.

"The *khoshever gast* doesn't know."

"The *khoshever gast* doesn't want to know," Goldman said. "It's a hundred times he's told this story already, Cohen, *nu?*"

"A *thousand* times," Cohen said. "Ask Horowitz."

"A million times," Horowitz said, and held out his glass for a refill.

"If the Lord didn't want it to rain, would it rain?" Solomon said.

"The rain has nothing to do . . ."

"If the Lord didn't want it should be thundering and lightening, would he *make* it thunder and lighten?" Solomon asked.

"The Lord works for Solomon," Cohen said. "The Lord does all these things only so Solomon can tell us about his Uncle Aaron in Bialystok."

"In Belopol'ye," Solomon said.

"Wher*ever,* and don't tell us again because it's time we all went home."

"In the *rain?*" Solomon asked incredulously.

"Better in the rain than your Uncle Aaron's story again."

"You want to hear it or not?" Solomon said. "Listen, if you don't want to hear it, believe me, I won't tell it."

"We don't want to hear it," Horowitz said.

"Do you want to hear it or not?" Solomon asked.

"He said already *no.*"

"Because if you don't want to hear it, I won't tell it," Solomon said.

"I already heard it," Cohen said.

"True, but did the *khoshever gast* hear it?"

"*Did* you?" Cohen asked Mullaney.

"No," Mullaney said, certain he had not.

"Perhaps *he* would care to hear the story?" Solomon said.

The men all turned to Mullaney. They wore entreating looks upon their faces, but none of their eyes pleaded so eloquently as Solomon's behind his magnifying lenses.

"Yes," Mullaney said gently, "I would like to hear about your uncle, Mr. Solomon."

"*Oi vei,* he's *meshuge,*" Horowitz said, and gulped his whiskey.

"It happened that my Uncle Aaron, he should rest in peace, was a no-good, always fooling around with women, cheating at cards, a regular gambler, anyway, which is forbidden in the Holy Book . . ."

"Where is it forbidden?" Cohen said.

"I don't know where, but it's forbidden, believe me. Otherwise there would be gambling houses in every Jewish ghetto, you think Jews don't like to gamble?"

"*I* don't like to gamble," Horowitz said, shrugging, "and it happens I'm a Jew."

"I once played a number, God forgive me," Goldman said.

"Well, my Uncle Aaron, he wasn't a once-upon-a-time numbers player because, first of all, in Russia they didn't have the numbers racket like here in New York, and also he was a cardplayer and a horseplayer from when they used to run the races."

"Where did they run the races?" Cohen asked.

"I don't know where, but in Russia in 1912 they had a big racetrack like all over the world, what do you think it was an uncivilized nation?"

"I'm saying where did they have a racetrack?"

"The Czar had a racetrack."

"Where?"

"In Moscow."

"Where in Moscow?"

"I don't know, I'll look it up. If the rabbi was here, he could tell you because it happens he's from Moscow himself."

"The rabbi, it happens, is in Livingston Manor," Cohen said.

"When he comes back, he'll tell you where the racetrack was. Do you mind terribly, Cohen, if I continue with my story?"

"Please continue, I only heard it already a thousand times."

"And a thousand times you made the same interruptions."

"Forgive me, Solomon," Cohen said, and executed an elaborate bow. "Forgive me, Melinsky," he said to Mullaney, and made another bow.

"So my Uncle Aaron, on this fateful day in 1912, he had been playing a game of cards with a couple of merchants from the village . . ."

"Bialystok, it happens," Cohen said, "is a big city."

"It happens," Solomon corrected, "that Bialystok is in Poland, whereas Belopol'ye is in Russia, and is a *small* village."

"Belopol'ye, it also happens, is a big city."

"We'll ask the *rov* when he comes back from Livingston Manor."

"We'll ask him," Cohen said.

"Anyway, my Uncle Aaron had been in a very large card game on Friday evening, continuing even until after the candles were lighted for the *shabbes,* and it was all over the village that the game was going on, but neither my uncle nor any of his friends would stop the game because very high stakes were involved. Melinsky, are you familiar with cardplaying?"

"A little," Mullaney said.

"The stakes can get very high," Solomon said.

"I know."

"So this game my uncle is in, with its very high stakes, is continuing on and on into the night—midnight, one o'clock, two o'clock, three o'clock . . ."

"All right, already," Horowitz said.

". . . four o'clock," Solomon continued, "five o'clock, still the game is going on, six o'clock . . ."

"Make it morning, please dear God," Goldman said.

". . . seven o'clock, and finally the game breaks up. So guess who's the big winner?"

"Your Uncle Aaron," Cohen said.

"Correct! And guess what he decides to do?"

"He decides to go to temple to thank the Lord for his good fortune."

"Correct!" Solomon said. "The sun had been up for perhaps an hour and a half by then, it was a beautiful spring day, it was April in fact, oh the sun was shining brightly and the cocks were crowing and all the animals of the field were making sounds in the early morning, the village very quiet . . ."

"A big *city!*" Cohen complained.

". . . and my uncle walking along the dusty road to the little temple, where are gathered for services several dozen old religious Jews like ourselves."

"This part I heard already," one of the men at the table said, and abruptly banged down his shot glass and walked toward the stairway.

"Mandel, wait!" Solomon called after him, but the man shook his head, and then made a shooing gesture with his palm flat and out toward Solomon, and quietly trudged up the steps. Solomon turned to Mullaney. His blue eyes behind their magnifying lenses were glowing with the pride of narration, the honest effort of building a story to a climax. Mullaney could hardly wait to hear what happened next. Solomon smoothed his trim white mustache under his nose, put a withered finger alongside his cheek and said, "The sun is shining bright, remember, when my uncle goes into the temple. He puts on a *yarmoulke* and a *tallis*—he is not carrying his own *tallis-zeckl* because this is the *shabbes,* and he is not permitted to carry anything, though his pockets are full of money that he won from the game . . ."

"*Tsah!*" Goldman said, and would have spit had he not been in the temple.

"Certainly," Solomon said, "I *told* you he was an evil man, I *didn't* tell you this from the beginning?"

"Still, to carry money on the *shabbes,*" Goldman said, and pulled a grimace, and touched the handkerchief knotted around his throat as if in affirmation. Mullaney suddenly realized that it was knotted there because he was not permitted to carry anything in his pockets today.

"Anyway, my uncle goes to put on the *tallis,*" Solomon said, "he is already saying the words, 'Bless the Lord, Oh my Soul! Lord my God, thou art very great,' and so on, when all of a sudden there comes a thing of lightning through the open window of the temple, it could blind you, and immediately afterwards there comes a boom of thunder like you never heard, and it starts raining. My uncle looks up and the lightning is still hanging there in the temple, it isn't moving, it's hanging just inside the window where it first came in, as if it's waiting there until it finds who it came in for, *farshtein?* And who did it come in for? Well, my friends, in the next minute that lightning starts to move around

the room, straight for my Uncle Aaron who's gambling and
fooling with women, who's carrying money in his pockets on the
shabbes, it chases him around that temple with the other Jews
running to get out of his way, and finally it chases him right *out*
the temple door into the street! And *there*, in plain sight of all the
people of the village, in plain sight so that everyone can see in the
eyes of God, *bang!* that lightning hits him right on the head and
kills him, and all the money he won in the card game falls out of
his pockets on the street! This is a true story, so help me God,
may I be struck down like my Uncle Aaron."

"I don't believe it," Cohen said.

"It's true," Solomon said, nodding.

"I don't believe it neither," Horowitz said.

"I believe it," Mullaney said fervently.

"You *do?*" Solomon asked, surprised.

"Yes. The exact same thing happened to my friend Feinstein."

"The *exact* same thing?" Solomon asked, astonished.

"Yes. Well no, not the exact same thing. Actually, it happened
in Las Vegas, outside the Sands, while Eddie Fisher was singing
inside. But yes, Feinstein *had* been gambling all night, and he *did*
get chased into the street, and he *was* struck by lightning.
Though later, of course, there was speculation about what had
really killed him, it being said a blackjack dealer had shot him
with a .45 automatic. I, personally, have always believed he was
struck by lightning, though witnesses claim Feinstein had been
praying aloud for aces all night long, which could have caused
the dealer to go berserk, I suppose, especially if he had no sense
of humor or was not as pious a man as Feinstein."

"Isadore Feinstein from Washington Heights?"

"No, Abraham Feinstein from the Grand Concourse."

"I don't think I know him," Solomon said, and suddenly turned
toward the stairwell.

The surprise was mutual and immediate, preceded only by the
creaking of a stair tread, the single harbinger that caused Solomon to turn. The stairwell was behind the rear wall of the

synagogue, and K and Purcell came around that wall cautiously, revolvers drawn, rather like bad imitations of television detectives raiding a numbers bank. Mullaney saw them at exactly the same time that they saw him, and all three men let out squeaks of surprise and almost leapt into the air, Mullaney in fear that he would be shot in the next instant, K and Purcell in delight at having found their quarry at last.

"There he is!" Purcell shouted—needlessly, Mullaney thought, since it was plain to see that there he was, and even plainer to see that there was no way out of this underground room save for the staircase which was now so effectively blocked.

Goldman, taking one look at the pistols in their hands, shouted, "Pogrom!" and all the other old men, cued by Goldman, remembering stories of atrocities in Russian and Polish villages, perhaps even remembering scenes from their own childhoods, began running around the room shouting, "Pogrom, pogrom!" coming between Mullaney and his two pursuers, who still stood near the stairwell uncertainly, the pistols ready in their hands, but not wanting to shoot a bunch of old men who were racing around the room holding their hands to their heads and their ears and shouting, "Pogrom, pogrom!" for the whole neighborhood to hear. Mullaney, who didn't want anyone to get shot either, least of all himself, picked up one of the folding chairs and threw it at Purcell, missing, he had never been very good at hitting people with folding chairs. The old men stopped running in that moment, perhaps because they realized Mullaney was the intended victim and not themselves, a realization that provided immunity and therefore power, perhaps because they remembered all at once that it did no good to run, it was more important to stand and fight even if the victim was only a stranger who had enabled you to pray publicly on the sabbath. Solomon seized the lighted candelabra from the altar, and with a bloodcurdling shriek worthy of an Irgun warrior, rushed K and struck him on the arm, sending the gun skittering across the floor, and also sending candles flying in every direction—oh my God, Mullaney thought, we're going to have a fire here.

"Run, Melinsky!" Solomon shouted. "Flee!"

But Mullaney could not run, would not run while candles were burning on the wooden floor. He began stamping them out, and saw that Purcell had turned from the stairway to level his gun at Solomon, who was bending over the fallen K now, ready to strike another blow, this time on the head perhaps. Cohen yelled, "Solomon, look out!" and then seized a whole handful of *talliths* from the rack and threw them over Purcell's head, the shawls covering him as effectively as a net. Mullaney kept stamping on the candles. A pistol shot rang out, shattering the stained-glass window, Purcell firing blindly from beneath his entangling silk shawls.

"We've got the situation!" Solomon shouted. "Flee, Melinsky!"

"Thank you!" Mullaney said, or perhaps only thought, and fled.

He fled into a city washed clean by the rain, her streets black and shining and smelling sweet and fresh, the sun poking through the clouds now like a religious miracle, great radiating spikes of dazzling light piercing the overhead gloom, reflecting in curbside puddles. A barefooted little boy stamped his feet in the water and shrieked in glee as Mullaney ran past him, turning left onto First Avenue, running uptown because uptown was where the library was.

The cessation of the storm had summoned everyone outdoors to sit or stroll. There was a holiday mood on First Avenue, partially because it was the sabbath and partially because this was the dirtiest city in the world and everyone was delighted that a rainstorm had carried away some of its soot and grime. Besides, it was spring, and city rain never succeeds the way it does in the spring, when it carries the aroma of unseen green clear across the canyons from Central Park, wafting gently on each crisp new breeze, cool and excruciatingly sweet. You can breathe in New York in the spring, Mullaney thought, you can suck great gobs of air into your lungs, especially after it rains. The clouds were scattering now, the sun was breaking through completely, putting the grey to rout, turning the streets to glittering obsidian. He ran not because he thought he was being chased, but only because he was beginning to enjoy running, feeling very much the way Jean Paul Belmondo must have felt on the Champs Élysées. In fact, when he spotted an old lady in a flowered housedress standing on the corner, holding a shopping bag, he ran up to her and threw the hem of her housedress clear up over her pink bloomers, "Oh, dear!" the lady said, and stared after him in wonder as he raced on past. The jacket was waiting for him at the library. The secret was nestling on the floor of that dusty vault where he had made love to Merilee, the secret to untold wealth, some of which he would lay on Jawbone's nose, oh what a lucky man I am, he thought, oh what a wonderfully lucky fellow to be running in this springtime city like Jesse Owens or Gunder Hägg.

But, being thirty-nine and very close to forty, he soon tired of all this springtime frivolity and, out of breath, panting hard, decided he had best try to rustle up twenty cents for a subway token that would take him to the library before he dropped dead of a heart attack right here on this lovely springtime street. He did not want to beg because it didn't seem fitting for someone as nicely dressed as he was to go around begging on First Avenue; that would hardly seem proper for someone wearing clothes that had belonged to a person ten times the man he was, or so Melanie had claimed, and he had no reason to doubt her word. And, as much as he detested the idea of stealing, he justified the plan that sprang full-blown into his head by telling himself that as soon as he made his killing he would come back and return the money he was about to pilfer—well, not pilfer, but certainly con out of an unsuspecting sucker.

He carefully cased the avenue, picking out the most crowded luncheonette he could find, and taking a seat at the farthest end of the counter, away from the cash register. He ordered a grilled cheese sandwich and a Coke, figuring he might just as well eat while he was at it, being very hungry. He ate leisurely and unobtrusively, keeping his head bent most of the time, avoiding the waitress's eye, and ascertaining what he had learned from his scrutiny of the place through the plate-glass window: that the cashier was a rather portly old gentleman wearing glasses and reading a copy of *Sports Illustrated*. When he finished his meal, he picked up the check the waitress had given him, walked toward the cashier, and then directly past the cashier and into the telephone booth. He lifted the receiver from the hook, pretended to deposit a dime, dialed Irene's number because it was the first number that came to mind, and then carried on an imaginary conversation with her while watching the cashier.

The cash register was on the extreme right-hand end of a long, glass-enclosed cigar display case. The cashier sat behind it on a high stool, turning to his right whenever a patron came to pay a check, adding up the items on it, taking the money and making change, and then turning to his left to skewer the check on the spike of a bill spindle that rested on the counter top to the left of the register. He then invariably went back to reading his magazine, leaning against the wall behind him, and looking up again only when the next patron arrived. Mullaney carried on his imaginary conversation with Irene, biding his time, waiting for the proper moment.

The proper moment arrived when three diners walked up to the cash register simultaneously, ready to pay their checks. Mullaney immediately came out of the phone booth, walked quickly to the register, and stood slightly apart from the people gathered there. The cashier turned to his right, took the check from the first patron, and then bent his head to add the column of figures. Mullaney swiftly and daringly thrust out both hands and stuck his own check onto the bill spindle to the left of the register, piercing the green slip, and then glancing quickly at the cashier to see if he had noticed the sudden move. The cashier pushed some keys on his register, opened the cash drawer, made change for his customer, a fat lady in a flowered bonnet, and then turned to his left and skewered the check on the spindle, covering the check Mullaney had just placed there. The only person who seemed to have followed the action was a hawk-nosed man with a heavy beard shadow, who glanced at Mullaney, shrugged uncom-

prehendingly, and then turned away. Mullaney waited until
everyone, especially the hawk-nosed man, had paid his bill and
left the luncheonette. Standing expectantly and patiently by the
register, he waited for the cashier to look up at him. The cashier
was now leaning against the wall again, reading his *Sports
Illustrated.* Mullaney cleared his throat.

"Yes?" the cashier said.

"May I have my change, please?" Mullaney said.

"What?" the cashier said, and looked up at him for the first
time.

"May I please have my change?"

"What do you mean, change?"

"I gave you my check and a five-dollar bill, but you didn't give
me my change."

"What do you mean, you gave me your check?"

"A few minutes ago. You stuck it on your thing there, but you
didn't give me my change."

"What do you mean, I stuck it on my thing there?"

"Well, take a look," Mullaney said. "I had a grilled cheese
sandwich and a Coke, it's right on your thing there."

"This thing here?"

"Yes."

The cashier pursed his lips, shook his head, and pulled the bill
spindle closer to the register. He studied the top check (which
had been given to him by the hawk-nosed man) and he studied
the check under that (which had been given to him by a man in a
grey sweater) and then he studied the check under that (the one
that had been paid by the fat lady in the flowered bonnet) all the
while muttering, "No grilled cheese sandwich here, you must be
crazy," and finally came to Mullaney's check, sure enough,
skewered on the long metal spike. He pulled it off the spindle,
shoved his glasses up onto his forehead, held the check close to
his face, peered myopically at it, and said, "Grilled cheese
sandwich and a Coke, is that what you had?"

"Yes, sir."

"You gave me five dollars?"

"Well, check your drawer there. I've been standing here for maybe ten minutes, waiting for my change."

"Why didn't you speak up?"

"Well, I saw you were busy."

"You should speak up," the cashier said. "You won't get no place in this world, you don't speak up."

"Well," Mullaney said shyly, and watched while the cashier rang up a No Sale, and then reached into the drawer for four singles and fifty-five cents in change, the grilled cheese sandwich having cost thirty cents, and the Coke fifteen cents, for a grand total of forty-five cents—"Four fifty-five," the cashier said, "is that correct?"

"That's correct, thank you," Mullaney said.

"Sorry to have kept you waiting," the cashier said.

"That's quite all right," Mullaney said. He walked back to the end of the lunch counter, left a twenty-five-cent tip for the waitress, and then nodded to the cashier as he walked out of the luncheonette, vowing to return with the money as soon as his ship came in.

He could not find the proper labyrinth.

He kept trying doors as he had last night, but somehow the magic was missing, he could not find the one that opened on the jacket's hiding place, the secret book-bound glade wherein he had claimed his maiden, promising her the world and then some. But then, at last, frantic and exhausted, he found a door that opened on what seemed to be a familiar passageway, and he followed it between rows and rows of books, the dust rising before his anxious feet, saw a red light burning somewhere in the distance, made a sharp turn, found himself in the remembered cul-de-sac, and immediately saw the jacket. Untouched, it lay on the dusty floor where he had dropped it, surrounded by the paper scraps that had been sewn into its lining.

His hands trembling, he picked it up.

There was nothing terribly remarkable about it, it seemed to be an ordinary-looking jacket, made of black wool, he supposed or perhaps worsted, which was probably wool, he was never very good on fabrics, FA–FO with four round black buttons on each sleeve near the cuff, and three large black buttons at the front of the jacket opposite three buttonholes in the overlapping flap, a very ordinary jacket with nothing to recommend it for fashionable wear, unless you were about to be buried. He opened the black silk lining again, and searched the inner seams of the jacket, thinking perhaps a few hundred-thousand-dollar bills were perhaps pinned up there somehow, but all he felt was the silk and the worsted, or whatever it was. He thrust his hand into the breast pocket and the two side pockets, and then he searched the inner pocket on one side of the jacket and then on the other, but all of the pockets were empty. He crumpled the lapels in his hands, thinking perhaps the real money was sewn into the lapels, but there was neither a strange sound nor a strange feel to them. To make certain, he tore a lapel stitch with his teeth, and ripped the entire lapel open, revealing the canvas but nothing else. He was extremely puzzled. He buttoned the jacket and looked at it buttoned, and then he *un*buttoned the jacket and looked at it that way again, but the jacket stared back at him either way, black and mute and obstinate.

He put the jacket aside for a moment and picked up one of the *New York Times* scraps, not knowing what he would find, or even what he was looking for, but hoping one of the scraps might give him a clue to what the jacket was supposed to possess. He began methodically studying each scrap, not actually reading all of them, but scrutinizing the newsprint to see if any word or sentence had been circled or marked, but none of them had. As he turned each scrap over in his hands, he remembered what McReady had said last night, "Let us say that where there's cheese, there is also sometimes a rat." Now what the hell was *that* supposed to mean? He sighed heavily; there were far too many bogus bills. He finally spread them out haphazardly on the library

floor, using both hands, and then only scanned them, making a
spot check now and again, picking up one bill or another to
scrutinize, and deciding on the basis of his sampling that none of
them had any of their corners clipped or trimmed or scalloped or
dog-eared or folded or anything.

Well, he thought, I don't know.

I just don't know what the hell it is.

He picked up the jacket and slung it over his arm, thinking he
might just as well hang onto it in the event he had a brilliant
inspiration later, which inspiration seemed like the remotest
possibility at the moment, and then decided he had better get
himself out to Aqueduct before the second race went off without
him. He didn't know what good it would do to be there, since he
now possessed only four dollars and ten cents. With subway fare
costing twenty cents, and admission costing two dollars, he
wouldn't even have enough left to lay a two-dollar bet on
Jawbone.

Well, he thought, we shall see what we shall see.

He left the library the way he had come in, though now he was
carrying the black-buttoned, black worsted jacket over his arm.
On his way to the IRT in Grand Central, he passed a department
store, and saw two pickets out front. One of them smiled, walked
over to him, and said, "Shopping bag, sir?"

"Thank you," he said.

The shopping bag was white with large red letters proclaiming
JUDY BOND BLOUSES ARE ON STRIKE! Not being a union man
himself, but being of course in sympathy with working men all
over the world, Mullaney accepted the shopping bag, dropped
the jacket into it, and hurried to Grand Central Station.

10. MONA GIRL

It took him forty-five minutes to get to Aqueduct from Grand Central via the IRT Lexington Avenue line to the Fulton Street–Broadway station where he changed to an IND "A" train that took him to Euclid Avenue in Brooklyn where he changed for a Rockaway train that took him directly to Aqueduct's own million-dollar station overlooking the racetrack.

He had been to the Big A more times than he could count in the year since he had taken the gamble. He felt now the same surge of excitement he experienced each time he approached the modern structure with its manicured lawns and blooming flowers, sprinkler systems going, a mild breeze blowing in off Flushing Bay. A smile erupted on his face. Still carrying the free shopping bag with its Judy Bond message, he walked jauntily up the wide concrete path to the grandstand entrance. He paid the man in the booth his two-dollar admission fee, bought a twenty-five-cent program and a copy of the *Morning Telegraph* from a hawker on the main floor, and then took the escalator up to the first floor. The track's ceilings were high and soaring, built to accommodate the huge, hanging Totalisator boards that blinked electronically with changing odds every few seconds, harmonious browns and beiges and corals blending to form a serene backdrop for the surging excitement on the betting floor.

It was only 1:10, and the first race (expected to start at 1:36, according to the tote board) had not yet begun. This meant that Mullaney had little more than forty-five minutes in which to raise whatever money he could in time for the second race. Anxiously, he scanned the faces in the crowd, searching for someone he knew. This was Saturday, though, and the gamblers (who normally composed perhaps ten percent of the track's daily attendance) were today spread even more thinly among salesmen and businessmen and out-of-town buyers, housewives who had saved their nickels and dimes, nine-to-five clock-punchers who were ready to blow their week's salary on a hopeful nag or two. There were present, too, gentlemen bettors with binoculars on their necks and blondes on their arms, college girls home for the spring vacation, servicemen on leave, Park Avenue ladies in slacks and mink coats, touts and tarts, bookies and bimbos, old Crazy Annie who would spend all day searching the vinyl tile floor for Win tickets mistakenly discarded, and even a juvenile delinquent in a black leather jacket with a skull and crossbones painted on its back (he had obviously seen the movie). Impossible to find anyone you know, Mullaney thought, unless you look very very hard, so he started to look and heard the track announcer's distinct, high, clear voice coming over the loudspeaker system, cutting through the din for only a moment: "The *hors*-es are *on* the track!"

That is marvelous, Mullaney thought. *They're* already on the track for the first race, and *I* haven't got the price of a two-dollar bet. He put down his shopping bag for a moment, leaned against one of the supporting girders, and opened his program. The second race was a six-furlong race with a $4,295 purse. It was limited to fillies and mares, four years old and upward, who had not won at least a $2,925 race since December 11th. The program noted that maiden, claiming, optional and starter races were not to be considered disqualifying, and then listed Jawbone as the number-3 horse, with morning-line odds of twenty to one, sure enough. She was owned by Targe Stables (whose colors were red polka dots on a white field, red sleeves, white cap) and she was to be ridden by Johnny Lingo, whom Mullaney knew to be an excellent jock. He nodded briefly, opened his *Telegraph* and scanned Jawbone's track record. Apparently, she worked well on a wet track, which today's track most certainly was, but she hadn't won on any of her last three outings, leading the field each time only to run out of steam in the stretch, failing even to place. She was up against some damn good horses, the favorite being the 4-horse, Good Sal, at two-to-one odds, and the next closest longshot being the 8-horse, Felicity, at ten-to-one, which was still a far cry from the steep odds on Jawbone.

She might do it, Mullaney thought. She especially might do it with a little help. And if she isn't about to *get* a little help, then why had his dice-player friend given him the tip as early as *yesterday*, and why had Jawbone then been scratched, and why had the tip carried over into today's second?

It looked very much to Mullaney as if that sweet filly had been set to receive a little help yesterday, but maybe some wires had gotten crossed, so she'd been scratched before 8:30 A.M., which was the official weekday time limit for scratching any horse. That meant that her owners had until 10:15 A.M. Friday to enter her in one of Saturday's races, and since fourteen horses could be

started in a six-furlong race, chances were she would draw a post
position unless the race was overfilled. It had apparently worked
just that way, and it looked to Mullaney as if she might just
possibly very definitely receive the help she needed today. A tip
doesn't carry from one day's race to the next, nor is it bandied
about by a hood with a stickball bat (no matter *what* the hell he
claimed it was—a broom handle, ha!) unless the fix is in there
tight, Charlie, unless that little help is going to be zinged in right
when it's needed, yessir, she looked very good indeed. He decided to play her, very definitely.

All he needed was some money.

He picked up his shopping bag, and began circling the echoing
betting floor, searching the lines at the cashiers' windows, seeing
a few people he knew (but not well enough to ask for a loan),
and then hearing the track announcer's voice saying, "It is now
post time," and then, "They're *off!*"

He walked out to the grandstand to watch the race without
interest, the announcer's voice drowned out in the yelling of the
crowd, "Come on, four! come on, Bidabee! come on, two!"
everybody wanting some horse or other to come *on*, when of
course none of the horses knew what anyone was yelling, and
even if they did would probably pay no attention since horses are
notoriously dumb animals who will bite you on your ass for no
good reason, he disliked horses intensely. The crowd jumped to
its feet as the 5-horse came streaking from fourth place to catch
and pass the frontrunners and take first. Mullaney watched all the
sore losers tearing up their tickets, and then looked at the tote
board and saw that the race had taken one minute and thirty-
eight seconds and that the present time was . . .

The electronically controlled figures changed as he watched.

1:39.

He had less than a half-hour to raise a stake.

He was delighted to see Lester Bohm in the crowd of gamblers
walking up from the reserved grandstand seats, and more delighted when he realized Lester wasn't tearing up any tickets but

was instead holding in his hand two ten-dollar Win tickets on the 5-horse. The tote board had already posted the official results, and the price quoted on the 5-horse was $17.20, which meant that a bettor would get that amount of money for every two dollars he had invested. Lester's ten-dollar Win tickets were each worth $86.00, so the possibility existed that perhaps he might be amenable to a small touch. Mullaney approached him confidently.

"Hello there, Lester," he said.

"Oh, it's *you*," Lester replied.

He was a short red-faced man wearing a colorful plaid sports jacket and a Professor Higgins hat. He always carried a cane, and it was rumored here and there that the cane served as the sheath for a rapier, and that Lester had once used it on a Chicago bookie who had welshed out on him. Mullaney could not believe this, however, because Lester seemed to him to be a very pleasant and personable fellow who would never dream of cutting up anybody, especially when he was holding two ten-dollar Win tickets in his fist. Lester had been married and divorced five times and was now working on his sixth wife—"My own personal Russian roulette," he was fond of saying with a grin. He was an excellent horseplayer in that he frequently won, but he also lost sometimes, though not often. He was a good man to meet at a track when you were in need of cash, or at least Mullaney hoped so; he had never asked Lester for a loan in his life.

"You're off to a flying start, I see," Mullaney said.

"Yes, I am," Lester said. "What is it, Mullaney?"

"What is what?"

"What do you want from my life?"

Lester's attitude puzzled him at first, until he remembered with something of a shock that Lester's opening words had been "Oh, it's *you*," with the stress on the word "*you*," as if something unspeakably vile had crawled out onto a white picnic cloth. Mullaney had never thought of himself as something unspeakably vile, and could not think of himself that way now. He was simply a gambler down on his luck, a situation that could be completely reversed this afternoon with a bet on Jawbone. But Lester's

attitude brought him up short, physically, so that he had to run to
catch up to him, and then felt somewhat foolish chasing this
dumpy roly-poly little man toward the Cash windows. He almost
gave up the chase then and there, almost said The hell with it,
there's nothing for me here, he's not in a moneylending mood.
But something else within him forced him to continue his pursuit,
the knowledge that he was *not* a vile and horrid insect that had
crawled out into the sunshine, and the desperate need to convince
Lester that he was not (although he could not imagine why
Lester thought he *was*). I'm a very nice person, Mullaney said to
himself. I'm just a little down on my luck, for Christ's sake, I just
need a few bucks to bet on a horse that's a cinch to win. Don't,
for Christ's sake, treat me like a loser.

I'm not a loser.

"Listen," he said, and Lester turned to him, lifted his face to
Mullaney's and pierced him with a cold, blue-eyed, frigid stare.
"Listen, I'm not a loser," Mullaney said, thinking he should not be
telling this to a little shit of a man who had stabbed a Chicago
bookie and made a mess of his life with his goddamn personal
Russian roulette, why am I telling this to *him?*

"So you're not a loser," Lester said. He stood leaning on the
cane, his round face turned up and blandly impassive. "So?" he
said. "So what?"

"I have a winner in the second race," Mullaney said.

"Everybody has a winner in the second race."

"This is a sure thing."

"Everything is a sure thing," Lester said.

"Lester, I've never asked you for a nickel in my life," Mullaney
said, "have I?"

"That's true, you never have."

"I need five hundred. This is a sure thing, Lester."

"Oh, all you need is five hundred, huh?"

"Lester, listen to me. I know I've been down on my luck lately,
but believe me this horse is a winner, I know it is, and I think you
know I'm good for the money."

"Oh yes, sure," Lester said.

"I've been down on my luck, that's all. You're a gambler, Lester, take the gamble."

"Five hundred, huh?"

"Yes, five hundred. I'll be paying you back in less than a half-hour, I'll pay you the five hundred and another five hundred besides. You can't ask for better than that, Lester."

"No, I certainly can't ask for better than that."

"Will you?"

"Will I what?"

"Lend me five hundred. I hate to ask, but . . ."

"Yes, I know, you've just been down on your luck, that's all."

"That's right, Lester. Lester, it hurts me to have to ask you for a loan, I mean it. Believe me."

"Yes, it must certainly hurt you to have to ask loans from all the people you've asked loans from in this past year, mustn't it?"

"It does."

"*Handouts* is what you mean, not *loans*. To my knowledge, Mullaney, you've never paid back a cent you borrowed, that's a very bad failing. I know a man in Chicago got stabbed for not paying the money he owed to someone."

"Lester, I'll pay back everybody I ever borrowed from, I've always intended to pay back."

"But never have."

"But will. Lester, what kind of person do you think I am?"

"Well now, I don't know, Mullaney. Suppose you tell me what kind of person you are."

"I'm . . ." He hesitated. He felt extremely foolish. "I'm a nice person," he said.

"Yes, I'm sure."

"Lester, lend me the five hundred."

"I'll lend you two dollars," Lester said, and reached for his wallet.

"Lester, look, don't kid around. Two dollars isn't going to . . ."

"All right, I'll make it four dollars. You can buy yourself two Win tickets, how's that?"

"If you can't go the full five hundred, make it four hundred, okay? I'll be paying you back right after the second race, four hundred plus another four hundred besides, as commission on your investment."

"My investment, huh? I'll give you ten bucks, how's that? You can buy yourself a real big ticket, Mullaney."

"Three hundred, okay? With the same . . ."

"Twenty bucks," Lester said, "and that's my limit. I won't go a cent higher."

Mullaney stared at him silently for a moment, and then shook his head.

"No, Lester," he said. "Never mind. Forget it."

"Okay, we'll forget it," Lester said.

"I still have my pride," Mullaney said, feeling more foolish than ever. "Don't forget that, Lester. I still have my pride."

"Yes, I'm sure," Lester said, and walked away toward the Cash windows.

"I still have my pride," Mullaney whispered after him.

He felt very small and very foolish. Oh, not because . . . well . . . no, no, not only because Lester had treated him like a beggar, had turned an honest request for a loan into a . . . a plea for a . . . a coffee-and-cake handout, like some wino coming up with an outstretched palm on the Bowery. God*damn* you, Mullaney thought, I once used to sell encyclopedias for a living, don't you *know* that? I never once stabbed a person in my life, I never once carried a sword in a cane, I've only been married *once*, you bastard, and I didn't divorce her because I stopped loving her, I divorced her only because I had to take the gamble, I had to get out here and live, don't you treat *me* like a bum, Lester, don't you ever dare treat *me* like a bum. But not only because of that, no, not only because Lester had swatted him flat on the picnic cloth causing him to ooze whatever dignity he had possessed until that moment—dignity, yes, and pride, yes—but also because he had come to Lester with a winner, had come with an absolute guaranteed winner, had come and said Look, I need five hundred, do you ask for five hundred on a *loser?* I'm going for the biggest prize, he thought, I came to you and asked for five hundred because this is my *life* on the line here, if I don't make it today, if I . . . if I don't make it, I'll . . . I don't know what I'll do. Can't you tell the difference between a simple loan when a guy only wants to win a few bucks on a horse, and a loan that is intended for a . . . a *life?*

My *life*, Lester.

My life.

His eyes were suddenly wet.

He dried them with his fist and thought Come on, come on, you're a grown man, stop it, come on. He sniffed. Still feeling foolish, he looked around to see if anyone had noticed him crying, but no one had, all the gamblers were milling about the floor in their own universes, studying the tote board blinking new odds every few seconds, completely unmindful of Andrew Mullaney or his need. He looked up at the board. The odds on Jawbone had risen to thirty to one. His nose was running. He reached for a handkerchief, his pocket was empty, I don't even have a god-damn handkerchief, he thought, and almost began weeping again in self-pity, but caught himself, forced himself to stand erect instead, his shoulders back and his head high, determined to find somebody in this crowd who would lend him the money he needed to put on Jawbone. Defiantly, he wiped the back of his hand across his nose (See the cop upon the corner) and dried it on his trouser leg (With the stripe upon his pants). Watch out, world, he thought, this is Andrew Mullaney here, rising from the picnic cloth where they thought, ha ha, they had swatted him flat, nossir!

Courage, he thought.

"The *hors*-es are *on* the track!" the announcer called.

Oh, he thought, give me courage.

He saw Merilee in that moment.

He saw her through the chain-link fence that separated the grandstand from the clubhouse section, saw her sitting with none other than Kruger, who had promised to kill him if he did not return with the money. She was wearing black, still wearing black though not the black velvet she had worn last night, which he had drawn up above her waist to spread her on the worthless jacket. He looked down at the shopping bag—JUDY BOND BLOUSES ARE ON STRIKE!—and at the crumpled jacket stuffed into it, and tried again to fathom its puzzle, and thought how much fun it would be to ask *her* for some money this time, thereby reversing the process of last night, "First the money," she had moaned, "First the money," and had only been screwed for her pains.

The tote board told him the time was now 1:55 and that post time was 2:06.

That is cutting it very close, Mullaney thought.

Even if I can catch her attention without Kruger seeing me, even if I *can* manage to do that without getting killed, how do I know she's got any money, all she had in her bag last night was her driver's license and a pearl-handled .22. Well, that is the gamble I must take, he thought, because the race is going to start in (he looked at the tote board again) exactly ten minutes, and the odds are now (another glance at the board) twenty-six to one, which means that the smart money is beginning to come in already, though it won't be bet heavily enough to change the odds completely. If it continues to come in at this rate, the odds should hold at maybe ten or fifteen to one, which are very good odds, especially on a horse who will be receiving a little help— how do I get her attention without also getting Kruger's?

Kruger put his binoculars to his eyes, watching the horses as they paraded on the track. Merilee, through instinct or because a Queens fly brushed her cheek just then, flicked her head to the right, looked straight into Mullaney's face where he was standing behind the separating chain-link fence, nodded only once briefly, turned away, touched Kruger's arm, whispered something to him, and then stood up. Her blond hair was wound around the top of her head, it looked like a neat golden *yarmoulke* similar to the white one Solomon had been wearing in the synagogue. Her black dress was cut low in the bodice, tight in the waist, flaring out over her long splendid legs, no stockings, black high-heeled pumps that clickety-clicked over the concrete steps as she walked toward the gate between the two sections. She was carrying a small black handbag in which Mullaney hoped there was something more than a driver's license and a .22. The guard at the gate stamped her hand with invisible dye so that she could later put it under the ultraviolet light when she returned to the clubhouse section, and she came through the gate, winked at Mullaney, and walked right on past him toward the steps, very quickly, her sweet little backside wiggling, her pumps clickety-clicking on the vinyl tile floor, he would never forget last night in the library, though she had said it was lousy.

He followed her up the stairs at a safe distance, first glancing over his shoulder to make certain Kruger wasn't watching, and caught up with her on the third floor, just outside the Man O' War Room.

"Hello, honey," she said, and smiled. "He's going to kill you," she said. "He's got George and Henry looking for you. You shouldn't have mentioned Aqueduct last night. He remembered your mentioning Aqueduct."

"Well, those are the chances one ofttimes takes," Mullaney said, thinking he sounded very much like K, and realizing that if he had mentioned Aqueduct to Kruger, he had doubtless mentioned it to K as well. It suddenly seemed terribly urgent to place the bet on Jawbone, collect his winnings, and get the hell out of here. "Do you have any money on you?" he asked.

"Yes, a little."

"How much?"

"Oh, a little. He gives me a little to bet. He's really very kind and generous indeed, though I can't stand him."

"Can you lend me some?"

"To get on an airplane to Brazil, do you mean?"

"No. To bet on a horse."

"Oh that would be a terrible mistake," Merilee said. "Lending someone money to bet on a horse."

"*This* horse is a sure thing."

"Besides," she said, "I never lend money to strangers."

"We're not strangers, Merilee," he said softly and sincerely. "We have been intimate."

"Oh yes indeed we have," she said, and smiled. "But still . . ."

"If the horse wins, I'll share the profits with you."

"You said it was a sure thing."

"That's right."

"Then why did you just say '*If* the horse wins'?"

"I meant *when* the horse wins."

"When you're making love," Merilee said, "you can say what you like. But when you're talking business, say what you mean."

"I meant *when* the horse wins, *when*."

"And how much profit will there be *when* she wins?"

"That depends on how much we bet and what the odds are when we bet it."

"Oh my," Merilee said, "it all sounds so dreadfully complicated."

"It's not complicated at all," Mullaney said. "How much money have you got?"

"A little," she said. "What will my cut be? Of the profits?"

"Well, let's say fifty percent," Mullaney said.

"No, let's say seventy-five percent."

"Sixty percent and it's a deal."

"Only because we once were lovers," Merilee said, and lowered her eyes modestly.

"How much have you got?"

"Three hundred dollars."

Mullaney glanced at the tote board. The odds on Jawbone had dropped to twelve to one. "Three hundred will have to do," he said, and looked at the board again. It was five minutes to post time.

"There are complications I can think of," Merilee said.

"Like what?"

"Like suppose the horse wins and they kill you before you can get to the cashier's window?"

"They would have to kill me in the next six minutes or so, and I feel certain they won't," Mullaney said, not feeling at all certain.

"Well then, suppose the horse wins, and you *do* collect the money, but they kill you before you can give me my share?"

"If that's bothering you, stay with me," he said.

"What do you mean?"

"We'll watch the race together. When the horse wins, we'll cash the ticket, and I'll give you your share on the spot. How does that sound?"

"Oh my it sounds very dangerous," Merilee said. "I told him I was going to the ladies' room. He's liable to send someone looking for me."

"We'll watch the race from inside the restaurant. It'll be starting in . . ." He looked again at the board. ". . . four minutes. He won't miss you in that time. Merilee, *please* give me the money. We've got to place the bet before it's too late."

"What's the horse's name?" she asked.

"The money first."

"The name first," she said.

It was three minutes to post time.

"Merilee . . ."

"The name," she said.

"Merilee, let's not . . ."

"The name."

Mullaney sighed. "No," he said. "I can't take that chance."

"I thought you were a gambler."

"I am, but . . ."

"One should always get the name first."

"This is not a cocktail party," he said, "it's a horse race." He looked at the tote board. "Merilee, the windows are going to close in two minutes, will you please for the love of God give me the money?"

"You're a very distrustful person," she said, but she opened her handbag and took out three hundred dollars in twenty-dollar bills, which she handed to him immediately. "Will you tell me the name now?"

"Jawbone," he said, and turned to run toward the hundred-dollar Win window.

"That's a nice name," she said behind him. "Jawbone."

He bought the three Win tickets and looked at the tote board a last time before they went into the restaurant. The odds were holding at ten to one. If Jawbone won, they'd get three thousand dollars, give or take, and his share would be twelve hundred, which was exactly twelve hundred more than he'd awakened with yesterday morning. Enough to break open a Harlem crap game, enough to buy a hundred good poker hands, enough to start the upward trend, change the course of this damn gamble and have it start paying off at last. The Man O' War Room was a sumptuous restaurant with twelve closed-circuit television receivers quartering the four walls of the room, enabling bettors to dine without missing any of the track action. Mullaney and the girl entered the restaurant just as the track announcer said, "It is *now* post time." They took seats at a table in the far corner, away from the entrance doors in case Henry and George were still on the prowl, and looked up at the nearest television receiver in time to see the horses breaking from the gate and the announcer shouting, "They're *off!*"

"Luck," Mullaney whispered.

"Oh yes indeed," the girl whispered back and covered his hand on the white tablecloth.

"It's a good start," the announcer said, "with no interference. Jawbone broke fast, God Sal is clear on the outside, Mercy's Baby is third by a length, Felicity in fourth place leading the field. Heading for the turn now . . ."

"It looks good," Mullaney said.

"Oh yes indeed," the girl answered. Her blue eyes were glowing. She kept licking her lips with her tongue, squeezing Mullaney's hand where it rested in a tight fist on the table top.

". . . it's still Jawbone in the lead, Mercy's Baby head and head with Good Sal, Felicity in fourth place on the outside . . ."

"Come on, Jawbone!" Mullaney whispered.

"Come on, Felicity!" someone at another table shouted.

"Rolling around the turn now," the announcer said, "it's Jawbone by a length, Good Sal, and moving up in there, Felicity,
getting into contention now . . ."

"Come on, Jawbone!" Mullaney shouted.

"Come on, Jawbone!" the girl yelled.

"It's still Jawbone by a head, Good Sal second, and Mona Girl
breaking away from the field, moving fast, moving up to fourth,
passing Felicity now, making a strong bid, head and head with
Good Sal . . ."

"Jawbone!" Mullaney shouted.

"Into the stretch," the announcer said, "it's Jawbone and Mona
Girl, the others beaten off . . . Mona Girl coming to the front,
Mona Girl in front by a length, Mona Girl leading by two
lengths, coming to the finish line, it's Mona Girl all the way,
Mona Girl by three lengths, Mona Girl is the *winner!*"

"Mona Girl?" Mullaney said.

"One should always get the name first," Merilee said, and
sighed.

11. ROLLO

"You are a loser," Merilee said, "oh you are very definitely a loser."

He thought about that while watching the tote board for the final results. Sure enough, it was Mona Girl first, Jawbone in the place position, and Felicity showing; his Win tickets on Jawbone were worth exactly the paper they were printed on, like the *New York Times* bills that had been in the jacket. He thought Yes, I *am* a loser on *this* race, on this *particular* race, Merilee, but that does not necessarily make me an all-time loser, I am just having a run of bad luck, that's all. But his run of bad luck seemed to take a decided downward turn in that moment because it was then that

George and Henry entered the restaurant and began glomming the room in twin intensity. Oh my, Mullaney thought.

He was feeling pretty depressed just then, truly feeling like the loser Merilee claimed he was, certainly too depressed to run again. Besides, he felt he had done quite enough running in two days, thank you, what had happened to that nice quality of unexpectedness he had initiated with the twins and used to such advantage? He decided to sit this one out, so he waited calmly at the table until the twins saw him, and then waited calmly as they walked over to him. Merilee, who had also seen them by this time, said only, "Oh my they are going to kill you, you are very definitely a loser."

He doubted very much that they would kill him in the midst of a crowded restaurant, no one was *that* dumb. The unexpected, he thought, that is the secret.

"Hello, boys," he said cheerfully, "nice to see you again."

"I'll bet," Henry said.

"I'll just bet," George said.

"I think you had better get up and come with us," Henry said. "Kruger would like to see you."

"I'd like to see him, too," Mullaney said.

"I'll just bet," George said.

They led him out of the restaurant and then over to the chain-link fence separating the sections, paid the attendant there (very nice of them) the difference between the admission prices for grandstand and clubhouse, and then led him over to where Kruger was sitting in the reserved section down front. The horses were already in the paddock for the third race, and Kruger was watching them through his binoculars. Mullaney sat down next to him, with Merilee on his right and with the twins taking seats behind him where they could shoot him through the head if necessary. Merilee crossed her legs, distracting some of the gamblers who were watching the horses in the paddock. She did not distract Kruger, however, who kept the binoculars to his eyes without turning to look at either her or Mullaney.

"You didn't come back," Kruger said.

"I know," Mullaney said.

"I trusted you, and you didn't come back."

"I promised to come back with the money, but there was no money."

"So Merilee has told me," Kruger said, still not taking the binoculars from his eyes. "What do you make of it?"

"Well, I don't know," Mullaney said. "I have the jacket here with me, if you'd like to look it over. You can take my word, however, that . . ."

"I will never take your word again," Kruger said. "You may not realize it, sir, but you hurt me deeply last night. Give me the jacket."

He put down the binoculars and took the shopping bag from Mullaney, who watched as Kruger carefully examined the jacket, turning it over in his hands, feeling inside the lining, searching the pockets, examining the buttons, and then finally crumpling it into a ball again and thrusting it back into the Judy Bond shopping bag.

"Worthless," he said, which ascertained what Mullaney had suspected all along: Kruger, no more than any of his fellows, knew why the jacket was important. Only K knew. K was the key.

"If you'd tell me what this is all about," Mullaney said, "I might be able to help."

"This is all about half a million dollars."

"In American money or Italian money?"

"In American money," Kruger said.

"Was it supposed to be in that coffin?"

"Yes."

"How'd you know that?"

"Why should I tell you anything when you've already broken trust with me?" Kruger said, offended, and put the binoculars back to his eyes.

"Because I may be able to help."

"How? You're a loser. Merilee told me you're a loser."

"When did she tell you *that?*" Mullaney said, turning swiftly to look at Merilee, who had not said a word to Kruger since they'd joined him, and who was sitting now with her legs crossed, her hands delicately clasped in her lap, her eyes on the horses in the paddock.

"Last night after your abortive love-making attempt," Kruger said, and Mullaney felt foolish.

"Well . . ." he said.

"Well, that also was not very nice," Kruger said, "making a pass at another fellow's girl."

"Well, I'm sorry," Mullaney said.

"Well, you should be."

"Well, I am," Mullaney said, thinking he was sorry about a great many things, but not necessarily about having made a pass at Merilee. Actually, he thought, if you *really* want to know, Mr. Kruger, it was a hell of a lot more than a pass, nor was it only an *attempt* at love-making, it was real and genuine, bona-fide and true love-making, *me* inside *her*, abortive or otherwise, though I don't imagine Merilee told you *that*. If she had told you *that*, you wouldn't have generously and kindly given her three hundred dollars to squander on the nags, which largesse she promptly turned over to the loser she supposedly claimed was me; she couldn't have thought I was very much of a loser if she was willing to trust me with three hundred dollars, what do you think about *that*, Mr. Kruger? She must have thought I was pretty hot stuff, don't you think, Mr. Kruger, no matter *what* she said to you or even to me, a pretty interesting and exciting fellow, if she was willing to give me three hundred dollars, which doesn't grow on trees where I come from. Think about *that* for a little while, Mr. Kruger, while you peer through your binoculars and examine the horses, what the hell do you know about horses, *or* women, or *me*, for that matter, a loser indeed!

But he could not justify her betrayal.

She had promised not to tell, she had promised to say only that he had escaped, and yet she had told all, or almost all, told enough to make him appear a fool. You shouldn't do that after making love, he thought, because making love is total exposure, and it only works if you can trust the other person enough to make a complete fool of yourself. Show and Tell is for kindergarten, he thought, not for lovers.

He suddenly wondered whether Irene (who had undoubtedly known other men since the divorce) had ever told any of them, for example, that he sometimes made muscles in front of the mirror, or that, for example, he had once said "Yum-yum" while going down on her, or that, for further example, he had once lain full-length and naked on the bed, with a derby hat covering his erection, which he had revealed to her suddenly as she entered the room with a "Good morning, madam, may I show you something in a hat?"—wondered, in short, if she had ever told anyone else in the world that he, Andrew Mullaney, was sometimes a fool, sometimes most certainly a horse's ass.

The thought bothered him.

To take his mind off Merilee's betrayal, off Irene's betrayal by extension, he turned back to the matter of the money again; there was always money to occupy a man's thoughts, there was always money to take a man's mind off the nagging knowledge that he was sometimes, perhaps often, a fool. "How did you learn about the money?" he asked Kruger.

Kruger lowered his binoculars, turned in his seat, and looked Mullaney directly in the eye. He was silent for a long time. Then, at last, he said, "I'm going to level with you, sir."

"Please do," Mullaney said.

"Someone in K's organization was in my employ."

"Who?"

"Gouda."

"Gouda," Mullaney repeated, thinking Where there's cheese, there is also sometimes a rat.

"Yes," Kruger said. "Unfortunately, he was killed in a terrible highway accident, as you may know . . ."

"Yes, I know."

"Yes, I thought you knew. In any event, he had outlived his usefulness."

"Was he the one who told you the money would be in the coffin?"

"He did more than that."

"What did he do?"

"He was responsible for putting those paper scraps in the lining of the jacket."

"Gouda?"

"Yes."

"I thought maybe McReady."

"No. It was Gouda."

"I see. In place of the money."

"Yes."

"What happened to the money?"

"He delivered it to us."

"I beg your pardon?"

"He delivered it to us."

"The five hundred thousand dollars?"

"Well, give or take."

"He delivered it to you?"

"Yes. I told you he was in my employ."

"He gave you the money, and substituted paper scraps for it, is that what you're saying?"

"That's exactly what I'm saying."

"Then you already *have* the money."

"No."

"No?"

"No."

"Who *does* have it?"

"K, I would imagine."

"But if it was delivered to *you* . . ."

"It was delivered to me, yes. But apparently someone *knew*

Gouda was working for me, someone *knew* Gouda would make the substitution, and someone very carefully worked out a triple cross."

"I don't understand."

"The money Gouda delivered was counterfeit."

"This is very confusing," Mullaney said.

"Yes," Kruger agreed.

"You mean they *knew* he was going to steal the money, so they . . ."

"Steal is a harsh word," Kruger said.

"They knew he was going to arrange a transfer," Mullaney said, "so they substituted counterfeit bills for the real bills, which counterfeit bills Gouda subsequently sto . . . transferred to you, leaving paper scraps in their place?"

"Yes."

"I don't get it," Mullaney said. "Why go to all the bother of shipping the coffin to Rome if they *knew* there were only paper scraps in the jacket?"

"I don't know," Kruger said thoughtfully. "But that's why we hijacked the coffin. When we discovered we'd been tricked, we assumed the real money was still hidden in the coffin someplace. As you know, it wasn't."

"Nor in the jacket, either," Mullaney said.

"Well," Kruger said reflectively, "it wasn't exactly a total loss. In my line of work, even counterfeit money is worth something." He paused. "Would *you* have any idea, sir, where the real money is?"

"No."

"I didn't think so."

"No, I have no idea."

"Mmmm."

"There's something else that's bothering me, though," Mullaney said.

"Yes?"

"Where'd all that money come from?"

Kruger was silent for quite a few minutes. Then he put the binoculars back to his eyes.

"Mr. Kruger," Mullaney said, "where'd all that money . . ."

"I think our business is concluded," Kruger said.

"I beg your pardon?"

"I think you will have to leave the track now in the company of Henry and George."

"What?" Mullaney said.

"Yes," Kruger said.

"But you said you trusted me!"

"No, I said I was going to level with you."

"That's the same thing!"

"Not quite," Kruger said. "Several men were killed in that highway accident yesterday, as I'm sure you know."

"Yes, but what's that got to . . ."

"Three men, to be exact. The police know only that a red pickup truck entered the Van Wyck Expressway, cut off the hearse, and shot three men to death. The fourth man unfortunately escaped through the bushes and brambles lining the parkway."

"That would be K," Mullaney said.

"Yes, that would be K. So you see, we do not wish the police to learn anything more about the accident than they already know."

"I see."

"We do not wish them to know, for example, that I or any of my fellows had anything to do with it."

"I see," Mullaney said again.

Kruger put down the glasses, turned to Mullaney, and smiled. Mullaney knew he was about to make a joke.

"Loose lips sink ships," Kruger said.

"I think I get your meaning," Mullaney said.

"I hope so."

"But you have nothing to worry about. I'm in trouble with the police myself, you see."

"Oh, are you really?" Kruger said drily, and put the glasses to his eyes again.

"Yes. So I would hardly go to them with information, you see, being in trouble with them myself, you see."

"I see," Kruger said.

"Yes."

"Yes, but in any event I think you will have to leave us now."

"You don't understand," Mullaney said.

"I think I understand," Kruger said.

"I'm telling you the *truth*," Mullaney said. "I really *am* in trouble with the police."

"Yes, I'm sure."

"I was arrested for *burglary*, in fact!"

"Take him away," Kruger said.

"The *hors*-es are *on* the track!" the announcer said.

"Do you see anything you like?" Kruger asked Merilee, lowering the binoculars.

"Mr. Kruger, look . . ." Mullaney said.

"Up!" George said behind him.

"I thought the seven-horse," Merilee said.

"Mr. Kruger, I assure you . . ."

"Let's go," Henry said, and prodded him with something that felt very much like a gun in a jacket pocket. Mullaney picked up his shopping bag.

"The terrible thing though," Merilee said, "is that I lost all my money on the last race."

"Do you really like the seven-horse?"

"Oh yes indeed, I think he's a cunning horse."

"Mr. Kruger, I wish . . ."

"Get him out of here!" Kruger said sharply, and Henry poked him again.

"All right, don't get tough," Mullaney said.

"Move!" Henry said.

"All right, all *right*," Mullaney said. Clutching the shopping bag to his chest, he began moving sideways out of the aisle, then stopped and turned to Kruger, who had the binoculars to his eyes again. "You haven't heard the last of me, Mr. Kruger," he said.

"I think I have," Kruger answered. "Which horse did you say?"

"The seven-horse," Merilee answered.

"Looks like a good horse," Kruger said.

"Looks like a *dog* to me," Mullaney said petulantly.

"No one asked you."

"And as for *you* . . ." Mullaney said, turning to Merilee.

"Yes?" she answered, looking up at him.

"I am *not* a loser."

"If you lose, honey," she said, "why then you're a loser, yes indeed."

"Move!" Henry said again.

Mullaney moved out of the aisle without looking back at either Merilee or Kruger, feeling the hard snout of Henry's gun against his back, and thinking how remarkable it was that you could always tell a gun by its feel, even when it was in somebody's pocket. He could not for a minute believe they were really going to kill him, and yet they all seemed so terribly serious about this, especially Henry and George, who solemnly led him to the escalator and then down to the exit and across the wide concrete path leading to the elevated train station.

"Shouldn't we take the car?" Henry asked.

"Kruger will want it," George said.

But that was all either of them said, leading him silently up the steps to the change booth, and buying three tokens (very nice of them), and passing him through the turnstile, and then taking him out onto the platform where they silently and ominously waited for the train going back to Manhattan.

"Where are you taking me?" Mullaney asked.

"Someplace nice," Henry said.

"Very nice," George said.

"You'll remember it always," Henry said.

"You'll take the memory to your grave," George said, which Mullaney did not think was funny.

When the train pulled in, they waited silently for the doors to open, and then got into the nearest car and silently took seats, Mullaney in the middle, George and Henry on either side of him. The shopping bag with the damn inscrutable jacket rested on the floor of the car, between Mullaney's feet.

"How should we do it?" Henry asked.

"I don't know," George said. "What do you think?"

"The river?"

"Always the river," George said disdainfully.

Mullaney, sitting between them, realized they were talking about him, which he considered impolite.

"You got any better ideas?"

"We could throw him on the tracks."

"Where?"

"In the subway. When we get back to the city. It'll look like an accident. What do you think?"

Henry thought it over for a moment. "No," he said, "I don't like it."

"Well, what do you feel like doing?" George said.

"I don't know," Henry said, "what do *you* feel like doing?"

"I saw a movie once where they were getting this guy with a laser beam," George said.

"Yeah, but we don't have a laser beam."

"I know. I was just saying."

"We could throw him off the Empire State Building," Henry suggested. "They'll think he jumped."

"I never been up the Empire State Building," George said.

"Me either."

"I hate to go someplace I ain't never been," George said.

"Me too."

"So what do you want to do?"

"I don't know. What do *you* want to do?"

"We could just plug him," George said.

"Yeah, I guess," Henry said.

"That's such a drag though."

"Yeah."

"What do you think?"

"I don't know. What do *you* think?"

"I read a book once, they had it fixed so it looked like the guy took an overdose of heroin."

"Yeah, but then we got to look up Garafolo, and maybe he won't even be holding, and then we get all kinds of heat from the narcotics dicks, it ain't worth it."

"Yeah."

They had passed perhaps three station stops by now, and were pulling into another one—Grant Avenue, Mullaney noticed. He thought he had better get the hell out of here quick because whereas it had not occurred to either Henry or George as yet, a very neat way of dispatching him would be merely to stomp him to death right here on the train. The way things were these days in New York, no one would pay the slightest bit of attention. He wondered when they would hit upon this best of all possible solutions, and saw the train doors opening, and calculated how long it would take him to reach those doors, and realized they could shoot him in the back before he'd run more than two feet from where they were sitting. The doors closed again, the train was once again in motion.

They changed trains at Euclid Avenue. There were a lot of people in the new car, reading their newspapers, or holding hands, or studying the carcard advertising, or idly gazing through the windows as the train clattered from station to station, making its way toward Manhattan. Mullaney wondered what would happen if he stood up and announced that the two men with him were at this very moment discussing ways and means of killing him, and guessed that everyone in the car would simply applaud and wait for him to pass the hat. He glanced across the aisle to the other side of the car, where a fat dark-haired woman sat with her button-nosed little daughter, and then looked beyond them through the open windows, watching the apartment buildings as they blurred past, wondering what part of Brooklyn they were traveling through. He suddenly realized he would be leaving the train by the doors on his right, in the center of the car, and he decided he ought to know how long it took for those doors to open and then close again. So he began counting as soon as the train stopped at the next station, one, two, thr . . . the doors opened, four, five, six, seven, they were still open, people were moving out onto the platform, others were coming in, eleven, twelve, thirteen, fourteen, the doors closed, the train was in motion again. Well, that was a very pleasant exercise, Mullaney thought, but I don't know what good it will do me when the time comes to make my break.

"What we *could* do," George said, "is throw him in that big garbage-burning thing they got on the East River Drive."

"I can't stand the smell of garbage," Henry said.

"Me neither."

"Hey, you know what?" Henry said.

"What?"

"We could take him to that little park they got there outside the U.N. building, you know that little park I mean?"

"Yeah?"

"Yeah, and walk him over to the river where that thing juts out over the water, you know where I mean?"

"Yeah?"

"Yeah, and hit him on the head and just dump him over the side there."

"Well, that's the river again, ain't it?" George said.

"Yeah."

"I mean, that's just the damn river all over again."

"Yeah." Henry seemed crestfallen. "Well, what do *you* want to do?"

"I don't know," George said. "What do *you* want to do?"

"Gee, I don't know," Henry said.

Mullaney heard the sound of an alto saxophone, and thought at first that someone in the car had turned on a transistor radio. New Yorkers were all so musical, always singing and dancing wherever they went, just like Italians, gay and light-hearted and singing, dancing, playing all the time. But as he turned toward the sound, he saw that a live musician had entered the far end of the car and was making his way, step by cautious step, toward where Mullaney and his potential assassins were sitting.

The man was blind.

He was a tall thin man wearing a tattered maroon sweater similar to the one Mullaney had worn all through college, dark glasses on his nose, his head carried erect, as though on the end of a plumb line, the saxophone mouthpiece between his compressed lips. The saxophone was gilded with mock silver that had worn through in spots to reveal the tarnished brass beneath. A leather leash was fastened to the man's belt and led to the collar of a large German shepherd who preceded the man into the subway car and led him step by step up the aisle, sitting after each two or three steps while the man continued playing a song that sounded like a medley of "You Made Me Love You" and "Sentimental Journey." The man, though blind, was a terrible saxophonist, miskeying, misphrasing, producing squeaks in every measure. The German shepherd, dutifully pausing after every few steps into the car, walked or sat at the man's feet in what appeared to be a pained stupor, a glazed look on his otherwise intelligent face. The blind man swayed above him, filling the car with his monumentally bad music while on either side people rose from their seats to drop coins into the tin cup that hung from his neck, resting somewhere near his breastbone, its supporting cord tangled in the leather strap that held the saxophone. The dog was similarly burdened, carrying around his neck a hanging, hand-lettered placard that read:

> MY NAME IS ROLLO.
>
> DO NOT PET ME.
>
> THANK YOU.

The blind man had reached the center doors of the car now. The dog dutifully sat again with that same pained and patient expression on his face, and Mullaney wondered why a nice-looking animal like Rollo would wear a sign asking people not to pet him. The train had pulled into another station, and people were rushing in and out of the doors, shoving past the blind man, who immediately stopped playing. But as soon as the doors closed and the train was in motion again, he struck up a lively chorus of "Ebb Tide," and then modulated into "Stormy Weather," which he played with the same squeaking vibrato and fumbling dexterity while the dog continued to look more and more pained. They were still coming up the aisle, slowly making their way toward where Mullaney sat. He had not thought to count the time it took for the train to go from one station to another, that was his mistake, he now realized, he had counted the wrong thing. The blind man and Rollo stopped, the swelling sound of the saxophone drowned out the speculations of Henry and George (they were debating the possibility of garroting Mullaney) and filled the car with horrendous sound. Coins continued to rattle into the tin cup, music lovers all along the car reaching gingerly into the aisle and dropping pennies, nickels and dimes in appreciation as Rollo and the blind man moved a few steps, paused, moved again, paused again, they were perhaps three feet away from Mullaney now. The dog is probably vicious, he thought, that's why you're not supposed to pet him, he's a vicious dog who'll chew your arm off at the elbow if you so much as make a move toward his head. The train was slowing, the train was pulling into a station, Rollo and the blind man were moving ahead again, two feet away, a foot away, the train stopped, and the dog sat in the aisle directly in front of Henry.

Mullaney begged the forgiveness of polite society, he begged the forgiveness of God, he begged the forgiveness of tradition, but he knew he had to save his life, even if the only way to do it was to take advantage of a blind man. He began counting the moment the train stopped, *one, two, three,* the doors opened, he had eleven seconds to make his move, win or lose, live or die. He suddenly grabbed Henry's right arm, cupping his own left hand behind Henry's elbow, pushing his own right hand against Henry's wrist, creating a fulcrum and lever that forced Henry out of his seat with a yelp. The dog was sitting at Henry's feet, and Mullaney, counting madly (*five, six, seven, eight,* those doors would close at fourteen), hurled Henry directly at Rollo's pained magnificent head, saw his jowls pull back an instant before Henry collided with the triangular black nose, saw the fangs bared, heard the deep growl start in Rollo's throat, *nine, ten, eleven,* he bounded for the doors as George came out of his seat, drawing his gun, *twelve, thirteen,* "Stop!" George shouted behind him, he was through the doors, *fourteen,* and they closed behind him. Through the open windows of the car, he could hear Rollo tearing off Henry's arm or perhaps ripping out his jugular while the blind man began playing a medley of "Strangers in the Night" and "Tuxedo Junction." George was across the car now and leaning through a window as the train began moving out of the station. He fired twice at Mullaney, who zigzagged along the platform and leaped head first down the steps leading below, banging his head on a great many risers as he hurtled down, thinking this was where he had come in, and thinking By God, he missed me! He heard the train rattling out of the station, and was certain he also heard applause from the passengers in the car as Rollo eviscerated poor Henry. He got to his feet the moment he struck the landing, began running instantly, without looking back, thinking I'm free at last, I'm free of all of them, and running past the change booth and then bounding down another flight of steps to the street, not knowing where he was, Brooklyn or Queens or wherever the hell, thinking only that he had escaped, finding himself on the sidewalk, good solid concrete under his feet, glancing up at the traffic light, seeing it was in his favor, and darting into the gutter.

He was halfway to the other side when he realized he had left the Judy Bond shopping bag on the train.

He stopped dead in the middle of the street and, as cars rushed past him in both directions, thought that Merilee's estimation had been correct, If you lose, honey, why then you're a loser, yes indeed. He had felt like a winner not a moment ago when he'd eluded the twins, but here he was bereft of the bag that still contained the jacket that held the clue to half a million dollars. He thought Well, the hell with it, easy come, easy go, and was almost knocked flat to the pavement by a red convertible that swerved screechingly away from him, the driver turning his head back to shout a few swear words, thereby narrowly missing a milk truck that went thundering past from the opposite direction. He did not think it would be a good idea to get hit by a moving vehicle as that might attract the attention of the police; there was still a Burglary One charge hanging over his head. So he stood exactly where he was, unmoving in the center of the street, waiting for the light to change again, and the traffic to ease.

When it did, he walked back to the curb and thought The hell with the jacket, I have had enough of this chasing after pots of gold at the ends of rainbows, and then was inordinately annoyed once again by the jacket's obstinacy. He liked to think of himself as a system player, and surely such a player was capable of piercing whatever stubborn disguise K and his fellows had concocted. The best system he had ever devised was based on the Martingale double-up or progressive system that expounded the theory of doubling your bet each time you lost, betting four dollars if you lost two dollars, for example, and then eight if you lost the four, and sixteen the next time out, and so on until— when you finally won—you were getting back all of your previous investment plus a two-dollar profit as well. Securely based on this premise, his own system (which he was thinking of putting into soft covers as *Mullaney's System,* if he could only find a publisher) was a variation of the theme, a sort of double-up retreat system, a sort of progressive-regressive system wherein he doubled his bet only four times if he was losing, and then began a process of reversal, halving his bet, and then quartering it, until he was back to betting only two dollars, after which he once again began doubling. The theory worked on the basis of simple gambling common sense: Mullaney knew that a run of bad luck could sometimes outlast even a very large bankroll. So he premised his system on the hope that enough winners, small or large, would come in over the progressive-regressive long run to allow a steady profit, enough to keep him in franks and beans, enough to keep him alive and betting.

Thus far, the system hadn't worked too well.

But a man who had devised such a scheme, a man who had painstakingly figured it out with pencil and paper, was surely a man who possessed the intelligence and ingenuity to crack the jacket's stubborn facade. Determined, he clenched his fists and marched up the steps to the subway platform, mindful that George or even poor Henry might get off at the next station stop, double back, and shoot him on the spot; well, those are the chances you have to take, he thought, if you want to get anywhere in this world.

The woman in the change booth was a very healthy person wearing a green eye shade and a tan cardigan sweater, the sleeves of which had been cut off raggedly at the elbows. She had muscular forearms that rippled with power as she arranged small piles of tokens on the counter top. One of her arms was tattooed with the name MIKE in a heart pierced by an arrow. Her hair was up in curlers, so Mullaney figured she was preparing for a heavy date later on that night.

"Excuse me, ma'am," he said, "but . . ."

"*Miss*," she corrected. She did not look up from arranging her little piles of tokens.

"I left a shopping bag on the train . . ." he said.

"Lost Property Office," she answered without looking up.

"Thank you." He started to walk away from the booth, turned, went up to the cage again, and said, "Where *is* that, miss? The Lost Property Office?"

"Phone book," she said without looking up.

"Thank you," he said. He found a telephone booth alongside the newspaper stand at the rear of the station, and quickly searched the Manhattan directory. He tried Interboro Rapid Transit System first and found *Interboro Time Clock Co* and *Interboro Trucking Co Inc* but nothing in between. So he decided to try Brooklyn Manhattan Transfer and found *Bklyn Mchy Warehse Corp* and *Bklyn-Manhatn Trial Counsel Assn Inc,* but nothing between those two, either. So he looked up Independent Subway System and found *Independent Subway Call NY City Transit System ULstr 2–5000,* which he called, but got no answer. He began leafing through the telephone book again, thinking there might be a listing for the Lost Property Office under New York City Transit System, but all he found was a listing for *NY City Transit Police Patrolmen's Benevolent Assn,* which he did not think would help him. He closed the book and walked back toward the change booth. The woman was still arranging tokens. She had made perhaps thirty little piles of tokens already.

"Excuse me," he said.

"Yes?" she said without looking up.

"I can't find it in the telephone book."

"New York," she said, "City of."

"I beg your pardon."

"New York, City of," she said.

"Oh, thank you," he said, and went back to the telephone book and found, just three pages before the *Transit Police Patrolmen's Benevolent Association* listing, a thousand or more New York City listings, including frequently called numbers like *City Prisons* and *Hack Licenses* and *Rent & Rehabilitation Admin* and—I'll be damned, he thought—a listing under TRANSIT AUTHORITY for *Lost Property Office, MA 5–6200;* he supposed a lot of people were losing things in the subways nowadays. He fished into his pocket for the dime again, dialed the number, and let it ring ten times before hanging up. He retrieved his dime from the return chute, went out of the booth, and back to the woman in the sawed-off cardigan. There were perhaps forty or fifty little piles of tokens on the counter now.

"Excuse me," he said.

"Yes?" she said without looking up.

"I called them and there was no answer."

"Who?" she said.

"The Lost Property Office."

"That's right," she said, "they're closed on Saturdays."

"Oh," he said. "Well, what am I supposed to do about my shopping bag?"

"Go fight City Hall," she said, and continued piling tokens.

"Thank you," he said.

"Don't mention it," she answered.

He walked away from the booth. Well, that's that, he thought. I tried. I really tried, so the hell with it. Well, he thought, you haven't really tried until you've exhausted every possibility, there is half a million dollars at stake here, or have you forgotten that? He reached into his pocket, extracted his remaining money and—spreading it on the palm of his hand—began counting it. He had exactly a dollar and fifteen cents in change. He wondered how far that would take him, and decided it would take him quite far enough. He went down the steps to the street, hailed the first taxicab he saw, and said to the driver, "Follow that el."

"What?" the driver said.

"Follow that el."

"You mean follow them tracks up there?"

"That's right."

"To where?"

"I don't know yet. I'm looking for somebody."

"Who're you looking for?"

"I'm not sure. Somebody with a shopping bag."

The driver studied him silently for a moment. Then he said, "I got to have a destination, mister. I got to write down a destination on my call sheet."

"Okay, write down Radio City Music Hall."

"Is that where you're going?"

"No, but you can *say* that's where I'm going. Then I'll change my mind as soon as I spot whoever has my shopping bag. I'm allowed to change my mind."

"That's true, you're allowed to change your mind."

"Okay, so write down Radio City."

"How you gonna find this person with your shopping bag?"

"Well, I don't know. I've got to keep my eyes open until we catch up with the train."

"What train?"

"The one up there heading for Manhattan."

"Mister, there are a *hundred* trains up there heading for Manhattan."

"Yes, but this one just left about five minutes ago. I'm sure we can catch it."

"Mister," the driver said, "I'll tell you the truth, I was just on my way in to the garage, you know? So why don't I just help you get another cab, huh?"

"No, this'll be fine," Mullaney said. "Here," he said, and handed the driver his dollar and fifteen cents. "This is all the money I've got. Just keep driving until the meter hits ninety-five cents, and keep the twenty cents for your tip. If we haven't caught up with the train by then or found my shopping bag by then, well, that's that, we tried, right? We can't go looking all over the city for that pot of gold, now can we?"

"Not on a buck-fifteen, we can't," the driver said.

"Right, so let's get moving, right?"

"This won't take you to Radio City," the driver said, pocketing the money and throwing the cab into gear.

"I know, but that's okay because I'm not going to Radio City, remember?"

"Yeah, yeah," the driver said.

"You forgot to throw your flag," Mullaney said.

"Yeah, yeah," the driver said.

"Do you know what time it is?" Mullaney asked.

"Quarter to four," the driver answered. "You know, don't you, that the minute I throw this flag, you got thirty-five cents on the meter right off."

"Yes, I know that."

"What I'm saying is this money ain't gonna take you very far. I mean, I don't know what kind of manhunt you got in mind here, but this money ain't gonna take you very far at *all,* if you know what I mean."

"Well, that's a chance I'll have to take, right?" Mullaney said. "Life's full of little chances one has to take, right?"

"If you say so, mister," the driver said, and lowered the flag, starting the clock on the meter.

"Please drive as slowly as you can," Mullaney said. "I have to look at the people. One of them may have my shopping bag."

"Mister, do you know how many people live in the borough of Brooklyn?"

"How many?"

"I happen to live in the borough of Brooklyn myself," the driver said, "and so I know whereof I speak. There happens to be 2,018,356 people living in this borough, and on a Saturday afternoon like this, with the sun shining and it so nice out, I'll bet you half of them are out here in the street. And I'll bet you furthermore that half of them that are out here in the street are carrying shopping bags. Now how do you expect to find . . ."

"Slow down, slow down," Mullaney said.

". . . a person carrying *your* shopping bag?"

"It's a very special shopping bag," Mullaney said.

"Oh? It has your name on it or something?"

"No, it has Judy Bond's name on it."

"Who's Judy Bond? A relation to James Bond perhaps?" the driver said, and burst out laughing. Undoubtedly thinking Mullaney had not heard him, he said again, "A relation to James Bond perhaps?" and laughed again. "You now have forty-five cents on the meter, mister."

"I see it," Mullaney said.

"That's almost half your ride," the driver said.

"I know."

The streets, as the driver had observed, were thronged with people, but Mullaney could not see anyone carrying a Judy Bond shopping bag. He was desperately hoping that the shopping bag was still on the train, and that he could catch up with the train before his meter money ran out. (The meter now read fifty-five cents, he noticed with rising despair.) He would then board the train (What would he use for fare? he suddenly wondered), retrieve the bag and figure out a way of tricking K into revealing the jacket's secret. That was his biggest hope, and he was gambling that his money would not run out before he could realize it. (The meter now read sixty cents.) But the possibility also existed that someone had picked up the shopping bag, disembarked from the train, and was at this very moment hurrying homeward with a supposed treasure trove, little suspecting that all the bag contained was a jacket with a torn lining. So he kept his eyes on the pedestrians scurrying past, shifting his attention from them to the meter and then back again, and suddenly hearing a siren somewhere up ahead.

He leaned forward tensely and peered through the windshield, noticing from the corner of his eye that the meter now read seventy cents and thinking I'll never make it, all is lost. There was a crowd of people milling about the steps of the elevated station stop ahead. An ambulance was parked at the curb, and the police car he had heard was just pulling up beside it.

"Slow down," he told the driver.

The driver obediently slowed the taxi as they came abreast of the ambulance. Two attendants were coming down the steps of the platform, carrying someone on a stretcher. Mullaney could not see the person on the stretcher, but he recognized George walking beside it, a grave, pale look on his face. That will be poor Henry on the stretcher, Mullaney thought, and grinned ghoulishly, figuring he would not have to worry too much about either of the twins for the rest of the day, what with hospital emergency rooms and all that. Even Kruger seemed only a remote menace now that his musclemen were out of the action. Still grinning, he said to the driver, "Scratch two."

"I beg your pardon?" the driver said.

"Drive on," Mullaney said, grinning. "And remember that a horse race isn't over until all the photos are in."

"Your particular horse race is gonna be over in exactly twenty cents," the driver said.

"Be that as it may," Mullaney said.

"Are you a cop?" the driver asked instantly.

"Oh no indeed," Mullaney said.

"Mister, there is now *eighty* cents on the meter."

"Yes, yes," Mullaney said, "well, that's the way it goes, you cannot win them all."

"Did you say a Judy Bond shopping bag?" the driver said.

"Yes. Why?"

"Because I just saw a girl carrying one."

"What! Where?"

"Up ahead there. You want me to pull over?"

"Yes, where is she? Where'd you see her?"

"Right over there, oops," the driver said, "she's gone."

"Let me out," Mullaney said.

"One moment please, sir," the driver said, and put his hand on Mullaney's arm.

"Look, I can't afford to lose that . . ."

"The fare is only eighty cents whereas you gave me ninety-five cents plus a twenty-cent tip," the driver said. "Now twenty cents is a more than sufficient tip on an eighty-cent ride, so if it's all the same to you, I would like to give you fifteen cents change."

"Fine, fine," Mullaney said. "Only please . . ."

"One moment please, sir," the driver said, and reached over for his change dispenser, pushing a lever in the dime section, and another lever in the nickel section, and then presenting both coins to Mullaney.

"Thank you," Mullaney said. "A *girl*, did you say?"

"Yes. Carrying that shopping bag you were talking about."

"Thank you," Mullaney said, and jumped out of the cab. He began running in the direction the driver had indicated, but he saw no one, male or female, carrying a Judy Bond shopping bag. He saw a lot of old women carrying plain old brown shopping bags or A&P shopping bags, and one carrying an Abraham & Straus shopping bag, but he did not see anyone carrying *his* shopping bag, the bag containing the goddamn jacket.

The trouble with New York City, he thought, is that there are too many people living here, and they all look exactly alike. Also, he thought, if you want to get right down to it, all the various boroughs of the city look exactly alike, too, with the possible exception of Manhattan and Staten Island. Take this sidewalk along which I am now running, pushing my way through the baby buggies and the kids roller skating and the old ladies gossiping and the teenagers giggling, take this street in the shadow of the elevated structure (whatever street it may happen to be, I haven't the faintest idea), but take it and add up all the butcher shops on it, the delicatessens and grocery stores, add up the shoemakers and dry-goods stores and luncheonettes, the record shops and jewelers and vegetable stands, the photography joints, and furniture stores and bakeries, add them all up and you no longer have a street in Brooklyn in the shadow of the elevated structure, you also have a street in Queens in the shadow of the el, and a street in the Bronx in the shadow of the el—they are all different and yet they are all the same. I could be searching for that girl with the Judy Bond bag on any one of those other streets as well (I never dated a girl from Brooklyn, what a pity, the Bronx is so very far away, my dears, the opposite end of the earth).

But identical.

Goddamn bloody well identical, he thought, and suddenly was stricken by a revelation so clear and so sharp that he almost forgot all about the shopping bag, stopped dead in the center of the sidewalk and allowed himself to be jostled by the crowds passing by, stood glassy-eyed and amazed and thought I'll bet by

Christ there are streets in the shadow of the el in Rome, or London, or Paris, not literally in the shadow of the el because they probably haven't *got* elevated structures such as these beauties that support our transit-system tracks, but I'll bet it's the same there, I'll bet the people look exactly the same there. I'll bet even in Yokohama—which *has* got an elevated structure because I once saw a movie—I'll bet even *there* everybody looks exactly the same, oh my God I feel like a carbon copy.

Is it this way in Jakarta? he suddenly wondered.

He saw his shopping bag going around the corner in a flurry of Saturday-afternoon humanity, a boy on a skateboard rushing past, two old ladies carrying groceries, a man wearing a straw hat and drinking beer from a bottle, he saw only the disappearing end of the bag as it rounded the corner and did not see who was carrying it, saw only a portion of a word, IKE!, and hurried to reach the corner, almost knocking over a man carrying a Christmas tree, a *what?*, turning to look back at the man—sure enough, he was carrying a goddamn *Christmas* tree in the middle of April—ran past the gardening shop on the corner, saw pines and spruces potted in tubs (is there Christmas in Jakarta? he wondered), said, "Excuse me," to a lady in slacks and high-heeled pumps, suddenly transported to Brentwood in Los Angeles 49, California, where Irene's aunt lived and where they had spent the entire summer of 1962 watching middle-aged ladies in gold lamé pants and sequined slippers shopping in supermarkets, all the same, all the same, reached the corner, turned the corner, saw a row of empty lots, a single huge apartment house—but not his shopping bag.

His shopping bag, carried by a girl he had not yet laid eyes on, had disappeared.

12. LADRO

He stood on the sidewalk and counted thirteen stories in the apartment building, and then started counting windows in an attempt to learn how many apartments there were, counting ten windows on each floor across the front face, and figuring another ten windows for each floor at the rear of the building, two windows to each room most likely. That would make it at least ten apartments on each floor, multiplied by thirteen (unlucky number) for a total of one hundred and thirty apartments. It suddenly occurred to him that the Judy Bond shopping bag he had seen might not be *his* shopping bag. Suppose he knocked on a hundred and thirty doors only to discover that the bag contained, for example, a pair of men's pajamas or a lady's bathrobe? Besides, even if it *was* his shopping bag, he still didn't know exactly why the jacket was worth retrieving. K and his fellows knew that, but the last time he'd seen them they were struggling with problems of their own. Except McReady. Mmmm, Mullaney thought, and immediately hailed another taxi, coldly calculating the petit larceny he was about to commit against the driver, but figuring *C'est la guerre,* and giving him the address of McReady's Monument Works in Queens.

This has got to be the end of it, he thought.

If that really is my shopping bag, then I know where the jacket is, or at least approximately where it is—there's only one apartment building on that block and the girl certainly didn't vanish into thin air. On the other hand, K and McReady and Purcell all know the secret of the jacket. So the ideal thing is to form a partnership, fifty-fifty, I tell you how to get the jacket, you tell me how to get the money, okay? Is it a deal?

No, they will say, and shoot me through the head.

But then they don't get the jacket.

I certainly hope they want that jacket.

"Have you been bereaved?" the cab driver asked.

"No, not recently," Mullaney said.

"I thought perhaps you had been bereaved, since you are heading for a gravestone place."

"No, I'm heading there to consummate a rather large business deal."

"Oh, are you in the gravestone business?"

"No, I'm . . ."

He hesitated.

He had almost said, "I'm an encyclopedia salesman," which he had not been for more than a year now.

"I'm a gambler," he said quickly.

"I take a gamble everytime I pick up a passenger," the cab driver said, which made Mullaney feel a bit uneasy. He had only fifteen cents in his pocket, and the meter already read forty cents.

"Really?" he said.

"Certainly. You'd be surprised how many times a year I get stiffed," the driver said. "You wouldn't believe how mean and rotten the people in this rotten city are."

"Really?" Mullaney said.

"I get guys in this cab," the driver said, "they look like respectable businessmen, nice, you know what I mean? Dressed neat, just like you. We reach where we're going, they get out and tell me they'll be right back, I should wait for them, *psssssst*, the great disappearing act."

"Really?" Mullaney said, and cleared his throat; he had planned a similar disappearance, but now he wondered whether he dared attempt it. "What . . . uh . . . do you usually do when something like that happens?" he asked.

"I wait."

"How long do you wait?"

"Five minutes, ten minutes, twenty minutes, sometimes a half-hour. By that time, I realize I've been stiffed." The driver shrugged. "So I drive away. What else can I do? It's a gamble, this whole rotten business. I wish I was in gravestones, like you."

"No, I'm not in gravestones," Mullaney said.

"That's right, you ain't," the driver said. "And you think hizzoner the mayor gives a damn about us? You got to fight tooth and nail for everything you get in this rotten city, we're like the coolies of the western world, they should give us them rickshas and them little straw hats and let us pull people around that way, it's the same rotten thing. What business did you say you were in?"

"I'm a gambler," Mullaney said.

"Horses, you mean?"

"Horses and other things, too."

"What other things?"

"Dice, cards . . ." Mullaney shrugged. "You know."

"Do you ever win?" the driver asked.

"Oh, sure," Mullaney said.

"What's the most you ever won?" the driver asked.

"Well . . ." He hesitated again. The most he'd ever won was a hundred and sixty-five dollars on the Daily Double at Yonkers Raceway. "I won . . . uh . . . almost three thousand dollars at Hialeah once. I was down there for the winter." He paused. "I go down there every winter," he said.

"That must be the life," the driver said.

"Oh, sure, it's a nice life," Mullaney said.

"You married?"

"No. No," Mullaney said.

"I got a battle-axe I'll let you have for a subway token," the driver said, and laughed. "I also got three miserable little bastards, one of them is playing around with boys, the other is playing around with pot, and the third is playing around with himself," the driver said, and laughed again. "I'll throw *them* in for the same subway token."

"Well, thanks," Mullaney said, and laughed, "but I like this free and easy life I have."

"Must be a free and easy life, huh?" the driver said.

"Oh sure, it's a very free and easy life."

"Three thousand dollars, huh?"

"I beg your pardon?"

"Down at Hialeah."

"Yes, that's right," Mullaney said. "I also won a lot of money at Churchill Downs once."

"That's in England," the driver said.

"No, Churchill Downs," Mullaney said. "That's in Kentucky. I go down there for the Derby each year."

"Oh sure, that's in Kentucky," the driver said. "You really get around, don't you?"

"Oh sure, I get around," Mullaney said.

"I envy you, mister," the driver said, "I really envy you. I get home the other night, my faggot son is sitting on some guy's lap, right in my own living room, I nearly killed him. I said you goddamn pansy get out of my house with your queer friends, you know what he told me? He told me What do you know about love, Pop? What do *I* know about love, who only *created* him, the little fruit."

"How sharper than a serpent's tooth," Mullaney said.

"You said it," the driver said.

They were coming around the perimeter of the cemetery now, fast approaching McReady's place. Mullaney did not want to add to the cab driver's woes, but he could see no way of leaving the taxi without stiffing him. He suddenly had a brilliant idea, or at least *told* himself it was a brilliant idea, completely ignoring the fact that he was about to compound his contemplated larceny.

"Listen," he said, "I'm going right back to where you picked me up, would you like to wait for me?"

"And get stiffed, huh?" the driver said, and laughed.

"Well, no," Mullaney said uneasily. "I really *am* going back. In fact, if you'd like me to pay you *before* I get out of the cab . . ."

"I think I can tell a gent when I see one," the driver said. "That's it up ahead there, ain't it?"

"Yes."

"You won't be long, will you?"

"Just a few minutes."

"I'll wait," the driver said. "I got to go back that way, anyway, because my garage is over on Sutter, you familiar with Brooklyn?"

"Not very."

"Well, that ain't too far from where I picked you up. But don't take all day, huh? It's already . . ." He looked at his watch. ". . . twenty to five, I should have been in ten minutes ago. Okay?"

"Fine," Mullaney said. He opened the cab door. "Thank you for what you said."

"What did I say?"

"About . . . my being a gent. Thank you."

"Come on, come on," the driver said, embarrassed, but he smiled nonetheless.

Mullaney went up the gravel walk, debating whether he should chance popping in on McReady without at least a preliminary phone call to announce the purpose of his visit. Suppose K or Purcell were in the cottage, suppose they all began shooting the moment he opened the door? He noticed that the window he had dived through the night before was still open, and whereas he didn't want to waste time trying to locate a phone booth, he saw nothing wrong with stealing over to the window and doing a little precautionary eavesdropping. He tiptoed across the gravel, ducked below the window, and then slowly and carefully raised his head so that his eyes were just level with the sill.

McReady was alone in the room.

He was standing near the Tutankhamen calendar, alongside which was a wall telephone. He had the phone receiver to his ear, and was listening attentively. He kept listening, nodding every now and then, listening some more, and finally shouting, "*Yes,* Signor Ladro, I under*stand!* But . . ." He listened again. "Yes," he said, "losing the body *was* inexcusable, I agree with you. But, Signor Ladro, I must say that I find this call equally inexcusable. I thought we had agreed . . . yes . . . yes, but . . . yes . . . what? Of *course,* the body was properly clothed. Yes, that *does* mean the burial garments were lost as well. *Including* the jacket, yes. But I told you we're making every effort to relocate the corpse. Yes, of *course,* the jacket as well."

Mullaney's eyes narrowed. Go on, he thought. Talk, McReady. Tell the nice gentleman—who is undoubtedly a member of your international ring, I can tell by the way you're using your finishing-school voice and manners—tell the nice gentleman all about the jacket.

"Eight," McReady said.

Eight, Mullaney thought.

"No, at five to six."

At five to six, Mullaney thought.

"Three, that's correct," McReady said.

Oh, it's *three,* Mullaney thought.

"No, ten, eleven, and nine, in that order."

Oh my, Mullaney thought.

"Signor Ladro, I really find discussing . . . yes, I can understand your concern over the delay, but we thought it best not to
contact . . . yes, I understand. But the matter is *still* a very
delicate one, here in New York at least. The . . . *accident* occurred only two nights ago, you know. One might say the body is
still very very warm. Good, I'm glad you do."

What is he talking about? Mullaney wondered. What the hell
are you talking about, McReady?

"Well, all I can do is assure you once again that we're doing
everything in our power to recover it. Yes, quite securely
fastened, there's no need to worry on that score. Besides, we had
arranged for a decoy, Signor Ladro, as you know. So we feel
confident that everything is still intact. Well no, we can't be
certain, Signor Ladro, but . . . what? We had them drilled. Yes,
each one."

How's that again? Mullaney thought.

"No, before they were painted," McReady said.

Now he's talking gibberish, Mullaney thought, frowning.

"Black, of course," McReady said.

Mere gibberish.

"That is correct," McReady said, "you have it all, Signor Ladro.
Please be patient, won't you? You will receive the coffin as soon
as we can correct the problems on this end. We understand that's
the family's wish, and we are doing everything possible to
comply. Well, thank you. Thank you, Signor Ladro. Thank you, I
appreciate that. It was good hearing from you, too, Signor Ladro.
Thank you. Please give my regards to Bianca. *Ciao.*"

McReady hung up, and then took a handkerchief from his back
pocket and wiped his brow. Mullaney, standing outside the
window, was thinking furiously. McReady had reeled off a string
of numbers, eight, and three, and nine, and eleven, he could
barely remember them all, were they some sort of code? He had
also said "At five to six," was that a time? Was he referring to a

specific time, and was it New York time or Roman time? Ten, that was another one of the numbers, what did *any* of them have to do with the jacket or with the paper scraps Gouda had substituted for . . .

Wait a minute. Didn't McReady say the accident had occurred two nights ago? In that case, he couldn't have been referring to the highway accident involving Gouda and the others because *that* had happened only yesterday afternoon, no, he had been referring to something else, something that was still very very warm, if I recall his words correctly, something that was still a delicate matter, here in New York at least, something that . . .

We had them drilled, McReady had said.

Each one.

Had he been referring to the three men who'd been shot on the highway? But no, how could he have been? It was Kruger's fellows who'd caused the accident, Kruger's fellows who'd done the shooting. Had there been *another* shooting as well, a gangland killing perhaps, a swap of assassinations, we kill somebody here in New York, you kill somebody there in Rome, even steven? But then why the need for a casual corpse picked up on Fourteenth Street, why not send the genuine item? Or items? There would have been more than one corpse because McReady had said "them," he had very clearly and distinctly said "We had them drilled," plural, *them*, not singular, him, her, or it. But why would anyone want to paint the victims of a shooting?

Black, he thought. McReady had said, "Black, of course."

Melanie is from the Greek, it means black.

Black.

The jacket was black, the lining was black, the buttons were black, the coffin was . . .

Oh my God, Mullaney thought, eight and three!

Oh my sweet loving merciful mother of God, oh you smart son of a bitch, Mullaney, eight at five to six, oh you genius Mullaney, you are once again sitting on a fortune, you have cracked the code, you have pierced the plan, you have tipped to what these fellows have done and are planning to do, you are a bloody blue-nosed genius!

Exuberantly, he rose from his crouching position outside the window.

The thing to do now, he thought, is get back to Brooklyn as fast as I possibly can and locate the girl who has my Judy Bond shopping bag. I don't need you any more, gentlemen—not you, Purcell, and not you, K, thank you very much indeed.

Need them or not, they appeared at the mouth of McReady's driveway just then, arriving in the same black Cadillac that had picked him up on Fourteenth Street the day before, and looking none the worse for wear after their bout with Solomon and his fellows.

He thought, I'm too close now to be stopped. I have doubled my bets and then retreated, doubled them again, and retreated further still, but this time I'm going all the way, straight to Jakarta where I will bet on cockroach races and sampan regattas, Mullaney's system, I am ready for the big kill, gentlemen, and you cannot stop me.

He ran for the taxicab waiting alongside the curb.

K and Purcell had already seen him and were backing the Cadillac out of the driveway as he threw open the door of the cab and hurled himself onto the seat.

"Those men in the Cadillac are thieves," he said to the driver. "Get me out of here! Fast!"

The driver reacted by putting the cab into gear and gunning it away from the curb, obviously delighted by this most recent of developments, and thinking how lucky he was to have found a diversion that took his mind off his three miserable sons.

"What did they steal?" he asked.

"They stole something worth half a million dollars in a certain foreign nation, Italy for example."

"That is a lot of cabbage," the driver said.

That is a whole hell of a lot of cabbage," Mullaney said. "My friend," he said, "if you can get me where I'm going safely, without those fellows in the Cadillac catching me and killing me, I will give you a reward of five thousand dollars, which is exactly one percent of the total, and which is the biggest tip you're ever going to get in your life."

"It's a deal," the driver said.

"Share the wealth," Mullaney said, "what the hell. Have you ever been to Jakarta?"

"I have never even been to Pittsburgh."

"Jakarta is better."

"I am sure," the driver said. "Where *is* Jakarta?"

"Jakarta is in Indonesia, and is sometimes spelled with a D-j," Mullaney said, recalling volume J–JO, *See Djakarta, volume* D–DR. "It is, in fact, the capital of Indonesia, which is the base of a triangle whose apex is the Philippines, pointing north to Japan. They have marvelous cockroach races in Jakarta."

"I have marvelous cockroach races in my own kitchen every night," the driver said.

"My friend, they are gaining on us," Mullaney said, glancing through the rear window.

"Have no fear," the driver said, and rammed the accelerator to the floor.

This is a fine exciting chase, Mullaney thought, if I don't get killed. It is almost as exciting as the finest most exciting chase I ever experienced, but that was a long time ago, and neither my life nor half a million dollars was at stake that time. The only thing at stake then was Irene. Irene was the pursued and I was the pursuer, and that was a fine exhilarating chase beginning on West End Avenue and Seventy-eighth Street, exactly where Irene lived, and ending in the Cloisters.

The chase started much as this chase had started, with the unexpected arrival of, coincidentally, two men. The two men who arrived that day at Irene's apartment were neither K nor Purcell, but a pair of U.C.L.A. philosophy professors whom she had met the month before on her yearly summer visit to her aunt in Brentwood, Los Angeles 49. This was July, I can remember the exact date, it was a Saturday, and it was July twentieth, and Irene had reason thereafter to remember the date, too, because we both made certain irrevocable commitments (we thought at the time) which later turned out to be as easily canceled as any peace treaty. But I did not know that, I only knew what was happening *then*, happening to Andrew Mullaney who was twenty-nine years old and still single, still living the carefree life of a bachelor. I had just started working for the Educational Encyclopedia Company, Incorporated, I remember, after having served two years in the United States Army, and then having completed my education (ha!) at City College, and having held a series of unrelated jobs in the intervening months since graduation. I had met Irene at a dance given by the Sons of Erin on Fordham Road, and had taken her out perhaps three or four times since that April night, had even escorted her to what was then called Idlewild Airport to put her on an airplane for her yearly visit to Auntie Brentwood (as we referred to her), little knowing she would meet these two very nice philosophy professors from U.C.L.A. *Certainly* never suspecting they would come to New York in July and naturally think of looking up the vivacious redhead whom they had tried to teach to surfboard at the Santa Monica beach one Saturday afternoon when Auntie Brentwood was out marketing in her gold lamé slacks and high-heeled slippers.

New York in July is a real summer festival, even without the unexpected arrival of two philosophy professors. The temperature on that July twentieth was seventy-nine degrees at eight o'clock in the morning, and was forecast to hit ninety-five before the day was done. The combined heat and humidity were intolerable (it ain't the heat, it's the humidity) even though the Weather Bureau had not yet created its "Discomfort Index," rare euphemism. Mullaney woke at ten-thirty in a sodden bed of tangled sheets, immediately called Irene to ask if she would like to go out to the beach, grinned when she said, "Oh my God, yes!" and went into the kitchen for a leisurely breakfast of orange juice, coffee, scrambled eggs and toast. He put on a pair of swimming trunks, pulled a pair of Army fatigues over them, went down to his old Chevrolet before the alternate-sides-of-street parking expired, and drove down to West End Avenue in time to see Irene leaving the building with two very handsome and bronzed young men whom he later learned (and didn't at first believe) were philosophy professors from U.C.L.A.

He could not understand why she was leaving her apartment without him even though he was more than an hour late (he was *always* late for dates; she knew that by now). The two men flanked her like storm troopers (Is she being abducted? he thought in panic), and led her to a blue Chrysler convertible parked illegally alongside a fire hydrant, its top down. Mullaney, pulling up to the curb, shouted, "Irene!" in shock and surprise, but when she heard her name, she only turned and smiled and waved at him, and then got into the Chrysler, which, Mullaney now saw, was sporting California license plates and a foxtail flying from the radio aerial. The radio erupted in that moment with what was undoubtedly the Country Western forerunner of today's Rock and Roll, the Emperor's New Music, erupted on that silent July avenue with all the bursting energy of a mortar explosion, *zooooooooom*, the Chrysler pulled away from the curb in a roaring California surfing-type rock and roll lousy handsome bronzed gods abductors of Irish maidens display of horsepower and *élan*, "Hey!" Mullaney cried out pitifully.

He climbed out of the decrepit Chevy and stood in the middle of the street watching the disappearing rear end of the convertible and thinking They are taking my girl away, and that was the beginning of the chase.

The chase roared up West End Avenue to Ninety-sixth Street, the battered old Chevy valiantly trying to keep up with the sleek and musical Chrysler, managing to do so only because the California professors (it took him three weeks to accept the fact that they really *had* been professors) were unfamiliar with the trip-light system in New York and kept getting stopped by red lights on almost every other corner while Mullaney kept his speed down, making all the greens, and steadily gaining on them, Mullaney's System in embryo. All the while, he kept seeing Irene's hair blowing free in the wind, Irene occasionally turning to look back, certain she knew he was following, certain she was urging her professor friends to step on the gas, enjoying this enormously while he kept swearing and mumbling under his breath and hoping his car would not overheat.

The Chrysler turned left on Ninety-sixth and hit the downhill straightaway to the Henry Hudson Parkway, almost leaving Mullaney in the dust, but shrieking to a stop when a gasoline truck unexpectedly pulled out of the garage on the right-hand side of the street, just before the viaduct, enabling him to gain on them again, but causing him to wonder what would happen when they got on the parkway and could really give their powerful machine its head. He pressed his own accelerator to the floorboard—the chase was beginning to get somewhat exciting now, he was beginning to think of Irene as some sort of rare woodland sprite captured by barbarians, the prize he must rescue, he had written sonnets about girls like this—and heard the valiant old Chevy rattling away on all six cylinders, and thought Come on, Bessie (he had never, before this, called the car anything at all), we've got to catch that submarine up ahead. The submarine up ahead, dispensing Country Western music that was assuredly being picked up on a shortwave radio hookup to some foreign land, perhaps California, flying its foxtail flag from the radio aerial, zoomed onto the parkway, and left Mullaney's Chevy rattling and steaming at the Full Stop sign.

They were very clever, those California hot-rod professors, but they forgot just one thing as they raced away on the parkway with the Hudson River gleaming in hot July sunshine on their left and the George Washington Bridge uptown spanning New York and New Jersey, they forgot Ford's Law, which stated that an automobile will continue to roll forward only in direct ratio to the amount of gasoline in its tank. They ran out of gasoline some five hundred yards short of the parkway's Mobil station, and both mad professors jumped out of the car and began running along the edge of the road, hoping not to get hit by the Saturday traffic, glancing back over their shoulders to shout words of encouragement to Irene, who was standing on the front seat of the Chrysler and cheering as Mullaney drove into view in the puffing Chevrolet. Keen of eye and strong of muscle in those days, Mullaney sized up the situation in a flash: The bronzed surfers had run out of gas and were jogging to the station for a replenishing gallon or two; Irene was alone in the automobile, wearing, he saw now, a bright-yellow shift, a yellow ribbon in her windblown red hair, a saucy impudent grin on her wide Irish mouth—she was daring him, the wench, she was daring him to kidnap her from her kidnapers.

Which he did.

He parked his old heap directly parallel to the sleek shining California submarine, threw open the door on her side, reached in and scooped her into his arms, skirts flying, white nylon panties flashing for an instant, she shrieking, he wanting to make love to her right there in the middle of the parkway, *zip,* he ran around the nose of the Chrysler, *zam,* he threw her onto the front seat of his own car, *whap,* he threw the car into gear, *whooosh,* he was off in a belching cloud of carbon monoxide. "Hey!" the surfers cried this time, "Hey!" their voices every bit as full of pitiable despair as Mullaney's had been outside Irene's apartment building. "Ho-*ho!*" Mullaney shouted as the Chevrolet rolled by, Irene laughing, her hair whipping about her face, green eyes sparkling, "I love you," he shouted, and she stopped laughing.

"I beg your pardon?" she said.

"You lovely wench, I love you," he said. "I'm mad about you."

"Well now," she said, and was solemnly quiet as he drove recklessly and wildly up the parkway, glancing now and again into the rear-view mirror for sight of the long blue submarine pulling out of the Mobil station. They do not know New York, he reasoned correctly, they are surfers from California, they do not know about such hidden nooks as the Cloisters, ah-ha, he thought, I will foil them.

"I will foil your surfboarding California friends," he said to Irene.

"They are professors," she answered.

"Ha!" he said.

The Cloisters was silent in mid-July heat, ancient rocks and stones baking in the sun, flowers blooming, insects droning lazily in the turreted stillness. He made love to her on a secret knoll overlooking the Hudson in the shadow of the timeless walls, feeling sacrilegious and daring and adventurous, telling her he was wild about her, "I adore you, mmm, I am stark raving mad about your mouth and your eyes and your legs and your pert tiny breasts . . ."

"Tiny?" she said.

"Oh, mmm, you are all peaches and cream, all soft and round and perfect, oh, I want to marry you," he said.

"When?" she said.

"Now," he said.

"*Love* me now," she said, "concentrate on that. You can marry me later if you like."

That was the chase, that was how the chase had ended, with Irene in his arms and the crisp yellow shift up above her waist, while perhaps the parkway traffic watched below, who knew or cared, though later, much later, she would not do it on a Ferris wheel. That day had been the most exciting day in his life, that day he first knew the dizzying excitement of her, that had been the most exciting day in his life until now, today, when he was being chased by two thieves in a black Cadillac, racing to retrieve a jacket worth half a million dollars.

"Are they still behind us?" the driver asked.

"No, I think we've lost them," Mullaney said, but was not at all sure.

13. MELISSA

He asked the driver to wait for him at the curb and then went into the apartment building, trying to decide where he should begin—top floor? bottom floor? middle floor? A clock in the lobby told him it was now twenty-five minutes past five, which meant that any self-respecting housewife was already preparing dinner for her spouse and children. He thought this might be a very bad time to go knocking on a hundred and thirty doors, but he could not think of a better time, what with K and Purcell possibly sniffing around and lending urgency to the situation. He was beginning to regret his promise to the cab driver. He had, after all, taken all the risks involved with locating the jacket;

he had figured out exactly why and how the jacket was valuable; he had been gambling on its worth since early yesterday; why in hell should he now give the cab driver one percent of the take simply for driving him from Brooklyn to Queens and back again? Well, he thought, we'll renegotiate that after I find the jacket, the first thing to do is find the damn jacket.

Ground floor? he thought.

Middle floor?

Top floor?

It is always best to start at the bottom, he thought, and work your way up, so what I'll do is go to the *very* bottom, which is the basement. In that way, I may catch some ladies still doing their wash, and thereby save myself the possibility of duplication; if I hit the basement last, I may run across some of them I've already talked to, yes, it's best to hit the basement first, that's exactly what I'll do. Something was bothering him, but he didn't know quite what yet. He found himself trying to decide whether he should take the money and go to Jakarta, or whether he should take it and go to Monte Carlo, or London (which is where it was happening, baby, all sorts of gambling action there) or perhaps Sicily where he could live like a king on two dollars a week, playing *bocce* for money with Mafiosi—all sorts of possibilities churned around in his skull, but of course he first had to find the jacket. And yet finding the jacket was not what bothered him, it was something other than that, though he could not yet put his finger on it.

Something though.

Something.

There was only one lady in the basement, taking her wet laundry out of the washing machine. He approached her and asked whether she had perhaps picked up a Judy Bond shopping bag on the train that afternoon, he being the rightful owner of the bag, and willing to offer a reward for its recovery since, well (using K's identical line), let us say it has sentimental value. The woman was a very pleasant type who looked as Irish as Irene, though nowhere near as pretty, thirty-five or thirty-six years old, with weary lines around her sharp blue eyes. Oh my, she said, I do wish I could help you, but you see I got up at five-thirty this morning to make my husband breakfast before he went off fishing in Long Island Sound, and then I did his breakfast dishes and woke the children and dressed them and fed them and got them ready to be picked up to be taken to Prospect Park where the school is having a picnic, and then I did *their* breakfast dishes, and vacuumed, and dusted, and my mother-in-law came over for lunch which I had to make for her, she loves fried chicken, and then I did *her* lunch dishes, and changed the slipcovers on the furniture, and tried to get the stain out of the living-room rug where the dog dirtied, and then had to wait for the electrician who was coming to fix the door on the refrigerator, the light won't go out when you close it, he didn't come until about three o'clock, and he finally got it fixed by four, it cost five dollars for a service call and a dollar seventy-five for parts, and my husband came home with some very nice flounder and blackies that I had to clean and put in the refrigerator, the light wouldn't go out again not ten minutes after the electrician had left, and then I came down here with my laundry at about four-thirty, and, as you can see, I'm just now taking the last load out of the washer, and now I'll have to go hang it up outside, and then go upstairs and prepare dinner for the family, the children are supposed to be home at six if the bus is on time, so you see I didn't have much time to ride the subway today, or to pick up a Judy Bond shopping bag with sentimental value, I'm terribly sorry.

Mullaney thanked her and was starting up out of the basement when he heard voices coming from one of the small rooms off to the side near the furnace. He approached the room confidently, expecting to find some more ladies chatting about the day's events, and was disappointed to discover only three tiny little girls sitting around a wooden table, playing jacks. The room, he saw, had been whitewashed and hung with cute little nursery-type cutouts of the Cat and the Fiddle and Old King Cole and the like. A bare light bulb hung over the wooden table, which had been shortened to accommodate the four tot-sized chairs around it. The table was painted a bright yellow, the chairs a bright pink. The three little girls were each perhaps eight years old, each wearing a pastel dress that blended nicely with the yellow table and pink chairs and whitewashed walls and cute nursery-school cutouts. They were shrieking in glee at the progress of their game and paid not the slightest bit of attention to Mullaney, who stood quietly in the doorway, watching. Unobtrusively, he turned to leave, and then saw something on the floor beside the pink chair of the little dark-haired girl who sat at the far end of the table.

The something was his Judy Bond shopping bag.

His heart lurched.

He recognized the girl at once as the button-nosed little tyke who, with her mother, had been sitting opposite him in the subway car. He took a step into the room, and then noticed that her small chubby fist was clasped firmly around the handles of the shopping bag. She glanced up at him as he abortively hesitated in the doorway, her dark brown eyes coming up coolly and slowly to appraise him.

"Hello," he said weakly.

"Hello," the other little girls chirped, but the dark-haired one at the end of the table did not answer, watched him intently and suspiciously instead, her hand still clutched around the twisted white paper handles of the shopping bag.

"Excuse me, little girl," Mullaney said, "but is that your shopping bag?"

"Yes, it is," she answered. Her voice was high and reedy, it seemed to emanate from her button nose, her mouth seemed to remain tightly closed, her eyes did not waver from his face.

"Are you sure you didn't find it on a subway train?" he asked, and smiled.

"Yes, I did find it on a subway train, but it's mine anyway," she said. "Finders, keepers."

"That's right, Melissa," one of the other little girls said. "Finders, keepers," and Mullaney wanted to strangle her. Instead, he smiled sourly and told himself to keep calm.

"There's a jacket in that bag, did you happen to notice it?" he asked.

"I happened to notice it," Melissa said.

"It belongs to me," Mullaney said.

"No, it belongs to *me*," she answered. "Finders, keepers."

"Finders, keepers, right," the other girl said. She was a fat little kid with freckles on her nose and braces on her teeth. She seemed to be Melissa's translator and chief advocate, and she sat slightly to Melissa's right, with her hands on her hips, and stared at Mullaney with unmasked hostility.

"The jacket has sentimental value," Mullaney said, trying to look pathetic.

"What's sentimental value?" the third little girl asked.

"Well, it means a lot to me," he said.

"It means a lot to me, too," Melissa said.

"It means a lot to *her*, too," her translator chirped.

"Thank you, Frieda," Melissa said.

"Well," Mullaney said, smiling, and still trying to look pathetic, "what can it *possibly* mean to you, an old jacket with a torn lining and . . ."

"I can do lots of things with it," Melissa said. She had still not taken her eyes from his face. He had thought only snakes never blinked, volume SN–SZ, but apparently Melissa was of a similar species, cold-blooded, with hoods over the eyes, never blinking, never sleeping, never relinquishing her coiled grip on the shopping bag.

"Name me one thing you can do with it," Mullaney said.

"I could throw it in the garbage," Melissa said, and giggled.

"She could throw it in the garbage," Frieda said, and also giggled.

"Throw it *where?*" the third girl, who was apparently deaf, asked.

"In the garbage, Hilda," Melissa said, still giggling.

"Oh, in the *garbage*," Hilda said, and burst out laughing.

The three of them continued laughing and giggling for quite some time, while Mullaney stood foolishly in the doorway, trying to look pathetic, and beginning to sweat profusely. There was no window in the small basement room, and he could feel perspiration on his brow and under his arms, trickling over his collarbones, sliding onto his chest.

"Well," he said, "if you're going to throw it in the garbage, you might just as well give it back to me, seeing as it has sentimental value."

"Then I *won't* throw it in the garbage," Melissa said.

"What will you do?"

"I'll cut off all the buttons."

"Why would you do that?" Mullaney asked.

"To sew on Jenny's dress."

"Who's Jenny?"

"My dolly."

"Well, you wouldn't want to sew those big ugly buttons on a dolly's dress, would you? Little dollies should have small bright shining buttons on their dresses."

"I could paint them bright and shining," Melissa said. "Anyway, it's *my* jacket and I can do what I want with it. Finders, keepers."

"Losers, weepers," Frieda said.

Hilda giggled.

"Look," Mullaney said, "I'll *pay* you for the jacket, how's that? I'm really very attached to it, you see, and I . . ."

"How much?" Melissa said.

"Fifteen cents," Mullaney said, which was all the money he had in the world.

"Ha!"

"Well . . . how much do you want?"

"Half a million."

"It's . . . it's not worth anywhere near that," Mullaney said, thinking the child was omniscient. "It's just an old jacket with a torn lining, it couldn't possibly be . . ." He wet his lips. "Look, Melissa . . . is that your name? Melissa?"

"That's my name."

"I'll tell you what I'll do . . ."

"Mister," Frieda said, "we're trying to play some jacks here, do you mind?"

"I certainly don't want to interrupt your game, but I don't think you understand how much that jacket means to me," he said, thinking I must be out of my mind trying to reason with a bunch of fourth-graders, why don't I simply grab the damn jacket and run? Sure, with Melissa's grubby little fist wrapped around it, miserable unblinking little reptile, I'll have to grab the jacket *and* the shopping bag *and* her in the bargain; I can just hear the unholy clamor *that* little gambit would raise.

"Mister," Frieda said, "why don't you go home?"

"Because I want my jacket," Mullaney said, somewhat petulantly.

"It's your turn, Hilda," Melissa said.

Hilda picked up the jacks, held them in her hand for an instant, and then dropped them onto the table top. There were ten jacks, each made of metal, each shaped like an enlarged asterisk. They fell onto the table top separately, or in pairs, or in small groups, tumbling and rolling and finally coming to rest. Hilda eyed them critically.

"Go on," Melissa said.

"I was examining them," Hilda replied.

"Don't be such an examiner," Frieda said.

"Examine when you come to foursies or fivesies. Don't examine so much on onesies."

"How do you play that game?" Mullaney asked suddenly.

"Oh mister, please go away," Melissa said.

"Seriously, seriously," he said, his eyes narrowing. "How do you play it?"

"You throw the ball up," Melissa said, "and it bounces, and if you're going for onesies, you have to pick up one jack each time before you catch the ball. When you're for twosies, you have to pick up *two* jacks each time."

"And so on," Frieda said.

"How do you win?" Mullaney asked.

"When you reach tensies," Melissa said.

"Tensies?"

"When you bounce the ball and pick up all ten jacks before you catch it."

"Are you a good player?"

"I'm the best player in the building."

"She's the best player in Brooklyn," Frieda said.

"Maybe in the world," Hilda said.

"Mmm," Mullaney said. He unbuttoned his jacket, took it off, threw it on the table top, and said, "You see that jacket? Easily worth fifty dollars on the open market, almost brand-new, worn maybe three or four times."

"I see it," Melissa said.

"Okay. My jacket against the one in the bag, which is torn and worthless, and which you're going to throw in the garbage anyway."

"What do you mean?"

"I'll play you for the jacket in the bag."

"Play me *what?*"

"Jacks."

"You've got to be kidding," Melissa said.

"She'll murder you," Frieda said.

"She'll mobilize you," Hilda said.

"My jacket against the one in the bag, what do you say?"

Melissa weighed the offer. Her free hand clenched and unclenched on the table top, her lips twitched, but her eyes remained open and unblinking. The room was silent. Her friends watched her expectantly. At last, she nodded almost imperceptibly and said, "Let's play jacks, mister."

He had never played jacks in his life, but he was prepared to play now for a prize worth half a million dollars—"I'll cut off all the buttons," Melissa had said, smart little fat-assed snake-eyed gambler. He sat in one of the tiny chairs, his knees up close near his chin, and peered between them across the table. "Who goes first?" he asked.

"I defer to my opponent," Melissa said, making him feel he had stumbled into the clutches of a jacks hustler.

"How do you . . . how do you do this?" he asked.

"He's got to be kidding," Frieda said.

"She'll *mobilize* him," Hilda said.

"Pick up the jacks," Melissa said. "In one hand."

"Yes?" he said, picking them up.

"Now keep your hand up here, about this high from the table, and let them fall. Just open your hand and let them fall."

"Okay," he said, and opened his hand and let the jacks fall.

"Oh, that's a bad throw," Frieda said.

"You're dead, mister," Hilda said.

"Shut up, and let me play my own game," he said. "What do I do next?"

"You throw the ball up, and let it bounce on the table, and then you have to pick up one jack and catch the ball in the same hand."

"That's impossible," Mullaney said.

"That's the game, mister," Melissa said. "Those are the rules."

"You didn't say the *same* hand," Mullaney said.

"It has to be the same hand," Frieda said.

"Of *course* it has to be the same hand," Hilda said.

"Those are the rules."

"That's the game."

"Then why didn't you say so when I asked you before?" Mullaney said.

"Any dumb ox knows those are the rules," Melissa said. "Are you quitting?"

"Quitting?" he said. "Lady, I am just starting."

"Then throw the ball, and start already," Melissa said.

"Don't rush me," Mullaney said. He eyed the field. This was surely a simple game if these little fourth-graders could play it, hell, he had seen little girls of five and six playing it, there was certainly nothing here that an expert dice thrower couldn't master. "Here goes," he said, and threw the small red rubber ball into the air and reached for the closest jack, and grabbed for the ball, and missed the ball, and dropped the jack, and said, "Oh, hell" and immediately said, "Excuse me, ladies."

"Your turn, Melissa," Frieda said.

"Thank you," Melissa said.

He watched her as she delicately scooped up the ten jacks in her left hand, watched as she disdainfully opened her hand to allow the jacks to spill onto the table top in a clattering, tumbling cascade of metal, watched as she coldly surveyed the possibilities, bounced the red rubber ball, picked up a jack, closed the same hand around the falling ball, bounced the ball again, picked up another jack, bounced it, another, bounced it, another, another, another, oh my God it is going to be a clean sweep, Mullaney thought, she is going to go from onesies to tensies without my ever getting another turn.

"That's onesies," Melissa said, and held the jacks above the table again, preparing to drop them. He watched very carefully as she opened her hand, trying to determine whether there was any secret to the dropping of the jacks, deciding that *this* part of it, at least, was all chance, and then concentrating on her technique for picking up the jacks. She worked so swiftly, bounce went the ball, out darted her hand like a snake's tongue (she is surely a pit viper or an adder, Mullaney thought), back it came in time to catch the descending ball, two jacks at a time now (that's right, she's going for twosies; *going* for it, my eye, she's almost finished with it), bounce went the ball again, out came the grasping hand, one unblinking eye on the falling rubber ball, pick up the jacks, catch the ball, "That's twosies," Melissa said.

"You've still got a long way to go," Mullaney said.

"She beat Selma Krantz," Frieda said.

"She even beat Rosalie Krantz," Hilda said.

"Play, play," Mullaney said.

"Threesies," Melissa announced, as though she expected to proceed directly from there to foursies (announcing it) and fivesies (again announcing it) and straight through to tensies, after which she would take the jacket bequeathed to him by a Negro ten times the man he was (or so the legend went) and go up to dinner, goodbye, Mullaney, unless you are ready to commit homicide.

The possibility intrigued him.

Melissa rapidly picked up three jacks, and then another three, and then another three, leaving a single jack on the table.

"What about that one?" he asked.

"If there's any left over," Melissa said, "if it doesn't come out even, you just pick up what's left over."

"Oh."

"Yes."

"Those are the rules," Frieda said.

"That's the game," Hilda said.

Melissa bounced the ball, picked up the remaining jack, and caught the ball in the same hand.

"If you drop a jack, you're out," she said.

"Those are the rules."

"That's the game."

"I see."

"Foursies," Melissa announced.

She went from foursies to fivesies to sixies with remarkable speed while Mullaney watched, figuring he had better learn this game damn quick because if she ever lost possession of the ball (which seemed highly unlikely) he would be called upon to perform once again, and his next chance would undoubtedly be his last and only chance. He began willing her to drop the ball, or to drop a jack, or to miss the ball, or to pick up only six jacks when she was supposed to pick up seven, but no such luck, *flick* went her hand, fingers closing on seven jacks, *down* came the ball into her open palm. Three jacks were left on the table now. She demolished those on the next bounce of the ball, and then announced, "Eightsies."

Mullaney wiped his brow with the back of his hand.

"It's very hot in here," he said.

"It's going to get hotter, mister," Melissa said, and giggled.

Hilda and Frieda giggled, too.

"Come on, play," Mullaney said irritably.

As Melissa picked up the jacks and opened her hand, dropping them onto the table top, Mullaney found himself praying that she would lose, the way he had prayed on the edge of too many dice tables in the past year—praying for the point when he was betting with the shooter, praying for a seven when he was betting the shooter wrong, praying that he, Andrew Mullaney, would win big just once, would pick up *all* the chips, *all* the cash, once, just once. With beads of sweat popping out on his brow, with his heart banging inside his chest, he prayed now that an eight-year-old girl would drop a jack, drop the ball, drop *dead* even, anything, so long as he won, so long as he *won*.

She scooped up eight jacks and caught the ball easily.

The remaining two jacks were spread rather far apart on the table top. Melissa eyed them with her same unblinking confidence, but he sensed she was in trouble because she was hesitating much longer than usual before bouncing the ball again. She was calculating the distance between the two jacks, he knew, the time it would take her to scoop up both of them before catching the descending ball. It would be a tight squeeze; *she* knew it, and *Mullaney* knew it, and he found himself smiling tightly for the first time since the game had begun.

"Go on," he said, "play."

Melissa nodded. Her tongue darted out (yes, she was most certainly a cobra, or at least a water moccasin), wetting her lips. The brown eyes looked from one jack to the other. She took a deep breath and threw the ball into the air. The ball bounced. Her hand shot out with dazzling speed, hitting one jack, sweeping it across the table top, pushing it ahead of her flat palm, the ball was coming down. She had shoved both jacks together now, her hand closed on them, she scooped them from the table top together, swung her hand to the left, clutched for the ball, and missed.

"You missed," Mullaney whispered.

"I know," she said.

"It's your turn," Frieda said.

"You're for onesies," Hilda said.

"And Melissa is still for eightsies."

"I'm going to win," Mullaney whispered.

"Like fun," Frieda said.

"I am going to win, little girl," he whispered. "For once in my life, I am going to *win*."

"Play," Melissa said.

He concentrated only on the jacks and on the red rubber ball. He ignored the malevolent stares of the little girls ranged around him at the sawed-off table, ignored the suffocating heat of the room and the discomfort of the tiny chair on which he sat, ignored too the knowledge that half a million dollars was at stake, concentrating only on the game, only on winning. He was a clumsy player. He seized the jacks too anxiously, clutched for the rubber ball too desperately, but he dropped neither jacks nor ball, and by the time he reached twosies, he was beginning to get the knack of the game. He did not allow his new confidence to intrude on his concentration. Twosies was the Daily Double, that was all, you picked the two nags most likely to win, and then you picked the next two, and the next two after that, and before you knew it there were only two left on the table, and you swept them up into your hand and reached clumsily for the falling rubber ball, but caught it, yes, clenched your fist around it, *caught* it, and were ready for threesies.

Threesies was merely picking the Win, Place, and Show horses in the proper order, three times in a row, and then there was only one jack left on the table, simple, bouncie bouncie ballie, scoop it up, catch the ball, there you are, my dears.

"I'm going to win," he whispered.

"Play," Melissa whispered.

He ignored their hard-eyed stares, their cruel silent devout wishes for his downfall, he ignored them and moved into foursies, it seemed to be getting easier all the time, all you had to do was scoop up four, and then four again, easy as pie, he closed his hand on the two remaining jacks, caught the ball, grinned at the little girls who were watching him now with open hatred, and said again, not whispering it this time, "I am going to *win*, my dears."

"You are going to *lose*," Melissa said flatly and coldly and unblinkingly.

"You heard her," Frieda said.

"You are going to *lose*," Hilda said.

"You are a *loser*," Melissa said.

"We'll see," he said. "I'm for fivesies."

"Play," Melissa said.

He dropped the jacks onto the table. He scooped up five, and caught the ball, scooped up the remaining five and caught the ball again.

"Sixies," he said.

He went through sixies in a breeze, feeling stronger and more confident all the time, not even noticing Melissa or her friends anymore, his full and complete concentration on the table top as he raced through sevensies, and eightsies, and ninesies, and then paused to catch his breath.

"Play," Melissa said.

"This is the last one," he said. "If I get through this one, I win."

"That's right," Melissa said.

"But first you have to get through it," Frieda said.

"First you have to win, mister."

"The game isn't over yet, mister."

"You can still lose, mister."

"Shut up!" he said.

The room went silent.

He picked up the jacks. I must win, he told himself. I must win. He dropped the jacks onto the table top. Nine of them fell miraculously together in a small cluster. The tenth jack rolled clear across the table, at least two feet away from the others.

"Too bad," Melissa said. "You give up?"

"I can make it," Mullaney said.

"It's a harder shot than mine was," Melissa said.

"I can make it."

"Let's see you," she said.

"All right."

The pile of nine first, he thought, then go for the one, and then catch the ball. No. The one first, sweep it toward the bigger pile using the flat of my hand, the way Melissa used hers, then scoop up all ten together and catch the . . .

No.

Wait a minute.

Yes.

Yes, that's the only way to do it.

"Here goes," he said.

"Bad *luck,*" the three girls said together, and he threw the ball into the air.

His hand seemed to move out so terribly slowly, hitting the single lonely jack across the table and sweeping it toward the larger pile, the ball was dropping so very quickly, he would never make it, the pile of ten was now beneath his grasping fingers, he closed his hand, his eyes swung over to the dropping ball, he scooped up the jacks, the ball bounced, slid his closed hand across the table and, without lifting it from the wooden surface, flipped it over, opened the fingers, spread the hand wide, caught the ball and was closing his hand again when he felt the ball slipping from his grasp.

No, he thought, no!

He tightened his hand so suddenly and so fiercely that he thought he would break his fingers. He tightened it around the ball as though he were grasping for life itself, crushing the ball and the jacks into his palm, holding them securely, his hand in mid-air, and then slowly bringing his fist down onto the table.

"I win," he said without opening his hand.

"You bastid," Melissa said, and threw the shopping bag onto the table top. She rose from her tiny chair, tossed her dark hair, and walked swiftly out of the room.

"You bastid," Frieda said.

"You bastid," Hilda said, and they followed Melissa out.

He sat exhausted at the small table, his head hanging between his knees, his hand still clutched tightly around the jacks and the rubber ball. At last, he opened his hand and let the jacks spill onto the table, allowed the rubber ball to roll to the edge and fall to the concrete floor, bouncing away across the basement.

The room was very still.

He turned over the Judy Bond shopping bag and shook the black burial jacket onto the table top. He fingered the large buttons at the front, and the smaller buttons on the sleeves, and then he picked up one of the jacks and moved it toward the center front button. Using the point of the jack, he scraped at the button. A peeling ribbon of black followed the tip of the jack. Flakes of black paint sprinkled onto the table top. He smiled and scratched at the button more vigorously, thinking There are three buttons down the front of the jacket (each about ten carats, Bozzaris had said), ten, eleven, and nine, in that order, scratching at the button, chipping away the paint; and there are four smaller buttons on each sleeve, eight at five to six carats each, I am a rich man. Mullaney thought, I am in possession of half a million dollars' worth of diamonds.

He had scraped all the paint off the middle button now.

He grasped the button between his thumb and forefinger, lifted it and the jacket to which it was fastened toward the hanging light bulb. It caught the incandescent rays, reflected them back in a dazzling glitter. This must be the eleven-carat beauty, he thought, it's slightly larger than the other two, I am a rich man, he thought, I am at last a winner.

"Hand it over," the voice behind him said.

He turned.

K and Purcell were standing in the doorway to the room. Mullaney had no intention of handing over the jacket, but it didn't matter because Purcell immediately walked over to him and hit him full in the face with the butt of a revolver.

14. IRENE

The sound of furies howling in the cemetery beyond, am I dreaming or am I dead, voices mumbling, K's and Purcell's, "should have made sure he was dead before you started for the airport."

"We thought he would suffocate in the closed coffin."

"He didn't."

"Nor did we expect the coffin to be hijacked and opened."

"You should have been more careful."

"Are you in charge here, or am I?"

"You are, but . . ."

"Then keep quiet."

"Here're the new trousers." Another voice, McReady's. He

dared not open his eyes, were they in McReady's cottage again? Proximity to cemeteries makes me somewhat ill, Mullaney thought, or perhaps it's only getting hit on the head so often.

"We wouldn't have to be doing this twice if you'd done it right the first time," Purcell said.

"We got the diamonds back," McReady said, "so what difference does it make?"

"This time we'll make *sure* he's dead," K said.

"Take off his shoes," McReady said.

"Why?"

"So we can get these pants on him."

"Is he still out?"

"Yeah."

"Drag him over here, near the coffin."

Someone's hands clutched at his ankles. He felt the floor scraping beneath his shoulders and back, heard the rasping sound of cloth catching at splintered wood. They had not bound him, his hands and feet were free, he could still fight or run.

He wondered how they had located him in the basement room, and then remembered he had left the cab sitting at the curb outside the building, that had been a mistake, a terrible oversight; I have been making a lot of mistakes these past two days, he thought, and I am very tired. Kill me and put me in the goddamn coffin, get it over with.

"Take off his pants," McReady said.

Purcell pulled at the pants he was wearing. It was cold on the floor of the cottage. He could feel the wind seeping under the front door, Why is it always so cold on the edge of cemeteries? he wondered.

"Polka-dot shorts," Purcell said, and laughed. "That kills me."

"Here," McReady said.

Purcell pulled the new set of trousers over Mullaney's feet and ankles, up over his legs.

"Doesn't he need a belt?"

"No, the jacket will cover the trouser loops."

"We're lucky the buttons are still on it," Purcell said.

"They're fastened securely," McReady said.

"We had a hole drilled through the pavilion of each diamond . . ."

"The *what?*"

"The pavilion," K said. "The part below the mounting. Doesn't he need a different tie?"

"A black one," Purcell said. "You could have cracked those stones, you know."

"An expert did the job. Don't we have a black tie, McReady?"

"If you'd cracked the big ones . . ."

"I know."

". . . the value would have gone all the way down."

"I'll look in the other room."

"We can't put him in the coffin with a striped tie," K said.

"How much did you say they're worth?" Purcell asked.

"The three big ones?"

"Yeah."

"Nine thousand dollars a carat."

"And the smaller ones?"

"Five thousand a carat."

"That doesn't come to half a million, does it?"

"No one ever said it did."

"*You* said it did."

"I said four hundred and ninety thousand dollars."

"You said half a million."

"I said not *quite* half a million."

"Are you getting that tie, McReady?"

"I could only find a black bow tie," McReady said.

"Do they bury people in bow ties?"

"Why not?"

"This is a nice bow tie," McReady said.

"I wonder what happened to his yellow shirt."

"Jasmine," McReady said, and chuckled.

"Jasmine," K repeated, and chuckled with him.

"Let's get the tie on him," Purcell said.

"We'll have to shoot him in the back of the head," K said. "Otherwise it'll show."

"Yeah," Purcell agreed. "I still say you should have done that in the beginning."

"I told you we didn't know the coffin would be hijacked."

"You should have figured it *might* have been."

"Why?" McReady said. "Gouda thought we'd already fenced the stuff and been paid for it."

"How do you fasten this tie?" K asked.

"Isn't there a clip or something?"

"No. Oh, wait a minute, is this it?"

"Yes, that's it," McReady said.

"I've never seen anyone buried in a bow tie," Purcell said. "Bow ties are for weddings."

"It'll have to do," K said. "You complain an awful lot, did you know that, Purcell?"

"I hate sloppy jobs."

"Gouda used to complain a lot, too," McReady said.

"Yeah, but I'm not working for Kruger."

"We *hope* not," McReady said.

"What's that supposed to mean?"

"Calm down," K said.

"Well, tell him not to make those kind of remarks."

"Don't make those kind of remarks," K said.

"It's not *my* fault you were careless," Purcell said.

"We were *not* careless."

"We *wanted* Gouda to think we'd received payment."

"We *wanted* him to steal the money."

"We *wanted* him to think we were innocently shipping half a million dollars in paper scraps to Rome."

"Yeah," Purcell said sourly, "the only trouble is it didn't work."

"It almost worked."

"Almost ain't quite," Purcell said. "The way four hundred and ninety thousand dollars ain't quite half a million."

"We had no idea Kruger would tip."

"The counterfeit bills were very good," K said.

"Excellent," McReady said.

"They were so good, I hated to part with them."

"Where'd you get them?" Purcell asked.

"Ladro's New York people supplied them."

"He was furious when I spoke to him," McReady said.

"Well, he'll be happy tomorrow morning," K said. "Let's get the jacket on him."

"Let's shoot him first," Purcell said.

"You think so?"

"Sure. Otherwise we'll get blood on the jacket."

"What do you think, McReady?"

"Either way, let's get it over with."

Well, how about it? Mullaney thought, and would have made his move right then, but something still was bothering him, the same elusive something that had begun nagging him back in the Brooklyn basement before he'd started gambling with Melissa, the same something that was eluding him now. You had better move, Mullaney, he told himself, you had better move now and fast and figure out what's bothering you later because if you don't you're going to be figuring it out in a coffin, dead this time, and I am told getting shot in the head is not a very pleasant death. Grandma told me that, however, and she has been proven notoriously wrong about a great many things.

"Lift him," K said.

"Why?" McReady asked.

"So Purcell can get to the back of his head."

"Oh," McReady said. "Yes."

McReady tugged at his hands, pulling him up into a sitting position. He could hear Purcell walking around behind him.

"Watch the angle now," K said.

"What do you mean?"

"Make sure you don't send the bullet through his head and into *me.*"

"Oh. Yeah."

"Point the gun up toward the ceiling."

"Right," Purcell said.

With his eyes still closed, Mullaney felt something hard and cold against the back of his skull.

"No, tilt it more," K said.

"Like this?"

"Can't you tilt it?"

"Not without crouching down."

"Then crouch down."

"You're behaving like an amateur," McReady said.

"Tell him to stop making those kind of remarks," Purcell said.

"Stop making those kind of remarks," K said.

The gun moved away from Mullaney's head. In that instant, he yanked his hands free of McReady's loose grip, and swung around in time to catch Purcell just as he was going into his crouch, knocking him back on his heels. There was a silencer on the gun, he saw, making it easier to grab, but rendering it none the less deadly. They can kill me here in this cottage as easily as whispering in church, he thought, and reached for the gun, missing. There was a short puffing explosion. A window shattered across the room. He clutched at Purcell's wrist, grasped it tightly in both hands, and slammed Purcell's knuckles against the floor, knocking the gun loose. He lunged for the gun, straddling Purcell as he did so, and then nimbly stepped over him and whirled to face all three men, the gun level in his hand.

"It is *now* post time," he said, and grinned.

"Give me that gun, Mullaney," K said.

"Ha-ha," Mullaney said, "you are very comical."

"Give me the gun."

"No. *You* give me the jacket." He extended his left hand.

"The jacket is ours," K said.

"Correct. Give it to me anyway."

"The diamonds are ours, too," K said.

"No, the diamonds belong to a jewelry firm on Forty-seventh

Street," Mullaney said, and suddenly realized what had been bothering him in the basement, what had continued to bother him all along. The diamonds were neither K's *nor* his. The diamonds had been stolen.

He frowned.

"I . . ."

And hesitated.

"I want that jacket," he said.

"Are you ready to kill for it?" K asked.

"What?"

"Because that's what you'll have to do," K said. "You'll have to kill all three of us."

He thought This isn't fair. He thought There's half a million dollars' worth of diamonds sewn to that jacket, what do I care whether or not they were stolen? I knew that all along, didn't I? These men are thugs, these men are hoods, these men are killers. I knew that all along, and it didn't stop me from making plans for Monte Carlo or London or Jakarta, why should I care now? Kill them, they're enemies of society, he thought, kill them and get out of here with the loot, who cares? You are a *winner*, Mullaney, you are holding the winning hand at last.

He was sweating now, the gun in his right hand was trembling. He could see the jacket draped loosely over K's arm, the middle button repainted black, an innocuous-looking burial garment that would be sent to Rome in exchange for four hundred and ninety thousand dollars, enough for a million and one Arabian nights, kill them, he thought, take the jacket, *win!*

Yes, Mullaney, he thought, kill them. You have done enough for possession of that jacket in these past two days, you have done enough over this past year, all of it part of the gamble, you have begged, you have borrowed, you have lied, you have cheated, you have stolen, you have Used, you have Taken, you have Grabbed, so what difference will it make if you perform one last slightly less than honorable act before you catch a plane out of the country, what the hell difference will it make?

Kill them, he thought.

Finders, keepers, winner take all, *kill* them.

He could not squeeze the trigger.

He stood facing them, knowing that he did not want to lose yet another time, but knowing he had already lost because he could not squeeze the trigger, he could not for the life of him commit this act that would finalize the gamble.

"No," he said.

"What?" K said.

"Keep the jacket."

"What?" Purcell said.

"But find yourself another corpse."

"What?" McReady said.

He felt like crying, but he did not want to cry in the presence of these international people with high connections in Rome and God knew where else, did not want them to realize he was truly a loser. So he kept his mouth very tightly compressed, a trick he had learned as a boy when his grandmother told him frightening stories, it was easier not to cry when your lips were compressed that way. He backed toward the door of the cottage, keeping the gun trained on the three men, opening the door with one hand thrust behind him, fumbling for the knob, feeling the cemetery wind as it rushed into the room. "I would appreciate it," he said, trying to sound calm and detached and debonair while knowing he had lost the final gamble, knowing he was a loser, "I would appreciate it," he said, "if you would drop the burglary charge against me."

K studied him solemnly for a moment. Then he said, "We'll see, Mullaney."

"*Ciao*," Mullaney said, and went out of the cottage.

He threw the gun into a sewer outside the cemetery and then began walking slowly, the first time he had walked slowly in the past two days, it seemed, slowly and calmly, hoping they would not follow him, and really not caring whether they did or not. He thought his parting shot had been a very good one, *"Ciao,"* he had said, losing the gamble, but showing what a sport he was anyway, a tip of the hat, a wave of the hand, *"Ciao,"* and it was all over. *"Ciao,"* and out the window went the past year, out the window went everything he had thought important, *"Ciao,"* goodbye to Monaco and Monte Carlo, goodbye to London and Epsom Downs, goodbye to Indonesia and Jakarta, where he had told the cab driver they ran cockroach races, though not at all sure they did. I'll have to look it up, he thought, and remembered that he had been locked out of his room, and wondered where he would spend the night now that the gamble was over, wondered where he would spend all the rest of his nights now that he was definitely a loser. Well, he thought, at least Irene will get a kick out of this, Irene will grin all over that Irish phizz of hers if she ever finds out her former husband has blown it all in little more than a year; she will certainly have a few laughs telling her new and doubtless winning suitors that her husband was a fool, and a loser to boot.

No, he thought.

Not Irene.

Perhaps she wouldn't do it on Ferris wheels, but he knew for certain she wouldn't laugh at him, either, would instead allow him to weep if he wanted to, which he felt like doing right now, but did not do, his lips still compressed. I'll bet any amount of money, he thought, I'll give you twenty to one, a *hundred* to one that Irene would not be happy about this, Irene would say, "Well, Andy, that's too bad, I'm terribly sorry to hear that."

He wondered if she had ever told anyone that sometimes he was a fool.

He went into a phone booth on the corner sidewalk, took a dime from his pocket and dialed Irene's number. At first he thought it might be too late to be making a phone call, but there were still lights on in the private houses bordering the cemetery, so he guessed . . .

"Hello?" she said.

"Hello, Irene?" he said.

"Yes?"

"This is Andy," he said.

"Andy?"

"Yes."

"Oh, hello, Andy," she said.

"I didn't wake you or anything, did I?"

"No, I was watching television," Irene said.

"What time is it?"

"About ten-thirty," she said.

"Oh."

"What is it, Andy? Why are you calling?"

"Well," he said, "you were right."

"About what?"

"Well," he said, "I blew it all, Irene. It took me a year, Irene, but I blew it all. I've got five cents in my pocket after this phone call, and that's it. I'm stone broke after that, though I've got to tell you I almost had half a million dollars just a few minutes ago."

"Really, Andy?" she said. "Half a million?"

"Yes, I could have had it, Irene, I really could have . . ." He stopped. "Irene," he said, "I never came close to having it."

"Well, Andy," she said, "That's too bad, I'm terribly sorry to hear that."

"I knew you would say that, Irene."

"Did you?"

"Yes."

The line went silent.

"Irene?" he said.

"Yes," she said, "I'm here."

"Irene, did you ever tell anybody about the time with the hat?"

"No," she said.

"Do you know which time I mean?"

"Yes, of course."

"Irene . . ." he said.

"Yes?"

"Irene, do you remember the night we got caught in the rain on Fire Island?"

"Yes," she said.

"Do you remember the time we were cleaning out cockroaches . . ."

"Yes, yes . . ."

". . . and found the Cache?"

"Yes, and got drunk."

"Yes," he said.

"And tried to make love."

"Yes." He paused. "Irene, would you do it on a Ferris wheel?"

"No," she said.

"Irene?"

"Yes?"

"Neither would I."

The line went silent again.

"Well," he said, and sighed.

"Well . . . well, what are you going to do now?" she asked.

"I don't know."

"Don't you have any plans?"

"No. I thought . . ." He hesitated. "I don't know what I thought."

"What did you think, Andy?"

"I don't know."

"Why did you call, Andy?"

"I guess to . . ."

"Yes?"

"To ask, Irene, if you would be willing to . . . to . . ."

"Yes?"

"Take a gamble."

"A gamble?"

"On me."

He said the words so softly that she did not hear him.

"What?" she said.

"On *me*," he repeated.

"Oh."

She'll say no, he thought. She'll say no, and I'll walk off into the night with a nickel in my pocket, fifteen cents less than I started with yesterday morning. Please don't say no, he thought. Irene, please don't say no.

"Irene?" he said.

"What is it, Andy?"

"Please don't say no. I know I'm a fool, I know I'm . . ."

"No, no," she said. "You're . . ."

"Irene, did you ever tell anybody I was a fool?"

"Andy, I don't think you're a fool."

"I am, Irene, I am."

"No, Andy." She paused. Her voice was very low when she spoke again. "Andy, you're a very nice person," she said, "if only you would grow up."

"Irene . . ." he said.

"Yes?"

"Gamble."

"I'm not a gambler, Andy."

"Neither am I," he said, and the line went silent. For a moment, he thought she had hung up. He waited for her to speak again, and then said, "Irene? Irene, are you . . . ?"

"I'm . . . I'm here," she said.

"Listen . . . listen, you're not crying, are you? Irene . . ."

"Andy, Andy," she said.

"Should . . . should I come there?"

She did not answer.

"Say yes, Irene."

Still, she did not answer.

"Irene? Say yes. Please."

He heard her sigh.

"Yes," she said.

"Yes?"

"Yes," she said. "I'm crazy."

"I love you," he said.

"All right," she said.

"I'll be there in a minute," he said.

"All right," she said.

"Well, not in a *minute,* because all I have is a nickel. It may take some time."

"Time we have," she said.

"Yes," he answered. "Time we have."

"But hurry, anyway," she said, and hung up.

He put the phone back onto the hook, and sat unmoving in the booth, feeling the April breeze that swept through the open doors, watching the eddying paper scraps on the floor. He sat that way for a long time, with the paper scraps dancing at his feet, and he thought about the gamble he had taken and lost, and he still wanted to weep. And then he thought about the gamble he was about to take, the biggest gamble of them all perhaps, and he simply nodded, and rose at last, and went out of the booth and began walking back to Manhattan.

THIS BOOK WAS SET IN
CALEDONIA AND LUCIAN TYPES,
PRINTED AND BOUND BY
AMERICAN BOOK–STRATFORD PRESS, INC.
IT WAS DESIGNED BY
LARRY KAMP